# KARMA CITY

## BY

## GARDNER M. BROWNING

Gardner M. Browning

Copyright © 2019 by Gardner M. Browning
All rights reserved
Del Sol Press

www.delsolpress.org

ISBN-13: 978-0-9998425-1-5
ISBN-10: 0-9998425-1-X

i

Karma City

*The city is half-dead. The decay is everywhere. Junkies and vagrants occupy once glittering skyscrapers. The waste in the streets thickens the air with the stink of rot. So many people sick, some wishing to die, and those like me who are left to do the killing.*

*I was only a kid when I kicked the dust from that dead place off my boots. Though as I wandered the years, I could not separate myself from the home I forever hated. What I lost there so long ago, I refused to abandon.*

*After decades of searching, drifting, chancing and fighting, I'm closer to the truth than I've ever been. Now, on a train and rolling through the night, there is no choice. I'm heading back to the one place I never wanted to see again...*

*Karma City.*

Karma City

# Chapter 1

Jameson Shoals crouched to keep his balance atop the speeding train. The wind beat against his leather jacket, scattering his collar length, brunet hair over his eyes like a frayed, muddy rag. The scalding steam and smoke puffing from the locomotive singed his nostrils. Raising his shotgun at the attacker standing only a few feet away, he shouted, "You're in a real heap of shit, pal."

The man glared at Jameson, with blond hair framing his gaunt face like tendrils of fire. His spindly legs backed to the edge of the train car roof with unnatural balance. "You should consider your own life," he hissed. Amber light burned in the man's hollow, jack-o-lantern eyes. "Detonation is imminent."

Before Jameson could shoot, the man leapt from the train, flipping backward and vanishing into the night.

Jameson dropped back into the passenger car through the rooftop hatch, concerned only about the possible explosive aboard. He found his partner, Luna Briggs, tending to the guard who had been struck unconscious by the strange man moments before.

Luna tucked a tress of her auburn hair behind her ear and her sea-green eyes met Jameson's. "Did you get him?"

"He jumped."

"What?"

"Forget it. We've got bigger problems." Jameson hurried to where the assailant had been sitting and found a shoe-box sized package wedged under the seat. A line of thin wires trailed from a digital timer taped to the top. The timer flashed, warning that a minute and a half remained. *Dammit; I can't see where the wires are going, definitely not touching this.* Jameson drew in a breath of courage and called to Luna, "Get ready for an early departure. There's a bomb!"

"This train's heading to Karma City Station! There will be hundreds of people there. We've got to disarm it."

"Luna, we need to get out of here." Jameson ran up the narrow aisle, snatching their bags from the overhead rack.

The guard stirred. His eyes rolled and blood trickled from his forehead. Luna helped him sit up. "Listen to me," she said sharply. "Call for the engine to stop."

Jameson forced open the car's door and yelled over the train's grinding wheels. "Luna, let's go!" The wind grabbed at him. The train raced over a towering trestle spanning the East River. In the distance, a cluster of high-rises raked the stars. The Karma City skyline shined in the night. For Jameson, it felt like a lifetime had passed since he had seen the majesty of Karma, the city of hope. He snorted a wad of phlegm and hocked it over the blur of the rails. *Bullshit. The city is a lie.*

The guard lost consciousness again and slumped to his side. Luna took his rifle and bandoleer of rounds and slung them over her shoulder. She rushed to Jameson, gripping him tightly around the waist.

Jameson felt her trust as surely as he felt the sway of the train. He leaned, timing their escape with the approaching river. "Ready?"

Luna nodded.

He held her with all of his strength and jumped.

The train and trestle erupted in a fiery, deafening blast. The collapsing bridge, hurling twisted iron and burning planks, splashed into the river.

***

*Minutes Earlier*:

"You've been sitting there for two hours," said Donna. "Why don't you take a break?"

Leaning back in his chair, Jack Halligan rubbed his eyes. The window beside his desk trapped his reflection. His ruffled, coffee-brown hair curled at his ears and hung just enough into his eyes to be irritating. The scratchy stubble shadowing his face, made him look like a panhandler rather than Karma City's most beloved writer. He still wore a collared shirt, but these days he only buttoned it halfway and rolled up the sleeves. Jack didn't think his style careless; it was a lack of inspiration that made him ignore the hairbrush and ditch the iron. "It's hard to take a break when you haven't accomplished anything. I just can't think of anything to write." He pushed himself away from his desk, cursing his illness, and moved across the small living room to join Donna on the couch. "Has it really been two hours?"

"Yeah," Donna leaned in and kissed his cheek. "But I don't mind." Jack savored the way her soft curls of strawberry hair swept over his nose. Lingering behind the sweet, floral fragrance that all women seemed born with, there was the lively, maple-waffle aroma of the diner that paid her bills. "You should have something to eat. Refuel a bit." Donna insisted. She went to the small kitchen, opened Jack's refrigerator and gagged. "Something die in here?"

Jack chuckled. "I know, I know. My fridge smells."

"Yeah," agreed Donna, pinching her nose. "Like old shoes and armpits. How do you live like this?"

He snapped his fingers in excitement. "There's an idea! Karma City is like my fridge."

Covering her nose with the collar of her shirt, Donna searched for food. "Is there anything edible in here?"

"There should be half of a sub."

"Found it." Donna slammed the door and returned to the couch. She handed the wrapped sandwich to Jack. "Now what's this about Karma and your nasty refrigerator?"

"Every time I put groceries in there, they come out ruined. Never fails. Things spoil in the blink of an eye. It's like every newcomer to Karma. They always wind up infected with the Malady parasite."

"That's some comparison."

Jack tore away the wrapper and brought the sandwich up to bite. He paused.

"What's the matter?" Donna asked.

"I can't eat this. It smells like my fridge. You see what I'm talking about? It's a cursed destiny for any food item that finds its way to my kitchen. Just like the travelers who journey across the Void Lands to this dump. They think that by living in Karma and being closer to Oasis Hospital, they'll have a better chance at staying Malady free. And let's not forget Graves Enterprises, lording over the entire city with its mind-numbing street drug, making addicts out of entire neighborhoods! People need to understand that the odds of catching the parasite increase in the big city. Basically, they're doomed to a rotten life in this festering fridge of a city." Jack, now boiling with inspiration, carried his spoiled meal to the window near his desk.

"What are you going to do with the sandwich?"

"I'm putting it back in 'the fridge.'"

He pitched it out the window.

As if he had tossed a grenade, an explosion from the area of the East River lit up the night, rumbling the buildings. Even in Jack's sixteenth floor apartment, glasses rattled and dirty dishes fell from the counter, breaking on the floor. A fire raged in the distance.

Jack and Donna held each other as they watched the orange blaze fill the night sky with smoke that blotted out the stars.

"What's going on out there?" Donna whispered.

"I don't know, but I bet it's going to make a great story."

***

Cracking open his eyes and licking his dried lips, Jameson woke to soft lamplight warming the hospital room's eggshell walls. The medicinal air reeked of bleach and withering windowsill lilacs. His bed felt as though it pitched and yawed over rolling waters. His body ached. Images of the explosion flickered in his mind like photos scattered in the wind. *Luna!* The thought of the only person he cared for jolted him from the pillow.

"Easy does it," urged a cheerful voice beside Jameson.

A man with short black hair, curly and unkempt, sat at the bedside sifting through papers. He wore a white lab coat and brown slacks. His tie was pulled loose and his collar unbuttoned. Small glasses, smudged like the clear panels of a bus stop shelter, hung from the tip of his nose.

"Who are you?" Jameson asked. "Where am I? Where's Luna?"

"Oh, good. The three typical concerns patients have when they wake up: names, whereabouts and friends."

"Answer me."

The man stuffed his papers in a worn satchel. "I'm Dr. Albert Walker. You're safe in Oasis Hospital. Luna Briggs is fine. She's in the room across the hall."

*Oasis Hospital in Karma City. I've made it! Got to get Luna and press on.* Jameson sat up and tugged at the hospital gown. "Where are my clothes, doc?"

Albert tapped the face of his wrist watch.

"My clothes," Jameson snarled.

Albert pushed his glasses up the bridge of this nose then pointed to a closet. "Take it slow. You've been through a lot. You've got some bumps and bruises, but no serious injuries. Your body was worn out from whatever traveling you've been doing; needed sleep the most."

"My travels aren't over yet," grumbled Jameson. "What time is it?" He swung his legs over the edge of the hospital bed. The charts on the walls, surrounding furniture and Albert's face kaleidoscoped, almost forcing him back to his pillow.

"It's early, only five-thirty in the morning; Monday."

Jameson pushed away the delirium, yanked out the intravenous tubing from his arm, then staggered to the closet. To his surprise, his clothes were cleaned and mended. His traveling pack hung from a hook on the inner wall. He opened the flap and inventoried the contents. *Sawed-off shot gun, Void Land map, hacksaw, rope, flashlight, lighter, cigarettes, knife, ammunition...where is it?* He rummaged through the bag for the one possession he valued above every survival item and gave a short sigh when he found it along the bottom seam; a worn photo of his father. He closed his pack and turned to Albert. "Thanks for looking after me. Not sure how I'm going to pay the bill." He swung the bag over his shoulder.

"I don't think any of the others who survived the explosion are going to be able to pay," added Albert. "And I don't care if they do or don't to be honest."

"Others? No one else was on the train."

"There was a tent town under the bridge along the river bank. Dozens of homeless people infected with Malady. The blast killed quite a few and injured many. We've been caring for them in the Malady Ward. Blood tests are mandatory for admission to Oasis

Hospital. Oh, and if you're wondering, you tested negative for the parasite."

"I'm not surprised," said Jameson.

"What do you mean by that?"

"Forget it."

Albert glanced at his watch again. "Boss-lady won't be in for a while," he mumbled, then grinned at Jameson. "You seem well enough; time for me to split."

"Shift over?"

"Sure. I'll go with that."

Luna's combat boots clopped down the hallway. Jameson turned to see her leaning in the doorway. Her hair fell on her shoulders in rusty brown waves partially hiding the deep scaring that marred the right half of her face. The shoulder-strap of the black AR-15 rifle crossed over her bandoleer of rounds. A hardened woman turned mercenary, Luna had stolen Jameson's heart. Her beauty was like that of a wise lioness—deadly, commanding and alluring.

He trusted no one more than Luna Briggs. For ten long months, they traveled the Void Lands and left their mark on the smaller settlements beyond Karma. Few endeavored to drift through the lawless wasteland, but the purpose of Jameson's quest kept him moving and it was Luna who kept him alive. She was more to him than a defender and traveling companion of like mind. Luna inspired him to believe in the possibility of good and beautiful things.

"I heard your voice," Luna said to Jameson. "And thought you'd be hungry. Here," she tossed him a brown paper bag. "Egg sandwich. Eat up. It's terrible." She smiled, and the flash of those small dimples sent a current through him that quickened his heart.

"Thanks."

Albert rubbed his hands together. "I do hope you've enjoyed your stay in the loving care of Oasis Hospital. Now, if you'll excuse me, I really must be going."

Luna put up her hand and blocked the doorway.

Jameson tore into the paper bag and bit into the sandwich. He spoke with a full mouth. "You're going to help us out, doc. You

6

see," he paused to chew and swallow, "We've come a long way to get to Oasis Hospital." He waved the sandwich around as he spoke. "A personal errand of mine, actually. Take me to the records room."

"The records room? Why?"

"I want information on a patient from twenty years ago."

"Those files are confidential. That's a violation of hospital policy." He checked his watch and shifted his satchel under his arm. "But who cares. I'm going by there anyway. Let's make it quick. I don't have a lot of time."

Luna moved aside to let the doctor lead the way. "There's something off about you," she said. "What's going on?"

"Nothing. I work the graveyard shift and I need to punch out. That's all. Overtime is another violation of hospital policy, you understand."

"You're a bad liar."

Albert shrugged. "I get that a lot."

The rising morning sun lit the wide windows, beaming off the polished floor. Head still aching, Jameson squinted under the brightness as he and Luna followed Dr. Albert Walker down the busy corridors of Oasis.

"I've never been inside this hospital," remarked Luna to Jameson. "Probably the cleanest place I've ever seen."

"How about a tour, then?" Albert cracked a sarcastic smile. "I'll start with the layout of the district, but I'll skip the East River since you've already become so well acquainted with it."

"Glad to see you've got a sense of humor," she said. "You ought to try leaping off a bridge sometime."

Albert stiffened in response to her gritty tone. He cleared his throat. "Staff and patients are safe here. Oasis is walled off from the Void Lands to the north. It's big place, three wings, and there's herb gardens, willow trees, and lily ponds to help with emotional treatment. I'd avoid feeding the koi fish though; they're little assholes sometimes. Anyway, the hospital is revered for its advances in the prevention of Malady. Oasis also provides free screening for early detection of the micro-parasite."

"Dr. Carmen Victoria still calling the shots?" asked Jameson.

Albert raised a playful finger, "Hey, was that a pun? It was great. 'Calling the shots.' Nice one."

Jameson shook his head and let out a calming breath. The scatter-brained doctor was getting on his nerves. He and Luna followed Albert down the halls. Jameson counted the rights and lefts instinctively while Albert blabbered on, obviously enjoying his role of tour-guide.

"Speaking of shots," said Albert, "Dr. Victoria's most acclaimed achievement was the formulation of an inoculation called the Victory Vaccine. It works only in the uninfected and only provides protection against Malady for one year. Second doses are ineffective, as the human immune system then fails to recognize the parasite's antigens as foreign; regardless, the temporary defense gives people a chance to isolate themselves from the infected population to safeguard their wellness. The Victory Vaccine isn't a cure, but it gives hope."

Karma City residents honored Oasis Hospital but for Jameson, the facility conjured only heartache. He heard the distant murmur of an ill child crying and remembered his own cries of panic, just a boy, running down these very halls in terror and desperation.

Luna's hand slipped into his. She knew his struggle and understood his pain; hers was not so different. Luna's tender grip felt small yet powerful, restoring Jameson's confidence as if he held a loaded gun.

Doctors and hospital staff carried folders into patient rooms. One doctor took a moment to ridicule Albert as he passed. "The ASAM team is really excited to hear more about your crack-pot theory."

"Laugh it up," Albert barked. "You'll all be sorry when the name 'Walker' is credited for curing the world."

The rival doctor burst with laughter.

Jameson noticed Albert's shoulders collapse. "What was that about?" he asked.

"No one understands my work. Consequently, they view me as a fool."

"What's the 'ASAM' team?"

"It stands for Advanced Science Against Malady. It's Dr. Carmen Victoria's personal team of scientists. I gave a presentation yesterday and they laughed me out of the conference room. Bastards." Albert led them down a stairwell to the ground level. They entered another hallway and stopped at a door secured with a digital keypad and card reader. He swiped his security card and entered his access code on the keypad. The door clicked and opened. "The records room is all yours, but I'd be fast with your poking around. The security office is just down the hall and the guards will be making rounds soon."

Before entering, Jameson gave Albert an appreciative nod. "Thanks for the help and good luck with your work."

Stepping into the records room, Jameson and Luna froze in place when a shrieking alarm blared throughout the hospital. A recorded voice repeated an alert.

*"Malady Ward breached. Malady Ward breached. Hospital lock-down in three minutes."*

The door to the records room closed automatically.

Jameson spun to catch the closing door and saw Albert's boot wedging it open. "Hurry," urged the doctor. "We need to evacuate, or we'll be trapped in the hospital."

"Dammit!" Jameson's fist hammered the door frame. "Give me two minutes. I've come too far to turn back now."

Screams and gunfire sounded from the floor above.

"Whatever you're after," said Albert, "it may have to wait for another day."

"He's right, Jameson." Luna clicked a magazine of bullets into her rifle. "With shots firing, we must keep moving." Hooking her arm through his, she pulled him into the hall with Albert.

Guards poured out of the security office, sprinting up the stairs toward the chaos with weapons drawn. Their radios squawked with calls of hysteria and pleas for help. The warning message blared over the loudspeakers.

*"Malady Ward breached. Malady Ward breached. Hospital lock-down in two minutes."*

Albert shuffled down the hall. "Jameson, Luna, follow me. The exit is this way."

Jameson shook his head. "I'm going to see what's happening upstairs. Maybe I've still got time. Luna, go with Albert and get to safety."

Luna's eyes narrowed in defiance. "I'm with you."

The two ran for the security office.

Albert rolled his eyes. "Wait for me."

A row of large monitors spread over the guards' desk. On the screens, Jameson watched the fighting as the security cameras captured it. The Malady Ward patients attacked the security guards, doctors and hospital staff, biting, clawing, beating them with lengths of broken furniture and choking them to the ground with electrical cords. Jameson leaned closer to examine the carnage. People, wounded from the explosion and wrapped in bandages, acted out in fits of wild rage. Bodies of medical personnel lay strewn about the halls and common rooms. Blood stained the walls. Jameson watched as a wave of Oasis guards ran into the fight wearing ballistic vests and face masks, shooting down the frenzied patients and aiding the victims.

Albert adjusted his glasses, staring intently at the monitors. Astonishment rattled his voice. "In stage three of its lifecycle, the Malady parasite is known to elevate hostility, even make people dangerous, but this is highly abnormal."

"And look at the guy in the middle of it," said Jameson, tapping one of the screens, "the skinny punk with the blond hair."

"It's the man from the train!" Luna exclaimed.

"He's staring at the camera," added Albert.

*He's staring at me,* thought Jameson. *Who are you?*

The warning message resounded through the hospital, hardly audible over the deafening pandemonium.

*"Lock-down in one minute."*

Albert clutched his medical satchel. "Can we please leave? Further delay will render us maimed, infected, dead or all three in that order."

"Luna, cover us," ordered Jameson.

Luna's ruddy lips curled to a smile as she aimed her laser sights on the feral mob trampling into the hall. The wild-eyed patients swarmed and Luna's rifle became thunder and lightning. She dropped the infected horde one by one, but the advancing attackers climbed over the bodies.

Albert, Jameson and Luna reached the exit. The security key pad beside the door flashed red and blinked the words: Building Locked.

"We can't get out!" Albert shouted. He wiped his sweaty forehead with the end of his tie.

Jameson drove his elbow into the key pad, shattering the device. Sparks flew and wires crackled. "Stand back!" He kicked the door with his heavy boot, breaking the latch from the frame. They escaped through the door, running across the parking lot. Jameson looked back at the unending crowd of killers. Luna kept firing as they followed Albert to an ambulance parked behind a large dumpster. He opened the rear doors. "Get in!"

With Jameson and Luna secured, Albert scrambled into the driver's seat and locked the doors. The ambulance sped off, rumbling down the parkways of Wolfgang Commons, toward East Main Street. Dense trees with low hanging boughs lined the park's road and swayed in the morning wind. Rays of silver sunlight shone in shifting beams, turning the sprawling green campus into a strange, landscaped jungle. Jameson and Luna sat in the back of the ambulance, on the floor, backs pressed to the wall.

"I was so damn close, Luna," huffed Jameson in frustration. "I just needed two minutes in that records room and I'd have found it."

"Maybe," replied Luna. "But at what cost? I didn't see that battle coming. I mean, a hospital? Who would guess a deadly riot would break out? We're lucky we survived."

Jameson took her hand. "You're right. Did any of them—"

"I'm fine," she answered, appreciation tensing her lips. "We've been through far worse than that."

"True. But if that was a taste of what Karma's become since I left, we're going to need more ammo."

"I see that look in your eye, Jameson."

"What look?" he asked playfully. "Oh, you mean the one when I'm worried about Malady-heads infecting you?"

"Exactly. Like I said, I'm fine. I'm always fine," she reached up and touched the side of his stubbly face, "thanks to you."

Albert turned on the interior lights. The ambulance had been converted to an open concept, mobile chemistry laboratory complete with burners, graduated cylinders, volumetric flasks and various tubes set on tiered racks. Graphs and charts covered the walls and a whiteboard depicted endless equations that looked more like the scribbled runes of a madman than precise mathematics. The doctor glanced back over his shoulder. "Thanks for getting me to safety. I've seen a lot of Malady-induced outbursts, but that was a nightmare! If not for your shooting, Luna, I'd be mashed potatoes."

Luna smirked from the doctor's odd expression. "No problem. Interesting ride you've got here."

"It's been a," his pause exposed his search for a believable lie, "side-project of mine for a while."

"You stole it," said Luna dryly.

Albert banged the steering wheel. "Oasis owes me for the crap they've put me through."

"I don't care what you're up to," Jameson interjected. "As soon as the way is clear, you can drop us on the roadside."

"I'm not dropping you off anywhere on campus. You saw how violent those patients became. It's too dangerous."

"I'm not afraid of the infected."

"I've noticed," said Albert. "People who live like you are normally far into their sickness. The more I think on it," Albert glanced back again, this time with a suspicious eye, "it is highly unusual, and statistically improbable, for a Void Land drifter to be so healthy."

"Just good at dodging bullets, doc."

"Why don't we just head to my—holy crap!" Albert jerked the steering wheel. The ambulance screeched as it swerved, barely missing a mass of people running into the road. Jameson hunched over the passenger seat and peered through the windshield at the crowd. The man with the white-blond hair and fiery orange eyes led the pack.

"Follow him," Jameson ordered. "Don't let him get away!"

"Are you insane?"

"Do it, or I'm taking the wheel and you're walking."

Albert stomped the accelerator. The ambulance lurched forward, engine revving.

Jameson hung out of the passenger window with shotgun in hand. The man looked over his shoulder as he ran, grinning with defiance.

Jameson opened fire but his shot missed when the man sprang upward, rolled in the air, and landed back on his feet in full sprint. He ran faster, moving with surprising speed. Soon, he was far ahead. The ambulance raced to close in.

"I've seen him before," Albert said. "He's from Graves Enterprises. I'm sure of it."

The man stopped suddenly and faced the ambulance, standing still in the road with knees bent and fingers hooked like readied claws. Albert locked the brakes, skidding to a short stop. Jameson fired again but the assailant leapt into the air, bounding from the vehicle's hood to the high branches of an oak. In the cover of the knotting boughs, the orange-eyed man disappeared from Jameson's view. Jameson slammed his fists against the roof and called for Luna.

The ambulance's rear doors flung open. Luna Briggs stepped into the road with her rifle poised. Jameson watched her pan the surrounding trees with her scope. He whispered through gritted teeth, "We're going to get you."

"I see him!" Luna called. She fired and the bullet ripped through a tree branch. "Dammit!" She switched on her laser sight and swept the red beam over the canopy of leaves.

The tree-tops rustled.

Luna fired, missing again. "He's gone."

Jameson climbed out through the passenger window and joined Luna in the road. Seeing her frustration, he put his arm over her shoulders.

"I never miss," she said. "He vaulted from the branches about twenty feet up, dropped to the ground, and then rolled out of view! I've never seen a person move like that."

"Where did he go?"

Luna pointed to a steep embankment that sloped to a muddy culvert. "Down there, into the storm drain."

Jameson dropped two shells into his shotgun and slid down the muddy hill, hurrying for the drain pipe. Luna followed.

Chasing after them, Albert called, "Where are you two going?"

Jameson didn't look back. "Hunting."

# Chapter 2

At the twenty-four-hour Greely Park Diner, Jack Halligan slid into his booth by the window, where he could watch the people of Karma City carrying on as best they could. A mother pulled her child away from a homeless man who crouched on the curb, coughing into gloved hands once outstretched for handouts. Another man in a suit and overcoat waited at the bus stop with a newspaper under his arm. He gave up his spot under the glass shelter so the woman and child could escape the cold wind. The man turned up his collar, shivering as the cars streaked by, blowing up litter on swirls of smoky exhaust. A smile passed between the man and woman. The bus arrived and collected the three, leaving the shelter free for the homeless man to claim for his camp. Jack knew the beggar would be there a long time. Days. Weeks. He would die there.

In the diner, a different world existed. A kinder world. Jack inhaled the comforting smell of stale, midday donuts and burnt home fries. *The smells of a new day*. Being a writer, the little details of city life—the scents, contrasts, and comparisons— colored the world around him. Then his eyes moved around the diner, examining the people. He counted a dozen new faces. Some looked tired and troubled while others stared into space, lost in their drug induced lethargy. *They're sick. Everyone's sick.* Still, there remained a positive energy in the diner and for Jack, that was the detail that mattered most.

The migration to Karma City became more apparent as newcomers took up residence throughout; the numbers often crowding once quiet pockets of town like Jack's community in central Karma, Greely Park. He shrugged. *Good for business, I suppose. But they just don't understand. There's no cure in Karma City.*

Jack poured cream into his coffee, watching tiny white clouds bloom like a brewing storm Listening to the patrons in the booth behind him gossip about the explosion, the destruction of the East River trestle and the horrendous murders at Oasis Hospital, Jack felt disturbed. Such violence at Oasis Hospital wasn't possible. Nowhere else in Karma City did a more peaceful place exist. And Jack knew that Dr. Carmen Victoria, passionate and dedicated to the people, must surely be grieving.

Donna came to his booth and gave him a hug. "Morning, Hun."

For a moment, Jack got lost in Donna's simple beauty. Her blue apron hugged her slender waist and her silky, red hair fell in loose curls around her rosy cheeks. Her almond-shaped hazel eyes warmed him more than any cup of coffee could ever do.

"Your new article is in print today," Donna said proudly, handing him a wrinkled copy of the day's paper. "The new folks have been chatting about it. They're finding it really helpful."

"That's good. Because when I pitched the concept to my editor, she was reluctant at first. I explained to her that while Malady is widely understood in Karma City, all the newcomers from the Void Lands either don't know how severe the sickness really is, or their present sickness is degrading their memory of it. I'm glad if my writing helps them."

"You do important work."

"So do you, Donna. You lift spirits. An almost impossible feat in this world."

The bells on the diner door jangled; a group of customers entered. "Guess the rush is starting," said Donna. "The usual today, Hun?"

Jack smiled. "Heck, yeah! But I'd like extra bacon, please."

She gave him a kiss and left to put in his order.

No other woman in the city compared to Donna Lynne. For seven years, Jack came to the Greely Park Diner for breakfast and every morning, Donna made sure a clean booth waited for him. He was her favorite writer and she enjoyed his articles in the *Karma Daily*. Jack enjoyed bouncing ideas off her and found her witty intelligence inspiring and motivational. What could possibly be better than starting the day with a great meal and in the company of this radiant, intelligent woman? Watching her greet the customers, serve their breakfast and refill their coffee, he counted the smiles she created.

Donna had a way with people that few could duplicate but all could appreciate. So many people outside the diner suffered with varying stages of the parasite. But Donna didn't keep count. She didn't care. At Greely Park Diner, people got the kindest service, the best food and most importantly, they got to forget about the microscopic worm inhabiting them, even if only for a little while. That's what Donna did for Jack, and that's why he loved her.

Jack unfolded the newspaper. His article covering the Malady pandemic made the front page.

*"Welcome to Town. Don't Get Sick"*
*By: Jack Halligan*

*A recent wave of inbound travelers has filled the already crowded streets with new faces, new hopes and likewise, new heartbreak. Natives of the Void Lands flock in caravans to Karma City, the brightest of the remaining big cities, believing this place to be a shining pillar of wellness only to crash against the horrific truth that there is no cure against the microscopic parasite called "Malady." The real tragedy is that many people do not understand the terms of their infection. For the parasite, this is just fine. Read on if you think you're ill, or if your sickness has made you forget.*

*Humans are the obligate host of this invading micro-worm. From the brain cavity, Malady affects a person in three stages. The larval stage brings the night terrors. The pupal stage brings memory lapse. I've just entered this stage. My memories are falling into a strange fog. During the third stage, adulthood, the host suffers from a serious and deadly depression. The three stages combined equal insanity.*

*Malady makes a monster of us all, but the parasite doesn't kill us. It's the effects of the parasitic lifecycle that render so many dead. One might get so tired from sleepless nights that he falls down the stairs. Another might forget to eat for weeks and starve to death. I once reported on a woman who became so paranoid in line at the store, that she turned on the man standing behind her and dug out his eyes with her nails. Bottom line: you can't live with Malady because Malady won't let you.*

*Over the near century of its known existence, Malady has caused the degradation of the human condition, collapsing cities far and wide, and turning neighborhoods to graveyards. Our world is one of lawlessness, chaos and crime. To every newcomer reading this, remember that infection is only one threat out there. STAY SAFE. I hope you enjoy your visit to the city, but I think you'll find that Karma's a bitch*

Donna brought a steaming plate of eggs, sausage and extra bacon.

"Thank you," said Jack. "Smells great."

"You look a bit distracted. Things okay?"

"Didn't sleep very well. That damn nightmare again."

Donna sat in the booth across from him and clasped her hands over his. "The one of your father?"

"Yes. Hard to believe he's been dead for almost twenty years."

"You were seventeen when he died. That's hardly old enough to understand, or accept, how sick he was," assured Donna. "His death was an accident. It wasn't your fault."

"I keep telling myself that." *But he wouldn't have gotten sick had I just listened to him.* Jack buried his father, but not the guilt. He often wondered if his own infection was his punishment. He took a bite from a strip of bacon. "You know what the most frightening part of the nightmare is?"

Donna shook her head.

"When I wake up, I can smell his cologne throughout the apartment."

\*\*\*

18

The white beam of Jameson's flashlight illuminated the twisting drain tunnel. The light bounced from the line of water coursing between his steps, sending eerie shadows up the curved, stone walls. He sorted through the unending jumble of echoes. The far-off rush of the subway and the moaning of the infected were bonded by the steady drip-drop of water—a sound that haunted as much as it soothed, like rusted bells and broken chimes.

"The risk of infection is moderate to severe down here," professed Albert. "I have gloves and masks if you'd like."

"I don't worry about Malady," stated Jameson matter-of-factly.

"I know you're not infected, but why so careless?"

"Not sure why you're following us."

"The man you're after, I've seen that man at medical conferences. He's one of Dr. Marcus Graves' lead researchers. Elliot Burroughs. He had some kind of influence on the Malady infected at Oasis. Scientifically speaking, this could lead to some profound discoveries. What's your interest in him?"

"He blew up the train," Luna added. "Even though I'm former Iron Tribe, I can't let him get away with that."

"I suspected you were a tribeswoman from the burn scars on your face," attested Albert.

Though the degradation in society perpetuated by the Malady parasite crippled advancements in industry and commerce, coal mining prevailed in the mountains and parts beyond Karma City, producing abundant fuel for steam engines and thermal power plants. As a result, the railroad had become the people's last lifeline. Two 4-8-4 steam locomotives, antiquated yet reliable engines, wheeled along cardinal tracks transporting people, medicine and goods back and forth from Karma, Rime, Lobos and many other unnamed stops in the endless Void Lands. The masters of these locomotives were the rifle-bearing men and women sworn to a life on the tracks— the cold-hearted, Iron Tribe. For them, nothing mattered more than the preservation of the monstrous "Mother Train" and her vast railway that carved the city and the lands beyond.

Though the Iron Tribe paid little attention to the affairs of the world beyond the tracks, they understood the value of the people as it related to their lifestyle. One only needed a ticket to board and the tribal guards would lower their weapons. Attacking the train or rails, however, meant death. Luna Briggs felt the old pride of the railway ignite her desire to bring the glowing-eyed man down for his crimes.

"What about you, Jameson?" asked Albert. "Why are you chasing this guy?"

Jameson ducked to avoid a low hanging pipe. "Not only did he almost kill us on the train, but that asshole ruined my chance at the Oasis records." He aimed his light so the others could avoid the pipe.

"Whose records were you looking for?"

"My dad's. Hold it..." Jameson put up his hand and stopped their trek. "I hear voices ahead."

Following the drain tunnel, they discovered a domed catacomb serving as an intersection for the various drainage channels of the city. Pipes, valves, and iron ladders lined the room. A group of homeless people huddled within the orange circle of a crackling trashcan fire, coughing and twitching. The scent of urine and body odor soured Jameson's nose. Despite the stench, other indicators warned of greater danger. Life in the Void Lands had given him the skill to spot the parasite in others. Malady revealed itself to Jameson in a number of ways: a haze in the eyes, hanging lower lip, a bouncing eyelid, fidgeting hands, nervous feet and jumpy knees. The worst was the boiling, blood-shot eyes that foretold violence. He pointed his flashlight at the group. The caged animal stare glared back at him. *They're all infected.*

Jameson warned Luna and Albert. "Those people are dangerous. Malady."

Luna stepped forward, calling out, "Hey! Any of you see a guy with blond hair come this way?"

A weathered old woman in a tattered gray mantle swayed over the fire, rubbing her hands near the flames. "Stop shouting, girl!" she croaked. "I hate your irritating echo."

"Answer the question and we'll be on our way," ordered Luna.

The hunch-backed woman slinked closer. She looked like a witch with snakes of hair clinging to her greasy, sallow skin. "Why should I answer you?" Her finger pointed like a threatening dagger of bone. "Leave me alone or you'll be sorry."

Jameson rolled his eyes and drew his shotgun. "Last chance, bitch."

Albert shuffled forward, waving for Jameson to lower his weapon. "Let me handle this," he pleaded.

"You're unarmed, doc."

"There's a better way." Albert addressed the woman. "Hello, ma'am. I'm a doctor and I notice that you're quite sick." He knelt down and opened his medical bag to reveal a small brown vial. "I've got some Quell. Trade you for a little information?"

Her eyes widened. "Quell, you say?" The others around the fire murmured in excitement.

"Yes. With the Graves Enterprises tamper seal intact. This is an un-opened, two-week supply. There's enough here to make you all feel better."

She hobbled over to Albert, who took a step back. "With all due respect, ma'am, that's close enough. I'm not infected, but I'd still like to help you." He placed the pill bottle on the ground and rolled it to her. She pounced for it and pried open the cap with her teeth. Albert pressed, "Your turn to help me. Did you see the man we're looking for?"

"Yes."

"Did he go up to the street?"

"No." She sat down and poured the small pills into her dirty palm. Her tree bark lips cracked when she sang, "Down, down to Undertown, where everyone is sick. Down, down to Undertown, the parasitic trick!" The old woman broke into a cackle. The others from around the fire swarmed her like hungry dogs, clamoring for the one medication that would relieve their suffering.

Jameson tugged Albert back. "Nice work," he said. "She probably would have jumped us and I would have had to shoot her. You might be handy to have around after all."

Albert pushed up his glasses. "There's always a better way, Jameson. And it's what makes us better people."

Jameson lit the dark throat of the tunnel with his flashlight. "Let's move."

21

The passage to Undertown sloped downward; the current of water flowing over the toes of Jameson's boots. As the group ventured below the surface of Karma City, the glow of artificial lights intensified, illuminating the entire passage. The dreary resonances of the drain system stirred to a clamor of shouts, laughter and jeers as they drew near the subterranean community. Jameson stopped short as the tunnel came to an abrupt end. The line of water he followed poured over the edge, raining down to a basin nearly thirty feet below. A vast stone chamber opened before him.

Undertown, a thriving city beneath the city, rooted itself around Karma's central subway station. The commuter trains rumbled the dozens of halls, tunnels and antechambers that stemmed from the station. Sparks sprayed from the electrified rails, parting the blackness of the tunnels. Leaning over the edge, Jameson found an iron ladder mounted to the stone wall. He signaled the others to follow.

After a slow descent, the three crossed a walkway spanning a drainage canal and entered the main thoroughfare. Businesses lined the common way. Workshops, salvage dealers, drug dens, brothels, gambling halls and hostels all advertised their services with bright signage and taunting workers. Jameson eyed a large mural painted over the damp brick wall. A depiction of Dr. Marcus Graves, founder of Graves Enterprises, stared back at passersby. His midnight black hair combed back above his flat forehead. The sharp nose, boney jaw and gull-white skin rendered thoughts of skeletons and vampires. The mural celebrated Dr. Graves with looping lettering framing the portrait, reading: Peace in the Mind—the Father of Quell.

"Outta the way, loser!" shouted a young man from behind.

Jameson side-stepped, quickly dodging the kid as he whizzed by on a skateboard. Jameson's temper flared and even though his nomadic life had taken him through plenty of strange settlements in the Void Lands, he struggled to understand what would tempt people to live like rats in a world of sewers and subways. Undertown's filth seemed immeasurable. Men and women enjoyed one another in dark alleys, while addicts indulged under the flickering light of the suspended lamps. The smell of human waste and mold permeated from the gutters.

Weaving through the crowds, Jameson and Luna asked the denizens of Undertown if any had seen the man they hunted. No one offered any information.

"This place is revolting." Jameson covered his nose with his shirt collar.

"I hear the Void Lands aren't very pleasant, either," stated Albert.

"At least there's open air out there. I feel like I'm walking in a giant toilet bowl."

"It's not so bad," replied Albert. "My new medical practice isn't far."

"You set up shop down here?"

"That's right. I opened for business not long ago and I just completed the assembly of the DNA sequencer I *purchased* from Oasis. It's marvelous and if you'd like to see it, I'd be—"

"First," interrupted Jameson, "tell me why you think it's a good idea to work in the Malady infested bowls of Karma City."

"I figure the best way to combat Malady is to surround myself with it."

Jameson gave a short laugh. "I get it. You were going to quit back at Oasis before all hell broke out. You've become a disgruntled thief and you only stuck around long enough to *acquire* the tech you needed for your lab. Am I right?"

"That about sums it up. But hold on a second, take a look around. This is a true parasite breeding ground. Everyone living beneath the streets of Karma City is infected and nearly all of them are Quell addicts. The world above can't care for them, treat them or be bothered to offer any empathy at all. There's no brotherhood of man in Karma City. If you're not infected, you shun those who are. If you are infected, you try to hide it, cope, or refuse to accept it. Time runs out for people above. And when it does, Undertown greets them with open arms. It's where they find me, ready to offer the care they can't get up there."

"You're nuts, doc. Have you had yourself tested for Malady?"

"I've been inoculated with the Victory Vaccine. That'll give me a full year to complete my work down here without risk of infection."

"I'm still not sold on your choice of real estate."

"One thing is certain," Albert professed, "there will never be a shortage of patients. Which presents countless opportunities for me test my theory."

"Fine, I'll bite. What is this theory of yours?" Jameson asked.

Albert fanned his hands in the air as if reading a billboard. "Malady-born."

"What the hell does that mean?"

He cleared his throat and adjusted his glasses. "I believe that the ASAM team and the scientists at Graves Enterprises have been unsuccessful in discovering a cure for Malady because they've been looking in the wrong place. The answer to finding a cure is not here in Karma City among its infected; it can't be. Malady thrives in Karma. Scientific efforts must branch out to the Void Lands and focus on the people who are born out there, born from infected people."

"I don't get it."

Albert raised a finger to accentuate his words. "What genetic information is hiding in the DNA of a baby conceived in a Malady infected woman?"

"I don't know."

"Exactly, no one does. My theory of 'Malady-born' proposes that there may be a genetic link occurring in the genome. Imagine a gene that is both parasite *and* human. If this Malady- born gene exists, I believe it can be the foundation for a cure."

"And how would this cure work?"

Albert paused and admitted, "I'm not there yet."

"Then why aren't you going on a trip across the Void Lands doing blood tests on kids?"

"It's not that easy. I don't think entering a hostile village and knocking on doors with needles will go over well. I'm safer down here, in Undertown. And I'm making progress. I've found that rodents and other paratenic hosts infected with the parasite sometimes produce offspring that resist Malady infection. And I bet the same thing is happening now, in people. It's groundbreaking stuff, Jameson."

"Okay, so you're hanging with Malady-heads and addicts in Karma's sewer-world and performing genetic testing on baby rats all in the hopes of saving humanity?"

Albert asked Luna, "Is he always such a jerk?"

Luna shrugged and fought the urge to laugh.

"Is this what you told the Oasis staff?" Jameson asked.

"Yes."

Jameson chuckled. "I see why you don't fit in."

"I'll tell you why I don't fit in, Jameson," Albert's face reddened. "Unlike the scientists of Oasis Hospital and Graves Enterprises, I have the gumption and courage to breach the boundaries of modern medicine to uncover the treatments these people so desperately yearn for. I, in so short a time, have become a practitioner of forward thinking, a scientific vanguard, a medical pioneer!"

Jameson glanced at Luna, who rolled her eyes. "Since you're so forward thinking," Jameson challenged, "answer me this, if you were a nut-job with glowing eyes that makes infected people go berserk, what would you be doing in Undertown?"

Albert waved a mocking hand. "Simple. I'd be trying to catch a commuter to gain as much distance between myself and those hunting me with guns."

Jameson grinned and slapped Albert on the shoulder. "That's it! Where's the next subway train leaving from?"

"Let's see..." Albert rubbed his shoulder and checked his watch. "Morning commute is running. Almost eight-thirty; the next outbound is leaving from Aces Wild Rock Club."

"Perfect. Lead the way."

Albert's brow dipped in worry. "Did you say *glowing* eyes?"

# Chapter 3

The stage fog and cigarette smoke melded to a purple haze over the crowd. Guest tables lined the large dance floor, where the rebellious and wild youth of Undertown stomped and fist-pumped to the electric music blaring from stacked speaker cabinets.

Jameson and Albert leaned against the bar while Luna took position further into the room. Jameson scanned the mosaic of people, searching for their evader. Albert's nerves made him fidget and ramble. "Based on what we've witnessed in Oasis Hospital," said Albert, "it's appropriate to assume that we're in a great amount of danger right now. Almost everyone in this establishment is infected with Malady. The man we're after seems to spark violence in the infected. The infected attack the uninfected. My surmounting concern stems largely from our present—"

"Shut up." Jameson cut off Albert, seeing Luna's hand signal. "Wait here and keep watch." Brushing passed Albert, Jameson cut through the crowd, joining Luna at the far wall.

Luna pointed to a row of cocktail tables lining the dance floor. "That's him. Second table from the left."

"How's your line of fire? Can you take his head off his shoulders right now?"

"For sure, and normally, I'd go for it. But twice we've attempted to shoot him down, and twice we've failed."

"Don't tell me you want to talk to him."

Luna smiled. "I don't. I want *you* to. Try it Albert's way. If that fails, I'll blow his head off."

"Deal."

As Jameson approached the man's table, he assessed his adversary by looking for unusual body contours or bulges under the clothing—indicators that might warn of hidden weapons or explosives. The man wore a long black coat that Jameson now recognized as a lab coat with the sleeves rolled up his forearms. His white collared shirt and black slacks were tattered and stained with droplets of blood. Jameson leaned on the table. "Mind if I join you?"

The man's eyes met Jameson's with an unflinching stare. He motioned for Jameson to sit across from him. For a long minute, the two men said nothing. They stared at one another like two boxers resting in their respective corners between rounds. The man broke the tension.

"I find it amusing that you've followed me," he said. "Though, I must insist that you make this confrontation quick, you see."

"Oh, I'm sorry," said Jameson smugly. "Got another train to bomb? Or maybe you're off to start another riot."

"Your interruption in my affairs will lead to dire consequences."

"It very well might." Jameson pointed to Luna, who waited behind the man.

Luna pressed her rifle's muzzle to the back of the man's head. "You're out-numbered," she said. "And I can't miss this time."

"Out-numbered?" The man laughed. "I could turn this nightclub on you with a single thought. They'd rip into you like ravenous wolves."

Jameson pretended not to hear the dark threat. "Who are you?"

"The easy answer is, you're looking at Elliot Burroughs."

"Why did you blow up the train?"

"To destroy the Lessers."

"The *what*?"

A sudden scream from a nearby club guest interrupted the confrontation. "Somebody help! That woman's gonna murder that man! Stop her!"

A large man leapt behind Luna and wrapped his arms around her chest, pulling her away from Burroughs.

Burroughs' eyes flashed with orange light. "Looks like we're done here." He overturned the table, sending it crashing atop Jameson, then darted into the crowd.

Jameson shoved away the toppled furniture, drew his shotgun and fought the man off of Luna, knocking him hard in the face with the gunstock. The man dropped to the floor, blood flowing in black streams from his crushed nose. Albert rejoined Jameson.

27

"Saw the whole thing," declared Albert. "Burroughs is heading toward the back exit, to the subway dock.

The crowd of club-goers broke into a panic at the sight of Jameson and Luna standing with firearms drawn. They peeled away in fear, allowing Jameson a path to pursue Burroughs. He waved for Albert and Luna to follow. The three ran through the panicked mob and pushed past the exit door, stepping into the subway corridor.

Jameson slid to a halt, holding the others back, when he encountered roughly twenty people slouching in torpor against the walls. Some rocked back and forth, mumbling. Others stared at their feet, heads drooped between their knees. "This hall is filled with the infected. Get ready."

Burroughs slithered down the hall, touching the shoulders of the listless citizens as he passed. He looked back at Jameson with fiery eyes. "Like ravenous wolves!" At once, the infected sprang to their feet. Burroughs pointed at Jameson, Luna and Albert. "They are Lessers. Kill them!" he commanded.

The Malady warped crowd charged down the hall with rage contorting their faces. Their cries for bloodshed echoed with the grind of an approaching train. Burroughs continued toward the subway platform.

Shotgun clenched, Jameson rushed the attackers head-on. He unloaded with a menacing blast radius, dropping two men with deafening shots. The spraying blood misted on his forearms. A frenzied man trampled over the bodies then leapt for Jameson's gun. Jameson swung the weapon around, clubbing the man in the mouth, caving in his jaw. Broken teeth became shrapnel, streaking out in all directions. Another hard hit to the throat collapsed the infected man, reducing him to a gurgling husk, frothing in a ball on the ground. Jameson pressed on, beating down several more of Undertown's malady-crazed vagrants.

The subway tunnel amplified the boom of Luna's rifle, turning the fearsome thunderstorm of bullets into a seismic eruption. Her trigger finger showed no mercy. Skulls burst like balloons. Bodies fell in contorted piles, granting Jameson further passage toward the enemy.

As Jameson chased Burroughs to the platform, the on-coming train's headlights pushed away the darkness of the tunnel.

Burroughs faced Jameson, his back to the tracks, fists like stone cudgels. The two stood mere steps from one another. Burroughs sniffed the air long and deep. "How strange," he said. "You are not like the rest."

Dropping two cartridges into his shotgun, Jameson readied for the kill. "I don't know what you're talking about." He aimed his weapon. "And I don't really care."

Burroughs vaulted into a handspring, wheel-kicking the shotgun from Jameson's grip. Jameson staggered from the force of the blow. Burroughs lunged onto Jameson's back, wrapping his arms around his throat. "You are not Lesser," snarled Burroughs, choking away Jameson's breath. "But you are not greater. Die!"

Jameson fought to peel this mysterious creature from his back. The boney arms clamping over his neck felt like iron bars. His head throbbed, darkening his vision. He fell to his knees, feeling his consciousness slipping away.

The subway screeched to a halt. The doors burst open. Men and women in long red coats swarmed the platform with pistols drawn. Jameson looked on, eyes blurring in and out of focus.

The apparent leader, a bald man in black sunglasses, pointed at Burroughs and ordered his men, "Shoot him!"

Gunfire broke out, illuminating the subway dock with bright flashes. A bullet ripped through Burroughs' coat sleeve, tearing his arm and breaking his grip on Jameson. Burroughs snarled and dove behind a support pillar. Jameson wheezed for air, watching Burroughs climb the pillar like a spider to the vaulted ceiling. *What the hell is he?*

The gunmen in red switched on flashlights, panning the cluttered apex of conduit, cables, ducts and pipes knotting overhead. Burroughs disappeared among the darkness of the underground.

"He's gone, sir," called one of the women. "But I hit him."

"Son of a bitch!" cursed the leader.

Jameson rubbed his throat. The gunfire had ended and Jameson watched Luna and the group of scarlet-clad soldiers scanning the defeated mob for movement; all were dead, but Albert emerged from the corridor, face white-washed from fear. Blood staining his clothes.

Luna took to Jameson's side and turned her rifle on the lead soldier in red. "Who are you?"

The man holstered his pistol and removed his sunglasses. "I'm Kurt Auger." He pointed to the four women and three men behind him. "This is my team of urban hunters."

Jameson rolled his eyes. *Another band of Malady hunters that will only end up dead like all the rest.* He'd encountered many of this kind as a young drifter hiking Route 88, the single highway stretching east and west across the Void Lands, disappearing over each horizon. Much like the railroad of the Iron Tribe, Route 88 served as the unbreakable thread holding the tapestry of fallen cities, deteriorated towns and ramshackle camps together throughout the Void Lands. "The Strange Highway," as Void Landers called it, became his guide as he searched for any clues about his missing father. The only thing to be found was Malady in all forms and in all the people of the Void Lands. Teams of hunters, prospectors, scavengers and raiders crossed Jameson's path more times than he could count and, because of his rough and merciless appearance, they seldom accosted him and often invited him to share their journey. He'd accept, seeing it more as an opportunity to learn of new dangers to avoid, new resources to obtain and most importantly, new places where his father might have gone.

The unions never lasted. The raiders would strike a camp of infected and go crazy from the worm. The scavengers would find an abandoned general store filled with contaminated goods and they'd go mad with Malady. The prospectors would swear that their maps had led them to 'the spot,' usually a forgotten suburb off the highway with extravagant homes filled with valuables left behind by Malady infected families. The parasite waited and it claimed them all. All but Jameson.

"Hunters, huh," said Jameson, his flat tone conveying his indifference. "Looks like we're after the same game. Glad you and your crew showed up when you did." He introduced himself and the others. "What do you know about Elliot Burroughs?"

"You're chasing this monster uneducated?" Kurt's forehead wrinkled in surprise.

"We're," he paused to cough, "learning as we go."

"First off," said Kurt, "That's not Elliot Burroughs. Not anymore. The thing that nearly killed you is the product of Dr. Marcus Graves' undisclosed genetic experiment, Project GEMNI. And that's what it calls itself—Gemni."

The subway chimed, indicating that the doors were about to close. Kurt signaled his crew to get back on. He put on his sunglasses and handed Jameson a white card with an address stamped in black ink. "Listen up, Shoals. If you plan to continue your pursuit of Gemni, I suggest you visit Professor Anthony Crimm at his home in Karma's lower east side. Tell the professor that *his sons* sent you."

Jameson watched the group in dark red trench coats board the subway train. The commuter pulled away, rattling along its electric rails and vanishing into the black tunnel.

Luna nudged Jameson. "Don't leave your shotgun lying around."

"Right." He returned to the area of his struggle with Burroughs and picked up his fallen weapon. A glimmer on the floor caught his eye. *Blood, and not mine. Has to be Gemni's.* "Hey doc, take a look."

Albert joined Jameson and stooped over the blood drops. He opened his satchel, put on some gloves, and produced a vial of what Jameson thought was blue ink. Albert dabbed at the blood with a cotton ball and administered a few drops of the liquid to the sample. The ink-like solution immediately effervesced and steamed. He threw the sample to the ground and took a quick step back.

Jameson rubbed the bridge of his nose in frustration. "What did you just do, and am I going to regret that I asked?"

"To answer your first question, I just applied a chemical agent, formulated by myself I'd like to add, that reacts to the presence of Malady in all stages of its lifecycle."

"That's damn impressive."

"As for your second question, while I don't know you well enough yet, your behavioral patterns indicate that what I'm about to tell you may...well, piss you off."

"Great," grumbled Jameson. "Just tell me what's wrong with that freak's blood."

Albert cleared his throat. "When we consider protein signatures, the baseline of detection directly correlates to—"

Jameson put up his hand. "Spare me the scientific presentation. Talk straight."

"Sorry. Here's the thing, my agent is only supposed to fizz. It nearly caught fire when I applied it to the sample. Whatever foreign body is in this blood is very potent. It's almost as if it's *more* than Malady." Albert dabbed another blood drop. He slipped the sample into a small plastic bag and tucked it in his satchel.

"If it's more than Malady, it's worse than Malady," asserted Jameson.

Luna put her hand on Jameson's shoulder to ground him. "Albert, have you heard of Project GEMNI?" she asked.

"No."

Jameson took another look at Kurt Auger's business card, and then stuffed it in his pocket. "You said you have a place in Undertown. Is it safe?"

"My medical center has clean beds, hot showers, and a cabinet stocked with munchies if that's what you're looking for?"

"Good. Let's get some rest and then we'll see what we can learn from this Professor Crimm guy."

***

Sitting at his kitchen table, Jack stirred his coffee while proof-reading his newest article.

Donna sat across from him, carefully painting chocolate icing onto a cake. "I don't want you cutting into this until your birthday."

Jack didn't respond.

"Hello?"

He looked up from his notebook. "Oh, sorry. The cake looks delicious, Donna. Thank you!" He reached his index finger toward the rim of icing. Donna slapped it away.

"Not until your birthday!"

Jack gave a playful pout and went back to reading his article.

*"Checking the Future"*
*By: Jack Halligan*

*Extraordinary news for the uninfected population! To strengthen Malady awareness, Dr. Carmen Victoria, of Oasis Hospital, has created what she simply calls "Checkers." A Checker is a small baggie that comes with a dropper filled with a tasteless agent and a tiny pouch of powder, no bigger than a salt packet. I had the pleasure of meeting with Dr. Victoria to discuss this breakthrough. She had this to say, "Test your food with the powder and drinks with the dropper. Any effervescence indicates parasitic contamination. I've devoted an entire wing of the Oasis Campus to the production and distribution of these consumables."*

*Being able to screen food and drink is a landmark turn for the better for residents of Karma City and parts beyond. Dr. Victoria's commitment to the people remains unshakable, and her personal struggles remain her guide. Here's a look into her past.*

*Dr. Carmen Victoria and her late husband, Wolfgang, were the leading scientists of Oasis Hospital specializing in methods for early detection and prevention. Dr. Marcus Graves' mastery of genetic sciences led him to join the Victoria's. The three doctors formulated the first temporary inoculation against Malady, The Victory Vaccine. This inoculation was only partially effective, but Karma City clung to hope; many believed the three doctors were close to a cure.*

*Goals and motivations collided. Graves felt that if they perfected the vaccine, it should be given only to deserving individuals to better society. The Victoria's felt everyone should receive it. Graves*

34

*decided to further his work independently. Wolfgang and Graves fought over two specimen vials and during the struggle, Wolfgang became infected. Graves severed his relationship with the Victoria's and shortly after, Wolfgang died from his infection.*

*Graves took ownership of a black high-rise on the western side of the city and named it Sable Tower. There, he established Graves Enterprises and formulated "Quell," the only drug of its kind capable of quieting the adverse effects of Malady. With the sick finally able to find respite, Dr. Marcus Graves had achieved what many have called a miracle.*

*Today, Oasis Hospital is still dedicated to wellness, prevention and sciences against Malady. Dr. Victoria's final comment for this article is, "If you aren't sick, visit Oasis and receive your temporary inoculation. Use the time it provides to move away from crowded places and establish a clean lifestyle. Stock up on Checkers and be safe."*

Donna opened Jack's refrigerator, then slammed it shut. "I'll keep your cake fresh at the diner until your birthday."

Jack laughed. "Good idea."

"How's the article, Hun?"

"Not bad. I just want people to understand what this city can and can't offer. I really wish I could have written about how addicting Quell is and how half the city is dependent on it. Editor warned against it."

"Graves Enterprises is helping families, Jack. People get a shot at living normal lives on Quell. There's a positive side to everything."

"Graves has Karma City in the palm of his hand. He owns the entire west side, collects monthly dues from registered Quell users citywide, and he's even got the Iron Tribe moving his medicine into the Void Lands by freight train. Let's not forget that massive vessel anchored off shore that no one seems to know anything about. It's a shame that good people suffering with infection have to sell their souls to Graves Enterprises for a batch of pills that don't even kill the parasite."

"I understand your point, Hun. But imagine how much worse this city would be if we didn't have Quell to manage the symptoms. Karma City couldn't last. At the very least, think of the kids. Many of them take Quell with their morning vitamins. Without it, they'd be...well..."

"You know, just last week I saw a bunch of kids peddling the stuff. Quell has become a form of currency in some sections of town. What frustrates me is that Marcus Graves is a genius. If he can manipulate the condition of the Malady parasite, then he's got to know how to kill it. I believe he's keeping people sick to keep them well. And through addiction, the people of Karma belong to him."

*You should worry about yourself, Jack.*

Jack locked his eyes on Donna's. "What did you say?"

"I didn't say anything."

"I thought I heard you say I should worry about myself."

"I wouldn't say a thing like that."

"I know you wouldn't." He shook his head and reached for his mug of coffee but accidently knocked it over. The hot drink spilled across his papers, splashed on his shirt and poured onto his lap. "Son of a—"

Donna snatched a dish towel and swooped in. "I've got this. Leave your papers and go clean up. I'll fix another cup for you when you get back."

Jack entered the small bathroom and peeled off his shirt. He closed the door and pulled a pair of dry pants from a hanging rack. As he changed out of his coffee-soaked clothes, a knock drummed against the door. "Be right out," called Jack.

"Take your time," replied a grainy, male voice.

*Who the hell?* Shirtless and with pants open, Jack barreled out of the bathroom. There was no one there. He called to the kitchen. "Donna, do we have company?"

"No one here but you and I." Donna came around the corner. Her concern made a row of wrinkles above her brow. "Are you feeling all right?"

Jack paused and took a slow look around the apartment. He smelled the unmistakable soapy-clean, musky cinnamon of his father's cologne. "Do you smell that?"

"Coffee. It's brewing now."

"No. Not the coffee."

"Jack, you're worrying me."

He took a deep breath. "Sorry. It's probably my Malady acting up."

"Or a wild imagination." Donna caressed his face and kissed him. "Writers are funny like that."

Donna returned to the kitchen. Jack hustled down the hall quietly, not wanting to further alarm Donna, and slipped into the bedroom. In the top draw of his dresser, a small gray pistol rested in a black holster. The gun felt cold in his hand. If someone was sneaking around his apartment, he'd be ready. He checked it...loaded.

"What's that for?"

Jack spun around and nearly fainted. Across the bedroom stood his father, but he did not look as he did in Jack's frequent dreams. The man wore a tattered flight suit and tall black boots. Various aviation patches adorned the shoulders and lapels. Half the rotting tissue of his face was missing, leaving only bands of dried muscle and exposed bone. Thin strands of straw-like gray hair stuck up from the top of his head. His colorless eyes shimmered with a coating of cloudy film and his lips flaked around his sagging jaw. *It's a corpse*, thought Jack. *It's my father's corpse standing in my bedroom!* The hand holding the pistol bounced in fear. Jack managed a few words. "What the fuck is going on?"

The corpse frowned. "Watch your mouth. You know better than to use language like that."

The room rolled around Jack. Nausea struck him, quaking his knees. He swallowed his rising vomit. *This is all just a hallucination. But he is so real! There is grave dirt all over my carpet for God's sake! Get a grip. You're sick, Jack. It's Malady.*

*Close your eyes real tight and take a deep breath. Deal with this.* Jack straightened and addressed the ghoulish visitor. "Listen up, Corpse-Dad. You're not real. But I'm going to treat you like you are until you go away."

Corpse-Dad's purple lips formed a ridiculous grin. "Glad to see you're feeling better. I thought you were going to puke for a minute there." He laughed. Dust blew from tears in his throat.

"What do you want?"

"Just paying my son a visit. I thought you'd be glad to see me. It's been a long time."

"You've been dead for nearly two decades."

"Which is why we shouldn't miss out on any more quality time." Corpse-Dad stepped closer to Jack with his arms outstretched. "How about a hug?"

Jack aimed the pistol. "That's close enough." His heart knocked in his chest. "I want you to go away. You hear me? I said get the hell out of here!"

"But, Jack, I don't have anywhere to go."

"Leave or I'll put a bullet in your brain."

"Please, listen! I'm just trying to help you."

Jack closed his eyes and pulled back the hammer with his thumb.

"You don't know what you're doing! DON'T SHOOT!"

He touched his finger to the trigger.

Donna's voice replaced Corpse-Dad's and screamed, "DON'T!"

*Donna?* Jack opened his eyes to find Donna cowering in front of him, her face wet with tears and pale from terror. He dropped the gun and snatched her in his arms. "Donna, I'm so sorry. I thought it was..."

She looked up at him, her glassy eyes quivered in terror. "I'm not sure how much more I can take."

"Please don't leave me. I need you."

"Jack, this has gone too far! You need medicine."

Jack broke down and cried into her shoulder, unable to hold back his sorrow any longer.

# Chapter 4

*Where are you? Please come back!* "DAD!"

Jameson woke to feel Luna's hand clutching his. She crouched next to his bed.

He took a deep breath and rubbed his eyes. "You're always there when I wake up. Why?"

"Because the only thing worse than a nightmare is waking up alone."

Jameson sat up and switched on the small lamp near the bed. The red lampshade warmed the white walls in a pink hue. The tiny guest room, one of three in Dr. Albert Walker's medical center, kept two beds and a table between them. "We were so close, Luna. After weeks of travel through the Void Lands, we finally made it to Karma City. The Oasis Hospital records were right in front of me." He cracked his knuckles. "Damn that Gemni, or whatever he's called."

Luna returned to her bed adjacent from his. She pulled her leather-bound journal and pencil from her pack and propped it on her knees. Her eyes, like wet pebbles of green ocean glass, fixed on his for a quiet moment. The rosy glow of the lamplight played on her face, washing away the scarring. Jameson saw the face that would be had her life been different: soft and symmetrical. He didn't like it. Her tribal branding showed her passion, might and the depth of her character. The scars ran deep, he knew. And though Luna's face represented principles she no longer valued, the scars made her beautiful in Jameson's eyes, more so than any other woman. He imagined getting up, crossing the room and climbing on top of her. How often he'd had the thought. And he knew she would fall beneath him, open for him, take him. His arms tensed, ready to lift his body to action but he froze when she spoke.

"Your father is lucky to have a son like you. You've never stopped caring about him. In this world where so many people forget, you hold on, you keep remembering."

"It hurts to remember sometimes. But it helps, too."

"Tell me something good."

A soft laugh rumbled in Jameson's throat. "All right. I remember Mom and Dad walking me along Center Avenue near Greely Park. I was just big enough to hold each of their hands. They'd lift me up and swing me between their steps. I'd laugh because it was fun and because my father laughed. Those were the good years when Mom was well. Dad was always there when I needed him. While Mom rambled in a Malady fit through the night, he read me stories at bedtime, making funny voices to distract me. I'd pretend to sleep when he cracked open my bedroom door in the middle of the night to check on me. Couldn't fool him. 'Go to sleep, Jamie,' he'd whisper. 'Mom's fine.' I can still feel his hands gently falling over my eyes, hiding the sight of mother lying on the bathroom floor, blood running from her wrists. That was the only time I saw him cry. When he knelt down to drape his bathrobe over the woman he loved, tears fell from the tip of his nose. But even then, like a superhero, he reached down and lifted her up. Dad carried her away and I just stood there, frozen in my grief. And that's where my childhood ended, in that bathroom doorway."

Luna frowned. "That started out good, then got really sad." She gave him a half smile to lift the gloom.

Jameson shrugged. "I've been called a downer, but I'm working on that."

"I think you're just a guy that has a lot he needs to talk about. And I don't mind listening."

"Thanks, Luna."

"We'll find your father, Jameson. Or at the least, we'll learn what happened to him. Our hunt continues in the morning. And now we're tracking two." She opened her journal and touched the pencil to the page.

Jameson watched her set to work. His curiosity piqued. "We've been running together a while and this is the first time I've seen that journal. I didn't know you wrote."

"I don't." She tossed the book to Jameson. He opened it and nearly gasped.

Elaborate sketches of rolling mountains, wide rivers, towering trestles and strange settlements filled the pages. He marveled at the detailed drawings of trains, railroads and steam works complexes. Deeper in the journal waited faces of men, women and children, all smiling with joy carefully rendered. After the mosaic of people, he found himself on a single page, a simple portrait she made without him knowing. In it, he sat beside a river, a smothered camp fire smoking behind him as he tied his boots. He remembered that day. "This was the morning after I dragged you from the river."

"I jumped the train that night, leaving the tribe, half-hoping to die. You saved me and gave me the chance to be someone better."

"Luna, don't talk like you owe me something. Cause you don't."

"I know that. But you deserve the same chance and I'm going to see that you get it."

Jameson looked back at the journal to distract himself from his rising passion. He wanted so badly to hold her against him and tell her every feeling of appreciation and love between a storm of kisses. His nostrils flared in private frustration. *Why can't I just do it?* He thumbed through the drawings again. "These are amazing, Luna."

"Thanks." She took back the book. "It's how I keep my memories. But only the good ones."

\*\*\*

Jack eased his motorcycle to an idle outside of Sable District's gates. He showed his *Karma Daily* press identification to the security guard and entered the district of Dr. Marcus Graves. The cool night air tore through Jack's denim jacket. The chilly nights and quick rains foretold the approach of autumn. He rolled the throttle, moving faster down the district roads.

He had come to Sable District to register for Quell. Jack knew that no other drug in Karma, or parts beyond, could quiet the effects of the Malady parasite. Over the years, he'd witnessed countless citizens fall deep into addiction, and the possibility of devotion to Graves Enterprises unsettled him. He sighed. *What other choice do I have? Can't put Donna in danger again.*

41

Soldiers in black armor patrolled the streets of Sable District with rifles, clubs and bright flashlights. Jack noticed black patrol vans roll down the street with spotlights sweeping the alleys. *Looks like they're searching for someone. Interesting.* He pushed the curiosity aside knowing that the Sable Guard kept committed to the swift apprehension, removal or destruction of anyone intending to harm the district, its people, or violate its regulations.

Families and businesses flourished behind the impenetrable stone walls fortifying the district. Arguably the safest community in Karma City, the wellness of Sable District remained an illusion. Only those individuals willing to register with Graves Enterprises and disclose their Malady infection were permitted to live in the district. Adhering to a strict regimen of Quell usage with routine medical examinations was the only requirement for residency. For the occupants of Sable District, this was a small price to pay for a sheltered and peaceful life.

Jack switched off the engine and kicked the stand into place. He dismounted and took a moment to gaze up at the dizzying building. Sable Tower, the one hundred and eight story skyscraper, dominated the Karma cityscape and could be seen for miles across the Void Lands.

"Must be some view at the top," he muttered.

His own words stirred something in the recesses of his Malady-deteriorated memory, something deeply forgotten. Shards of remembrance glittered around in his mind like a broken mirror reflecting distorted truths. He thought of beautiful landscapes seen from high above the clouds. *Flying with Dad. The airplanes. I was a boy.* Memories or dreams? Malady deceived him, only allowing a long-dead past that he could not recall and could not escape.

Jack entered the front lobby of Sable Tower. Armed guards watched as he approached the front desk. A young, female receptionist with curly yellow hair greeted him. "Good day and welcome to Graves Enterprises at Sable Tower. How may I help you?"

Jack took off his hat and tucked it under his arm. "Yes, hi. My name is Jack Halligan. I'm here for a nine-thirty appointment."

She typed his name into the computer and twirled her hair while waiting for the system to locate his information. "Are you *the* Jack Halligan? From the *Karma Daily*?"

He gave a playful bow.

With a beaming smile, the receptionist handed Jack a clipboard. "Please fill out this registration form and the nurse will call you to the examination room in a few minutes. Need a pen?"

Jack pulled a silver pen from his pocket. "Nope." The prying writer in him took over. He pointed to the guards. "What's with all the firepower around town?"

The receptionist glanced at the Sable Guardsmen and Jack clearly saw the fear fall over her innocent eyes. She gave a scripted reply. "Due to increased security concerns, Sable District is under enhanced community-focused protective services."

Jack stepped away from the desk and sat in a chair against the lobby windows. *There is definitely something off in Graves' district. Maybe it has to do with the outbreak at Oasis Hospital. Probably trying to prevent that from occurring here. But why would that woman seem so afraid? There's something more.*

Jack hated the thought of relinquishing personal information to Graves Enterprises. More interested in the strange mood overcasting the district, he made light of the registration form. *Eyes...two. Hair...thinning. Hereditary issues...I'll ask my dead father next time I see him.* He set aside the form and took out his pocket notepad to jot down his curious observations. *Armed guards patrolling streets. Searching? Nervous residents. Behavioral switch in receptionist after questioning. Fearful of surroundings. Being watched.*

Minutes later, a nurse entered the lobby and welcomed Jack. He followed the woman to a small examination room.

"Good evening, Mr. Halligan. It's nice to meet you," the nurse held out her hand.

Jack accepted. "Call me Jack."

"I must say, I enjoy your articles very much."

"Thank you."

"Please have a seat on the examination table. I'll be taking some blood in just a moment." She looked over his registration form and smiled. "Nice work."

Jack shrugged. "I didn't see any magazines in the lobby so I had to entertain myself somehow."

"I understand. Tell me, what's this about seeing your dead father?"

Jack waved a hand. "Oh, just a joke."

"Is it?"

Jack's shoulders crumbled. "No. I've been having hallucinations of my father's corpse. He talks to me like I'm a child and he's so real that I can smell him." Jack looked into her eyes. "So, how crazy am I?"

"Sounds like you're suffering from Stage Two Malady, Jack."

"Great."

"But Malady affects people differently. The mind-altering affects are unique to the individual, based on personality and coping skills. Some people, like the young, timid or elderly, fall harder to the parasite because they just don't have the resolve, experience or courage to persevere."

"My condition will worsen in time, right?"

"Yes. As it does in everyone. Stage One typically lasts three months. Stage Two can be longer depending on the parasite's activity; some people remain in Stage Two for up to year. Stage Three is expected to be diagnosed after a year and a half of infection."

"Damn." Jack sighed. "Then I've got roughly another year before I go completely nuts."

"A regimen of Quell will greatly slow the parasite's advancement. Jack, you can regain, and possibly maintain, control. At least, that's the goal and the belief here in Sable District."

"How does Quell work?"

"Through the science of osmobiosis, we are able to force an organism to fall into a state of cryptobiosis, or 'living death' as some call it, by a chemical reaction. Quell makes Malady sleep in the host's brain, slowing its production of harmful waste toxins that corrupt the functions of the brain's limbic system."

"That's amazing; a little frightening, but amazing."

"You don't need to be afraid of Quell. It's helped so many people take back their lives. Nearly everyone in Sable District is proof of that. *I'm* proof of that."

"You have Malady, too?"

"Yes. I've been infected for four years."

"But you seem so healthy."

She gave him a comforting smile. "I feel healthy, which means I *am* healthy."

Jack thought of Donna and of the gun in his hand that almost killed her. He blinked hard but could not erase the scene from his eyes. "There's side effects, right?"

"Yes. But they're manageable with appropriate dosage. Expect a little drowsiness as your body acclimates to the drug. There's a little nausea, too."

"I don't want to be addicted. Let's face it, Graves has the damn city doped up and it's made him the sovereign of Karma. I don't want to feel sick anymore. I don't want to hallucinate. I don't want to become a danger to my girlfriend but dammit, I don't want to lose who I am to a bottle of pills." He let out a calming breath, as if venting a smoldering fire in his core. His head hung between his shoulders.

"You're right to feel this way, Jack. But only irresponsible people become addicts. Look," she paused and folded her hands in front of her. "You're sick and need medicine. That doesn't make you a junkie or promise you'll become one. Quell should be used as needed. Graves Enterprises understands that the severity of symptoms varies from person to person. You control the intake. You control your health."

Donna's sentiments echoed in Jack's heart. *People get a shot at living normal lives on Quell.* He cast aside his opinions of Grave's Enterprises and decided that preserving his life with Donna was far more important; he needed a shot at normal. "Sign me up."

The nurse flipped over the registration form. "Now, we do need an address so we can ship your medicine. The train takes shipments to town twice a week; Monday's and Thursday's.

Tomorrow's only Tuesday so I'll send you home with a supply to hold you over."

"My address is six twenty-five Center Avenue, Greely Park District. Floor sixteen. Apartment two-o-two."

While the nurse penned his information, Jack wondered how she'd react to questions about the condition in Sable District. "Speaking of the train, did you folks hear the train bridge explosion over the East River? It rattled my apartment all the way in central Karma."

"Yes. Did they ever find the people who jumped?"

*People who jumped from the train?* Jack wondered. *Interesting.* "Uh, no, actually," he answered, pretending to be in the know. "They're still investigating."

The nurse became animated, excited to gossip. She rolled up Jack's sleeve and swabbed his upper arm with a disinfectant wipe. "Crazy thing, huh? My brother said people just started killing. He works at Oasis Hospital and escaped; oh, and he saw two people— a man and a woman with guns—flee the scene in an ambulance with Dr. Albert Walker."

"Walker. The name sounds familiar. Yes, I've read about him. A real nut-job, huh?" Jack played along, hoping to get more leads.

"No kidding. Anyway, my brother says there's been no sight of Dr. Walker or the two mystery people since. Are you following the explosion and riot for a story?" The nurse injected the needle. Jack winced as she drew a blood sample.

"Sure am." *Sure am now.*

# Chapter 5

The midday sun flashed between the tenements and high-rises as the ambulance sped through the crisscrossing roads and alleyways. Jameson Shoals sat in the passenger seat and noticed his reflection in the side mirror. His face looked different from Karma's citizens, harder, unyielding. *I remember this place. The only thing that's changed is me.*

The buildings of brick and stone wore brandings of graffiti while broken windows— some boarded, others agape and glassless—added to the bleak reality of the times. The decay of the neighborhoods stemmed from the alleys, spilling into the streets, contaminating places once beautiful and proud. Litter tumbled like autumn leaves, filling potholes, and packing gutters. Streetlamps leaned, winking as if clinging to life like the rusted cars that sputtered and choked. People wandered, people begged. They slept on the sidewalks beside the warm subway vents. They sipped coffee in bus stops and huddled around trash fires. Abandoned homes stood like monuments but to what, none cared to recall, or even *could* recall.

Jameson rolled down the glass, but the city air wasn't fresh. Rotting garbage and carbon monoxide curdled his nose. He asked Albert, who drove the ambulance, "Do you even know where you're going?"

"It should be around here somewhere."

"You've gone up and down this street four times. Find a place to park. I'm getting tired of driving around."

"Someone's grumpy today."

Albert parked in front of a general store. Jameson noticed his reflection again, this time in the store-front window. The stock of his shotgun protruded from his backpack, rising above his right shoulder. His leather jacket foretold his travels and warned of his volatile nature like the stripes of a deadly snake. "I'm grabbing some supplies," he told the others. "Be right out."

The bell on the glass door jangled when he stepped inside. The store smelled of lemon cleaner and bleach. The clerk behind the counter labored with a rag and spray bottle, scrubbing the register area with passion; prevailing in his personal war against the micro-parasite. He paused his chemical assault and gave Jameson a nod. "Welcome. What brings you in?"

"I need water, bandages, and Checkers."

"Water is in the cooler," the clerk pointed with his nose, "back that way. Bandages are down in the center aisle, just ahead. You can get your Checkers from me when you cash out."

Jameson moved down the center aisle. There, a woman and her young child shopped. The woman carried a basket and struggled to keep her little boy by her side. The boy, who Jameson guessed to be about six years old, whined and tugged a small red water pistol from his mother's hand. "But I really want it."

The mother shook her head and took back the toy. "I told you, I just don't have the money for that. I wish I could buy it for you. Really, I do. Maybe in a few weeks."

"It might not be here in a few weeks." The boy pouted and stomped his feet.

Jameson couldn't ignore the hurt in the mother's eyes as she tucked the water pistol out of the boy's reach. He stepped in, taking the toy in his callused hand.

The boy looked up at him, upset. "No! Don't take it away."

Jameson crouched down. "I'm not taking it away. I'm going to buy it for you."

The boy's eyes lit up. "You are?"

"If your mom says I can."

The woman nodded, her eyes misting and her lips trembling with happiness.

Jameson handed the toy gun to the boy.

"Wow! Thank you so much!"

"You're welcome. Now, be good for your mother. Protect her."

"I will."

The mother thanked Jameson and continued shopping. Jameson took a few packs of bandages from the shelf and moved toward the back coolers for the water. He smiled when he heard the boy laughing and 'ka-powing' as he pretended to shoot. Then, Jameson paused when he heard the clerk shouting.

"I've told you a hundred times, I don't serve sickos. I won't be having Malady contaminating my store. Now get your infected ass outta here!"

Jameson whirled around to see a dirty man in rags pacing near the front counter. He could smell the body odor from across the room.

"Ka-pow! Ka-pow!" the boy shouted at the man.

"How dare you point that thing at me?" The infected man lunged. "Give me that!"

"No! It's mine!"

He pulled a rusted knife and pressed it under the boy's chin. "I said give it to me!"

The mother wailed. "No! Please don't!"

The boy screamed in terror. Jameson sprang to action, rushing down the aisle. He raised his shotgun, turned it around and clubbed the attacker in the head. Blood sprayed across the floor. The man fell to his back, his eyes glazed from the blow.

"Get the boy out of here," ordered Jameson to the mother. "Now!" The mother pulled the boy close and hurried out the store without a word or a moment of hesitation.

Jameson heard the door's bells jangle again and felt satisfied that boy was safe. He looked down at the groaning man and pressed his boot onto his throat. "You're the worst kind of person."

"Why?" The man struggled to speak under Jameson's boot. "Because I have Malady?"

"Because you would hurt a child."

"Hurt?" The man choked on his guiltless laughter. "I'd KILL the Lesser! I'll kill ALL the Lessers!"

Jameson stomped as hard as he could, caving the man's throat and shattering the bones of his neck. A quiet minute passed as he stood over the corpse, lost in the fog of his ire.

"JAMESON!" Luna's shouting pulled Jameson from his darkness. "Shit, what happened? Are you okay?"

"I didn't come in here for this. But I always seem to find some crazy fucking bastard that I have to put down like a mad dog." He put his shotgun away and his shoulders fell under the weight of his actions. "I've been killing since I was that boy's age. I saw myself in him."

"I know, Jameson."

"There is no crime in killing to save those who can't save themselves. Malady is the predator and you and I refuse to be prey." She pointed to the dead man on the floor. "That's not an innocent person. That's Malady right there. And it's dead. You did the right thing. You always do."

Jameson drove the ambulance through the labyrinth of intersections, bringing the group on the correct path to Professor Crimm's address. As he suspected, Albert was way off.

Luna sat with Albert in the back, giving Jameson a moment of quiet focus as he navigated the streets of Karma.

Albert whispered to Luna, "Jameson's pretty rattled and I know it's not because I got us lost. What happened in the store?"

Luna sighed and held up a finger, telling him to wait a moment. She asked Jameson, "How about some tunes? A little music to clear the head."

Jameson switched on the radio and turned up the volume. A rock song with a fast, wailing guitar, filled the ambulance. Luna moved close to Albert and spoke softly. "Back at the store, one of Gemni's psychos was about to murder a child."

"What?"

"Jameson took care of the problem. He killed the bastard. But when there's a kid involved, it gets to him."

Albert eyed the Void Land drifter driving his ambulance, then looked back at Luna. "What's his deal, anyway?" he asked, still whispering. "Honestly, he scares the shit out of me sometimes."

"He's had it rough, Albert. His mother suffered from Malady and died when he was little. His father was his world, but he lost him."

"He died, too?"

"No. When Jameson turned ten years old, he and his father, Eric, were playing catch in Greely Park, you know, enjoying the birthday. Well, four Malady punks surrounded them. Quell junkies, dealers. Eric refused to buy any drugs and the men got pissed. They pulled knives and jumped Jameson's dad, right in front of him."

"That's terrible."

"Gets worse," added Luna. "Eric was armed. He pulled his gun and shot the men dead, saving his and Jameson's life. But Eric had a nasty wound on his arm and the two hurried to Oasis Hospital to check for Malady infection. The nurses pulled Eric in for immediate testing while young Jameson played at the playground in the Oasis courtyard."

"Was his dad infected?" asked Albert.

"Don't know. Jameson stayed at the playground all afternoon, but his father never came back for him."

"You're kidding? Where did he go?"

"Like I said, don't know."

Albert snapped his fingers. "That's why he wanted to search the hospital records."

Luna nodded. "That's why we came back to Karma. He believes there's a trail that he is now wise enough to find."

"What do you think?"

The ambulance came to a jarring halt. Jameson turned down the radio and said, "We're here."

Luna secured her rifle and nudged Albert. "I think it's time to get back to business."

They walked up the front steps of Crimm's apartment building and entered. Years of neglect made the hallway swampy, with mold and ancient air layered in ashy dust. The staircase creaked under their weight and Albert gripped the banister with both hands, fearing a sudden collapse. He said quietly, "I'm kind of nervous about meeting Professor Crimm."

"Why is that?" Luna asked. "You two are scientists. That's common ground."

"He's special. He's the only scientist who works for both Oasis and Graves Enterprises. Dealing exclusively with Carmen Victoria and Marcus Graves. He's highly trusted."

"But why?" pressed Luna. "What's he bringing to the table that others don't?"

"He is the man who taught Graves about genetics and the place we all know as Oasis Hospital used to be his academy. He sold the grounds to the Victoria's and helped them design the hospital campus. Karma City owes a lot to Professor Anthony Crimm."

"If he's so great," piped Jameson, "why does he live in Karma's ghetto?"

Albert pushed his glasses up the bridge of his nose. "Good question."

Jameson knocked on the door.

"Who's there?" the old man called from inside.

"Jameson Shoals. My crew and I were sent by your 'sons.'"

Latches and locks clicked open. The door squeaked on its rusted hinges. A man with fluffy white hair, curling mustache and oversized bow-tie greeted them with a quick smile. His pin-striped slacks bunched over his scuffed brown shoes. He adjusted his small glasses. "Hurry up and come in." A tea kettle whistled from within the apartment. He scurried through the cluttered living room, waving the group to follow. "Close and lock the door behind you."

The professor's apartment, though messy with stacked books and papers, was a combination of a laboratory and residence. Couches, end tables, book shelves and picture frames surrounded a computer desk that held burners, vials, tubing, gauges and various charts, bottles and flasks. Professor Crimm returned from a small pantry to the right. He carried a tray bearing a decanter of hot tea, clean mugs and small pastries into a small sitting room. He put the tray down on a nearby table and regarded his guests. "Please have a seat and help yourself to tea and tarts."

The three sat around the small table. Jameson replied, "Thank you kindly, professor."

Crimm sat in a wide recliner and leaned back. "If my sons sent you that means you're all here regarding the one called Gemni."

"We were told to see you for information," affirmed Jameson.

Crimm stared at them over the rim of his glasses. "Introductions first."

Albert chimed in. "I'm Dr. Albert Walker. And I must admit, sir, it's an honor to meet you and to be sitting in your home. And these tarts look delicious and the tea smells great. I enjoyed your publication on transposable elements and I had some thoughts about—"

Crimm cut him off. "It's nice to meet you, Dr. Walker." He pointed to Jameson and Luna. "You two would make fine additions to my team of hunters."

"Kurt and his crew look capable enough," said Jameson. "Luna Briggs and I recently encountered Gemni on a late-night train. He attacked the tribesman and detonated a bomb, destroying several cars and the East River Bridge. We ended up in Oasis Hospital and, as luck would have it, Gemni turned up there, too, somehow making the Malady Ward turn on the hospital staff. We tracked him to Undertown but lost him for a third time. We want to know what he is and how to stop him."

"I can tell you exactly what he is. But first, I need to know if I can trust the doctor." Crimm shifted his eyes to Albert. "Tell me your involvement in this, Dr. Walker."

Albert squirmed in his chair. "I've recently resigned from Oasis Hospital to further my independent research against Malady. After witnessing the devastation at Oasis, I've been assisting Jameson and Luna in their pursuit of Gemni. I've made a discovery that has only created more questions." He reached into his medical satchel and pulled out the specimen baggie. "My initial field examination indicated the presence of the Malady parasite in Gemni's blood but in a bad way."

Crimm pointed to the microscope standing on the nearby desk. "Have a look, Dr. Walker."

Albert put on some gloves and wiped the blood onto a microscope slide, then placed the slide under the lenses and studied the sample. He gasped and switched on a projector connected to the microscope. After a few flickers, the projector threw an image on the wall. Jameson looked at the glowing scene of a magnified parasitic worm writhing around, noticeably agitated.

"This is a Malady parasite," said Albert. "But it's too active. Malady normally cysts outside of a host."

"What does 'cyst' mean?" asked Jameson

"It means it curls up in a little ball and catches some Z's while it waits to infect a host it can feed off of. Malady can remain in a cystic stasis for ten years outside of a host. That's why it's such a problem in the world today. This parasite is nearly an adult bordering stage three development; which is of great concern."

Professor Crimm challenged Albert. "Why do you say that?"

Albert glanced up from the microscope. "If this entered your body, it would invade your brain cavity like a wrecking ball. You'd be thrown into an irreversible state of madness."

Crimm went to a glass cabinet marked: CAUTION-PARASITIC SPECIMENS. He retrieved a small tube and removed the seal. The professor moved Albert aside and hunched over the microscope, working the tube's invisible contents onto the slide. The group watched the projected image. There, two parasites reeled.

"The bigger one on the left," Crimm explained, "is the Malady parasite you recovered from Gemni's blood. The smaller one on the right is a common Malady specimen. Now watch closely."

Gemni's parasite thrashed about, as if communicating with the common Malady beside it. The common Malady slowly moved closer until it touched Gemni's. The smaller parasite remained at the side of the larger, appearing submissive and protected.

"I've never seen two Malady parasites bond before," Albert admitted. "Very strange."

Crimm retrieved another vial and added its contents to the slide. "It's about to get stranger, Doctor."

A third parasite, with a serpent-like body twice as long, fell in with the others. Immediately, it attacked Gemni's parasite. In a matter of seconds, it tore it in half. The smaller common Malady jolted as if in panic but was quickly ripped apart under the light of the microscope.

Jameson whistled in amazement. "I enjoy a good ringside bout, but what the hell just happened?"

Crimm grinned and returned to his recliner. He took up a cup of tea and a tart. After a few slow bites, he began his explanation. "The two parasites, Gemni's Malady worm and the killer that I introduced, are twins; both engineered by Marcus Graves in his genetic experiment, Project GEMNI. GEMNI stands for 'Graves Enterprises Malad-X Neural Implant.' The killer parasite is called 'Malad-X' and it has one purpose."

Albert pushed his glasses up his nose and stared at the image of the monstrous parasite. "To destroy Malady."

"Indeed," Crimm confirmed. He took another bite of his tart.

Jameson stood up and paced the room. "So, Graves has made a twisted cure for Malady? One worm to kill the other, is that it?"

"That was the goal of Project GEMNI, yes. But the first breed of Malad-X was technically a failure. The lead researcher for Graves Enterprises and trial host, Elliot Burroughs, was sick with Malady and offered to be the first human to receive Malad-X. The parasite awakened and took over his mind and body."

Jameson ran his fingers through his tousled hair. "Awakened? I don't get it."

A glob of raspberry filling dripped onto Crimm's shirt. He muttered to himself as he dabbed at it with a napkin. "Initially, Malad-X was created to enter a sick patient and kill the Malady, then die from exposure to the Malady waste toxins. That's not what happened in Burroughs. The new parasite bonded with the Malady already present, as you've just witnessed, and from this union, was further enhanced to a kind of super-Malady."

Albert clapped his hands. "A transmutation!"

"In a way, yes. The first Malad-X parasite developed into a breed of Malady stronger than I can express. It merged its neurons with Burroughs,' enabling domination of the mind and body. With a full neurological bond complete, this terrible Malady parasite assumed full control, and astonishingly, consciousness!" Crimm looked at Jameson. "It awakened."

"Unbelievable!" Albert whispered incredulously.

"I thought so, too," agreed Crimm. "I was further astounded when I witnessed Burroughs, or Gemni as he now calls himself, escape Sable Tower. I saw the first *turning* with my own eyes."

"Turning?" Jameson fought to catch up in the conversation.

"Yes," concurred Crimm. "He can compel people with Malady to follow his commands."

"We've seen that first hand," added Jameson. "At Oasis, in the subway and again with the man in the store. He really can make the Malady-heads go nuts."

"Yes. He turns them through mental pulses, an intense outward neural synapse that makes the Malady parasites in others bond to their host's limbic system, which affects their behavior in the ways Gemni desires."

Jameson sat back down and urged Crimm to continue. "What happened in Sable Tower?"

"Well, I should start with honesty." Crimm cleared his throat. "Many years ago, I assisted Marcus Graves in the early genetic designs of Malad-X. The thought of creating a stronger parasite to kill the weaker was too ingenious to ignore. I worked the concept on the side while assisting the Victoria's in establishing Oasis Hospital. In those days, I wanted to contribute to both efforts against Malady, prevention and eradication, in any way I could.

"Two weeks ago, I received a call from Marcus Graves. He said that at long last, the first Malad-X worm was ready and that implantation in his patient zero was to commence. I doubted this claim but nonetheless, raced to Sable Tower. I was delayed at a railroad crossing and was too late. When I entered the lobby, Elliot Burroughs emerged in a hospital gown, with intravenous tubing and EKG wires hanging from his limbs. He looked like a feral cat, wild-eyed and ready to slash. The Sable Guard surrounded him with weapons drawn but he raised his hands, as if ready to stop their bullets with his palms."

Jameson noticed Crimm's hands shaking. The tea cup rattled in his grip. The old man's lower lip quivered as he carried on.

"As is the case with most citizens of Sable District, the security guards were already sick with Malady. Gemni sensed this and by his command, they aimed their guns at each other and fired. Gemni's eyes glowed with a demonic orange light as their bodies fell lifeless. He knocked me down with incredible strength and ran out into the night.

"Moments later, Marcus Graves found me on the floor. He helped me up and for a long while, we stood in the lobby of his tower, neither of us knew what to say. But I recognized the severity of what we'd accidently created and I decided what I must do."

"You came to this unlikely neighborhood," finished Albert, "to establish a place where you could work to unravel Graves' science."

Crimm put down his cup. "And I am doing so as secretly as I can, Dr. Walker. Marcus Graves still thinks I am working with him on perfecting Project GEMNI, he believes that Burroughs will perish in the city, like so many unfortunate infected do, and sees no reason to go after him."

"Project GEMNI is still ongoing?" Albert asked.

"Yes. Graves believes the answer to ridding the world of Malady is through releasing Malad-X into the population to turn the infected on the infected. And Dr. Walker, you were right. If it enters the brain, it will be like a wrecking ball, turning the host into a ruthless killer."

"There is something missing here, Professor," Albert added. "Marcus Graves is valued for Quell. Why would he want to create a cure for Malady? No one would need Quell anymore and he'd be out of business."

"How astute of you. Twenty years ago, I discovered that the Malady parasite is growing resistant to Quell. There are still many people who remain uninfected but choose to use drugs to satisfy their own addictions. These addicts contract Malady and the parasite matures in them to release offspring that have developed in a body where the chemicals of Quell are present."

Albert snapped his fingers. "Of course! And the parasite's offspring are born Quell resistant and are spreading. Quell is becoming less and less effective."

"Correct again, Dr. Walker," said Crimm. "I reported this discovery to Graves who immediately sought to combat this evolution. He increased Quell's potency in response to the parasite's evolving tolerance, then turned to genetics to remove the gene responsible for Quell resistance. In attempting this, he inadvertently heightened the aggression of the tampered Malady parasite, making it desire the destruction of any lesser forms. This served as the inspiration for the conception of Malad-X and the start of Project GEMNI so long ago."

Albert frowned, shaking his head. "Graves is keeping people sick to keep them well. And you've condoned it? Why?"

"I'm old, Dr. Walker. I'm lucky to have lived as long as I have. I hope you get to as well, and I hope that you'll do whatever you have to do to stay alive to further scientific advancement against the horrible condition plaguing us all. There are sides in science, just as there are in this big city. You'll choose one, then another. You'll make lines in the sand that others will cross. And the day will come for you, as it has for me, when you'll ask yourself if science truly allows for creation for the betterment of mankind. You'll ask yourself if you ever really helped anyone. I hope you can say yes."

Jameson sighed. "Let me see if I have this straight. Marcus Graves created Malad-X to kill Malady. His first Malad-X worm backfired and converted itself to a super Malady worm that took over Burroughs' mind and became Gemni, who is now loose in the city and making the Malady infected under his control?"

"Yes."

"Now, Gemni is out there making Karma's infected population side with him to kill off the healthy people because he thinks humans are 'Lesser' and need to be wiped out."

"That's right."

Jameson pointed to the projected image of the Malad-X parasite. "Graves still wants to release Malad-X on the population so the Malad-X infected will kill the people with Malady."

"Correct, Mr. Shoals. And Graves has already begun the next phase of his project—human testing. This time, however, he has moved Project GEMNI off site. It is not occurring at Sable Tower. I'm trying to learn the whereabouts of his experiments now. Furthermore, I've enlisted the finest urban hunters to track and kill Gemni. I've named my team 'the Crimsons,' and they are devoted to shutting down Graves Enterprises." Crimm stood up and went to his apartment window. He opened the blinds. Beyond his silhouetted form, the Karma cityscape scraped the gray sky.

"Doom is swiftly eclipsing the city." Crimm took off his glasses. "Will you help me save the people of Karma?"

Jameson plopped back into the chair, snatched up a tart and bit into it. He said with a mouthful of raspberry, "My team and I need to talk it over."

# Chapter 6

Jameson and Luna met on the rooftop. Luna stood with one foot propped on the ledge and her rifle slung over her shoulder. Clouds bloomed overhead, sending the wind whistling through the surrounding buildings. Voices murmured from the streets below. She looked at the citizens ambling along the streets and alleys. From the rooftop, they looked like tiny figurines or wandering insects. Sounds of traffic and the far away clatter of the train united the noise of the city, turning it all into a strange music. She tied back her hair to keep it from blowing into her eyes and turned to face Jameson, who stood nearby eyeing the skyline of Karma City.

"You told Crimm you wanted to talk it over with the group," she said, "but I know you meant 'talk it over with me.'"

Jameson sighed. "Yeah. You've been risking your life for me since we hooked up. You don't need to keep doing that."

"We keep each other alive."

Jameson paused. Luna watched his eyes squint to a piercing gaze across the city. He reached into his pocket and pulled out a pack of cigarettes and a lighter. He lit one and puffed in quiet thought. "We really don't need this. We can just go."

"Go where?"

"Back into the Voids. We can wait it all out then rake up the spoils of whatever bullshit war is about to break out."

"What about your father?"

Jameson flicked the cigarette butt over the edge of the roof. "Maybe I missed my chance. Or maybe we come back another time. There's always maybes."

A group of children ran down the sidewalk. They hooted and jeered at one another and their playful laughter echoed through the streets.

"Poor kids," Jameson muttered. "Do you think the kids today know how bad the world is?"

"Did you know?"

He shrugged.

"I think kids always know," said Luna. "But their innocence allows them to cope in ways we no longer can. When it rains, kids wait for rainbows. Adults just get depressed."

"You're right, Luna. And the hard part is the truth. Those kids down there, all of them, are likely infected."

"Jameson, we can't leave now. We can't let Gemni or Graves get to them."

Jameson offered a soft smile. "Then you think we should keep going? Take down Gemni and Graves?"

Luna looked into his bottomless, diamond-hard eyes. There, she saw that primal strength she found so empowering. Jameson forged a sense of power and determination for himself over years of loneliness. The passion that sparked in the depths of his eyes revealed itself when she needed it. And she needed it now because so much unknown lay ahead of her. Since leaving the rigid life of the Iron Tribe, the world beyond the rails opened for her and without Jameson, Luna knew she would have been devoured like a lost cub in a bloodthirsty jungle. *This city is a jungle. Now it's my turn to protect the innocent.* "If not us," she answered, "then who?"

Albert approached. "Forgive the interruption, but I just wanted to let you know that you can go on without me if you want."

Luna noticed the doctor wringing his hands. He was scared. "Why do you say that?" she asked.

"It's just that I don't know how to shoot. And I don't want to know. I don't think I ever could. I'm afraid I won't be much help if trouble comes our way again. I'd hate to be baggage."

Jameson slapped him on the back. "I thought you'd be too scientifically intrigued to pull out now."

"I certainly am, though I—"

"You're sticking with us, doc. Our schedule just opened up, so we decided to head out and save Karma. We're going to need you."

Albert looked to Luna. "Really?"

"You are strong because you *don't* use a gun, Albert," answered Luna. "You understand the threat in a way that Jameson and I can't. We need your help. The city needs your help."

She offered a smile of sincerity.

Albert stood taller. "Thank you. I'm honored and I'll just stay low when the bullets start to fly."

Jameson laughed and Luna gave a playful nudge.

"Well then," continued Albert, "I also came up to tell you that I've received further directions from Professor Crimm. We're to meet Kurt Auger in an hour. He's going to fill us in on the next move against Graves and Gemni."

Albert drove the ambulance toward an athletic park a few blocks from Professor Crimm's apartment building. A red traffic light prompted their ambulance to stop at a crowded intersection. As citizens crossed the road, Luna felt the ambulance shake. A deafening horn blared, echoing off the buildings and through the alleys. A chill rippled down Luna's spine.

"What the hell is that?" Albert asked.

The shaking in the road intensified. Luna watched as the citizens ran in fear, some screaming, others ducking their heads. Windows rattled, businesses closed their doors. People dashed into buildings or crouched behind parked cars; though, some remained on the curbside, peering down the street in ignorant anticipation.

Jameson drew his shotgun.

"Put that away. Now!" Luna ordered.

"Sounds like a train is about to rip through here," Albert said, "but we're miles from the rails."

Luna shook her head. "Not a train, but you're pretty close. It's Baby Boy."

"Excuse me?"

Luna pointed. A colossal eighteen wheeled truck rolled into view. Its black body panels wore swatches of rust along riveted armor plating. The wheels held dreadful blades that diced the air as the studded tires turned. A menacing steel grill looked like the deadly grin of a lion. The horn sounded again, this time reverberating through Luna's chest. Sunlight beamed off the towering chrome exhaust stacks. Black smoke curled upward from the pipes like two smoldering volcanoes, filling the street with a sooty haze. The truck hauled a long trailer expertly fitted with thick armor panels and dotted with firing ports. Mounted to the trailer roof, a large machine gun turret rotated, aiming its sights over the panicking crowd. The machine gun fixed its sights on their ambulance. Luna's heartbeat quickened in remembrance. "That's Baby Boy. It's the Iron Tribe's AFV."

"AFV?" Albert questioned.

"Armored Fighting Vehicle. The entire big rig detaches and reattaches to the Iron Tribe's train. It drives onto the tracks and hinges to the caboose couplings. Railway wheels drop down from the truck's undercarriage so it can roll on the tracks."

"Impressive," Albert remarked nervously. "W-What do they use it for?"

"Baby Boy is a death dealer. The trailer houses a team of foot soldiers, weapons cache and radio communications deck. The Iron Tribe deploys the truck from Mother Train in the spirit of vengeance. They're on the hunt."

"For who? I hope it's not us!"

"Relax, Albert," said Luna. "Baby Boy is reserved for those marked as true enemies of the Iron Tribe."

"Then why do they have that huge gun pointed at us?"

"We're about to find out."

Five men in weathered, brown dusters emerged from the trailer. Wide brimmed hats shadowed their scarred faces. Each man carried an AR-15 rifle and wore a bandoleer of rounds. They surrounded the ambulance, dreadful combat knives clanking at their hips as they took formation.

Luna whispered, "Do not speak unless ordered. Do as they say or we're all dead."

Baby Boy idled in front of them. The machine gun turret locked its position, ready to shred the ambulance to scrap metal. Luna saw the driver emerge. His raiment differed from the others. His duster was black and trimmed with silver chains and metal studs. His physical size matched the girth of the semi. His tree trunk neck, barrel chest and boat-ore forearms made him look like a terrible ape in menacing urban clothes. "Get out of the vehicle and lay on the ground! Faces down!"

The group obeyed, hurrying out and dropping to the ground. Baby Boy's driver walked around them; his chunky boots clopping like the hooves of a minotaur. "Listen up!" he barked. "I seek the one who bombed the Mother Train and destroyed the trestle. An Oasis Hospital Ambulance driven by drifters is unusual."

Luna hoped Albert would not open his nervous mouth.

"Your identities will be verified," said the driver. "If you are found to be responsible for the bombing, you will be executed."

One by one, the driver forced them to roll over onto their backs in the road. He stared at their faces with rifle ready. Albert whimpered in fear. Luna was the last inspection. The driver nudged her with his boot and she rolled over. Her hair fell from her face, revealing her scars.

"Who are you?" the driver asked.

"Luna Briggs. Former gunner and scout. Honor to you, brother."

The driver lowered his rifle. "Honor to you. You may all stand." He shouted to his tribesmen, "Clear. Return to Boy."

Luna and the others stood up and dusted themselves off.

"Do you know of the one we seek?" asked the driver.

"Yes," answered Luna "We are after him as well. He is called Gemni. He is dangerous and has proven difficult to apprehend." Inspiration overcame her then. A powerful idea filled her mind so rapidly that she had to act on it. She lifted her chin, standing firm with shoulders back and eyes set on the driver with purpose. "Let's join forces. We have knowledge. You have the strength."

"We seek no outside alliances in our mission."

"Outside alliances? I am," she paused, "*was* Tribe."

His razor eyes cut her down. "Exactly." He turned from her abruptly and walked toward the waiting big rig. Luna's sudden shout escaped her, unable to be contained.

"You won't find Gemni. Not like this."

The driver stopped but did not turn to face her. She knew he listened. She knew he might kill her there in the street.

"You have to change the way you think," continued Luna, "the way you see. Or—"

"Or what, Briggs?" growled the driver. He spun to face her. His eyes wide with astonishment over her bold position.

"Or you'll die. That's what goes on here in the city. There are no rules. There is no code. People are sick, they're hostile, they kill and they die. Some people get to live and watch it all go down in heaps around them. You're not the hunters now. Neither is Gemni. The city is the predator and you're driving right into its jaws. Help us and we'll help you."

"We serve the Mother Train. No one else."

Luna shook her head. "You need to serve the people." She thought she saw his eyes soften in a brief flash of confusion.

He smirked. "And why should I do that?"

"Because if not, you'll lose your way. And no one deserves to be lost. Not in Karma, not on the tracks and not in the Voids." She signaled for Jameson and Albert to get back in the ambulance.

The driver walked back to the black semi. *Maybe I'll see him again. Maybe not.* Soon, Baby Boy thundered away, scraping against parked cars and smashing over trashcans. Half of her heart yearned to return to her old life. Seeing the warriors of the rails depart without her was surreal. *You're different now, Luna. You're not in the tribe anymore,* she reminded herself. *You left because of your sister. Don't ever forget what you did to her.*

The group pressed on to find Kurt Auger. At the entrance of the athletic field, Luna paused to survey the surroundings. She looked for signs of aggravation or tension among the people. Finding only common revelry, she pressed on, following the others into the park.

Crowds gathered in the bleachers around the field to watch two rival soccer teams collide. Families of Karma City cheered as their beloved heroes of Karma Thunder battled on the home field against The Lobos Express. Applause, heckles, and referee whistles filled the sporting park with honest excitement.

They passed a vendor stand and Albert gave her a nudge. He sniffed the air and pointed. "Hot dogs! Hungry?"

"No."

Albert raised an eyebrow. "Well after being waylaid by the Iron Tribe I could use a little happy food. I always get hungry after nearly shitting my pants."

Luna smiled at the comment.

"Tell you what," said Albert. "I'll get you a hot dog anyway. Oh, and they have smoothies! Just what I need to take the edge off."

Luna giggled and the sound startled her. How long had it been since she felt such innocent happiness? She watched him awkwardly purchase the food from the vendor and couldn't contain her laughter. There he stood, brilliant yet frantically searching his pockets for enough change, rifling through his satchel in near panic, papers fluttering in the breeze, swears escaping him, yet a pause to signal her with a cool and collected thumbs up as if he had it all under perfect control. She knew he wanted to perform an act of kindness, maybe chivalry of sorts, and get the lady of the group some food, and he just wouldn't let her down. Nothing came easy for Albert Walker, not even buying lunch. Still, Luna saw the depth of his compassion and the extent of his determination. With the hotdogs paid for, pride spread over the good doctor's face. She watched him swagger back to her side. He held out the hotdog, "There you go!"

She shifted her rifle strap to the other shoulder and took the food.

"You look like you've never seen a hot dog before," Albert remarked.

"I have. Just never ate one." She pinched the brown meat, pulling it from the bread.

"Whoa, hold it! You're violating sacred hot dog rules. You leave it *in* the bun and enjoy it that way. Geez, Luna, you almost gave me a heart attack!"

She laughed again and that was when she decided that she'd return his kindness in the only way she knew how; by protecting him. Albert Walker's company felt refreshing. This odd, quirky little man had a way of talking, a way of being, that reminded her of her life before being a warrior, of a time when simple joys were all that mattered; he reminded her of what it was like to think in a way that allowed for good feelings to be commonplace.

She thought she'd be playful. "What else do I need to know concerning hotdogs?"

"Mustard and relish are the real companions. Some would say ketchup is key, but they'd be wrong."

"Dr. Walker would know."

"Indeed."

Jameson led the group to the high bleachers that stretched under the tall scoreboard. There, Kurt waited in his long red trench coat. He sat with a copy of *The Karma Daily* newspaper opened on his lap and a pair of binoculars around his neck. Luna noticed the bulges of his firearms tucked at his waistline. He regarded the group and motioned for them to sit. He said to Jameson. "I was hoping you'd join us."

The crowd hailed as the soccer game carried on. Luna was captivated by the deep green of the grass, the painted white lines and all the people surrounding the event, no one seeking to harm anyone else. Her thoughts tangled. *There is peace here. In the middle of Karma City, where so many are sick, the people still come together in peace. How is that possible?*

Luna looked back to Jameson, hoping to find the answer but found only the man who hated Malady more than anything else. Though always calculating, always staying ahead of the dangers of the world, the parasite had stolen everything he loved, everything that mattered to him. Everything except her.

Like stone to clay, her shoulders softened in the sunlight. There on the bleachers, she relaxed and sighed. *Peace.* What a foreign feeling. Unsettling at first, but wonderful. She wanted to share this serenity with him.

She read Jameson's tension. The crow's feet at the corners of his eyes, the way he cracked his knuckles with his thumb, how his brown hair fell into his eyes and he didn't care. She wanted to take his hand and pull him down to the bleachers to sit beside her for a while. *Just relax. Just be here with me for a minute or two and let's be happy. Let's pretend that things are different, that we are different. Doesn't he see that Malady can't take away the sunny afternoon or the pretty park? Just see it like I do, Jameson. Just once, please see it and understand that Malady cannot take your heart.*

That was the answer.

Kurt's serious tone sounded out of place. "You met with Crimm?" He peered into his binoculars. Luna reasoned he was searching the crowd for Gemni.

"He gave us the full story," answered Jameson, "and hired us to help you. Something about how you aren't as tough as he thought."

Kurt looked up. "Very funny, Shoals. Tell me, what are your qualifications in terms of urban hunting?"

Jameson scratched his stubble. "For starters, I've traveled the Void Lands for most of my life, lived with scavengers, raiders, and villagers. I've trekked Rte. 88 to Brody and beyond. I've spent years in the lawless town of Lobos and I've killed more Malady-heads than you've killed mosquitos. If that isn't enough for you, I've got her." He pointed to Luna. "Luna Briggs is ex-Iron Tribe and still in good with the masters of the rails. She and I have made a habit of moving through this shit-hole of a world and coming out on top. Question is: do you have the Iron Tribe on your side, Kurt?"

Kurt bowed his bald head. "Impressive. You have my respect. But what about Malady? You infected? On meds?"

"Not infected. I don't worry about the worm," remarked Jameson.

"Oh, I see," scoffed Kurt. "Another one of those 'too good to get sick' types."

"It's a lot less complicated than that. And it's none of your damn business. Now please tell me you're not here to see Karma Thunder take on The Lobos Express."

"No. The Crimsons are scattered throughout Karma City," Kurt explained. "We're watching for Gemni and protecting the public while Crimm secures additional resources for the next mission. I assume you and your team *are* the resources."

"What's the plan?"

"We're trying to learn where Marcus Graves is conducting human testing of Malad-X. Crimm has learned that the Malad-X lab has been moved from Sable Tower to his vessel."

Albert interrupted. "You mean the Graves Enterprises Shipping Vessel? That's not a research ship. It exports Quell to places beyond Karma."

"We've now learned," said Kurt. "that Graves has built a laboratory aboard and we believe it's where he's keeping his containment of Malad-X and his advanced test subjects. Furthermore, recent intelligence from Crimm has revealed that Graves is renting a warehouse on the docks. We need to find out which warehouse and determine if in fact human testing of Malad-X is occurring. If so, we strike and shut it down."

"Do you realize," Albert questioned, "that Karma's docks are owned by a powerful man named Mr. Eduard Gabriel?"

"Yes. We don't care."

"You don't care?"

"What am I missing, here?" Jameson asked. "Who is Mr. Gabriel?"

"He's best known for his pleasure palace in Karma's Red-Light district," Albert explained. "It's an extravagant brothel called Eden. He is also a major drug runner. He manufactures street drugs from resources gathered in the Void Lands."

Kurt stood up and tossed his newspaper onto the bleachers. He tied his trench coat closed. "Your mission is twofold. First, infiltrate Eden's security offices and access Gabriel's computer system to obtain a copy of his database of clientele. This database will tell us which warehouse Graves is renting out. Once you've done this, report to the docks. I will meet you at an abandoned boat house near pier forty."

Jameson nodded. "And the second part?"

"Destroy the Graves Enterprises vessel."

***

Marcus Graves' fountain pen slowed to a halt on the page of his notebook. The black ink blotted as he looked over the rim of his reading glasses to the open balcony. The moon bathed his private study at the one hundred and eighth floor of Sable Tower in ghostly white light. A figure waited on the balcony. The moonlight stretched the visitor's shadow across the room and over Graves' desk. "How did you get up here?" Graves asked.

Gemni stepped off the balcony and entered. He gave a half grin. "Would you believe that I climbed?" Gemni pointed to the notebook. "I do hope I'm not disturbing any late-night work."

Graves stood up behind his desk. "It can wait." He walked to the fireplace on the other side of the study. The fire's light turned to oil on his ink-black hair. He stared at the flames as he spoke. "I'm surprised you've survived out there so long, Mr. Burroughs."

"I am Gemni."

"Call yourself what you wish. What do you want?"

"I command you to stop your work on Malad-X."

"Command?" Graves snickered. He took up a fire iron and twisted to face Gemni. "You can do things that even I could not have foreseen. You are faster than man. Stronger. Your senses are immeasurably acute. And most remarkably, you turn Malady infected into your submissive, raging puppets. But that won't work on me."

"I can smell the Malady parasite. And I smell it in you." Gemni pointed his gnarled, claw-like hand at Graves. "Your sickness is mine now. Be awakened and do as I say!"

Graves approached Gemni, leaning on the fire iron like a cane. "You can't *turn* me." His cold laughter sounded like the mournful caws of a crow.

Gemni took a step back, hunched in apprehension like a cornered cat. "You're infected. I command you to stand down!"

"You cannot control me." Grave's face darkened with fury. "I made you from the offspring of *my* Malady. You may very well be Malady supreme, but in truth you remain nothing more than a ruinous experiment. I am going to dash your brain about the carpet and put the failure behind me." He lifted the fire iron and pounced.

Gemni hurdled over him, flipping in the air to land in front of the fire place. He reached into the flames and pulled a length of burning wood. Wielding the crackling shard like a torch, he shouted, "I won't allow Malad-X to spread and empower the Lessers. From the ashes of your 'ruinous experiment' has risen the evolution of humanity!" He blew into the fire, coaxing it hotter. "Let's create more ashes."

"Put the fire down!" Graves shouted.

Gemni's eyes glowed brighter than the flames. He threw the fiery board across the room. It knotted among the silken curtains lining the balcony. The flames engulfed the fabric, blooming up to the ceiling. Gemni streaked toward Graves and snatched him by the throat. "You can die now or do as I say."

Graves pulled a syringe from his coat pocket and stuck Gemni in the neck. Gemni whirled in sudden delirium and staggered across the room.

"What have you done to me?" screeched Gemni, reeling under the Quell's potency.

Graves followed, stalking him with murder in his eyes. "Quell. Knocks unruly parasites to the ground." Graves chuckled. "You can't win, Gemni. Malady can't win. I will cross-infect the population and the Malad-X carriers will slay those with Malady. And guess what they'll all turn to for clarity? Quell. And who controls that? Me. The scope of my power is quite clear."

A sprinkler system activated overhead. Water sprayed over the room, extinguishing the flames.

Graves laughed as the water rained down. Gemni charged, but the drug swung the balance of the fight in Graves' favor. The enraged scientist grappled his attacker, hurling him into his desk, smashing the lamp and knocking stacked books to the floor. Gemni crawled behind the furniture. Graves picked up the fire iron and pursued but found no one behind the desk.

Gemni, poised for escape, called from the moonlit balcony, "Get ready for war!" He held up Graves' notebook and fanned the pages, absorbing the text with incalculable speed. "Ah, I see Professor Crimm is involved in Malad-X. Not for long." He bowed in a mockery of triumph, fanned his arms and leapt from the one hundred and eighth floor.

***

The subway shuddered to a halt. Jack closed his notebook and tucked his pen in his shirt pocket. He looked through the dirty window to be sure this was his stop. A large sign over a wide stairwell to the streets above read: Oasis District-Hospital Station. The subway doors parted and the passengers crammed the aisle as they filed out and onto the station platform. Jack exited and took in the early morning smells of breakfast stands steaming with pots of nutty coffee beside racks of powder and chocolate donuts, still warm and sticky. The cold wind of the subway tunnel wafted around him as the small train pulled away. A voice shouted to him from one of the food stands. "Morning, son! How about a donut? They have jelly! You love jellies!"

Jack's heart sank. Corpse-Dad waited with a juvenile grin. The zombie-like figure waved for Jack to join him. *This isn't going to stop, is it? Where the hell is my Quell?* Jack's fingers found the small amber bottle in his coat pocket. He popped the cap, poured out a pill and swallowed it down. *First time. I guess I'm in the club now. Just have wait for this stuff to kick in.* Jack looked around, nervous that others might see the grotesque man calling out for him but he shook away the worry, reminding himself that this nightmarish visitor was only for him. He took a deep breath to cool his nerves and met the coffee vendor, trying his best to ignore his dead father.

"Large cup, please. Cream only."

The vendor held out an open palm. "Two bucks."

Jack handed him the money and sipped the coffee.

"What about breakfast?" Corpse-Dad asked.

With his notebook tucked under his arm, Jack walked up the stairs to the street, clutching the hot cup in both hands. Corpse-Dad followed.

"Hey son, I was thinking, if you're not busy today, maybe we could go to the airfield and watch the planes. You used to love that! What do you say?"

"Airfield? I don't know what you're talking about." Jack muttered, "The Quell better work its magic soon."

"Until it does, I'll keep you company."

"Thanks."

The Wednesday morning sun bobbed in and out of passing clouds. Tall willow trees swayed in the subtle breeze, their sweeping, curtain boughs twinkled with dew. The thick grass carpeted the Oasis Hospital campus in a deep green hue. Jack's shoes clopped on the stone walkway leading to the hospital's main entrance. Corpse-Dad's steps scraped along with Jack's.

"My goodness," Corpse-Dad said, "Oasis. I haven't been here since they partnered with my aviation business. Wait, that's not true. They brought my body here after our little 'accident,' didn't they?"

Jack turned on his heels to face him. "It's clear to me that you're going to keep turning up. So, here's how this is going to go. Don't talk to me. Don't expect me to talk to you. In fact, just be a good hallucination and stay imaginary. Thanks to you, I'm on the fast track to becoming a Quell addict. Do me a favor and try to be as little of an interruption to my life as possible!"

"I think I understand what's going on. You're embarrassed by your old man. I get it."

"No, you don't!" Jack yelled.

A patrolling Oasis guard approached. Jack regained his composure. He straightened his tie and blew the steam away from his hot coffee. The guard frowned. "Sir, I need to ask you to control your outbursts on the premises."

"Yes, I'm sorry. It's just that..."

"It's apparent you're suffering with Malady. Do you need help checking in to the hospital?"

"No. I'm not here to check in. I'm here on business."

The guard looked him over. "What might that be, exactly?"

Jack cleared his throat. "My name is Jack Halligan and I'm—"

Corpse-Dad interrupted, "You know, the famous writer!"

"What the hell did I just tell you?" Jack barked. "Shut your damn mouth!" Corpse-Dad pouted and faded away. Jack felt his knees tremble as the Quell took effect. The drug dissolved the Malady-induced confusion in his mind but knocked him off balance. He fell to his hands and knees. His coffee spilled, but he managed to catch his notebook. The ground tilted and dipped beneath him; he dug his fingernails into the walkway as if struggling to keep atop a bouncing raft. The guard knelt to help him up. Jack leaned on him for stability while the Quell settled in him. *That's some powerful stuff.*

The guard lifted Jack back to his feet and asked, "Halligan you say?"

"Yes." Jack took a few deep breaths. "From *the Karma Daily*. Listen, I just popped my first Quell pill a few minutes ago and it really packed a punch."

"I understand. What can I help you with today, Mr. Halligan?"

"I'm here to inquire about the survivors of the train explosion, the two allegedly seen jumping from the train. I want to meet them; get their story."

"I'd love to help you. But the recent incident is being carefully—" A radio hanging from the guard's belt crackled. "Hold on a sec, Mr. Halligan." The guard turned up the radio and answered, "This is Officer Brooks, go ahead."

"This is detective Carl Wright," replied the distorted voice. "We've got a serious situation down in Karma's lower east side."

"I'm listening, detective. Go ahead."

"I'm standing in an apartment full of dead bodies. I need any available officers to report to three-seventy-six East High Street immediately. I'm sending a report to Dr. Carmen Victoria now."

Brooks rolled his eyes. "Sounds normal for the lower east side, sir. There were five other corpses found there this month alone. Why trouble Dr. Victoria with it?"

"Because Professor Anthony Crimm is among the dead."

Jack recognized the name. His heart quickened as the story knotted in his head. *Train explosion. Jumpers. Hospital riot. Dr. Walker fleeing with mysterious armed people. Now Professor Crimm is murdered.* He opened his notebook and scribbled the address.

Brooks regarded Jack before running off. "Go easy on the Quell, Mr. Halligan, and stay safe out there. Sorry I couldn't help you with your story." Brooks hurried for a parked cruiser.

"East High Street, here I come," whispered Jack.

The detective and his team had taped off the building. Jack showed his press identification and was permitted inside. He ventured up the stair well and into the apartment. The putrid stench of death filled Jack's nose. He pulled up his shirt collar to keep from vomiting when he saw the remains of the old professor scattered about the room. Blood painted the walls and stained the furniture. Crimm's insides trailed the apartment. His mangled corpse lay strewn atop a blood-blackened couch near his desk. Jack counted eight other bodies in the room. They were men and women, all strangely wearing red trench coats.

Jack noticed Officer Brooks reviewing some photographs with other detectives. Brooks eyed Jack, and with a look of disapproval, crossed the room. "You're a slippery one, aren't you, Mr. Halligan?"

"Chasing a story, is all. Don't mind me."

"Listen, this is a very tragic and very serious situation. Take notes but don't disturb the scene. Got it?"

"No problem."

Brooks rejoined the other officials, leaving Jack alone with his notebook.

Maybe it was the calming effect of the Quell in his veins, maybe it was the unexpected thrill of the moment or just his morbid, journalistic curiosity; Jack wasn't sure what drove him to want to poke around. He stepped over the chunks of entrails and puddles of blood, making his way to the professor's desk. He opened drawers, sifted through papers and combed through stacks of files. *Nothing interesting.* A shattered glass cabinet caught his attention. Its doors were closed and shards of glass littered the floor beneath it. A closer examination revealed that the cabinet was still locked. Whoever murdered Crimm broke the glass to obtain the contents. *Now that's something.* Next, Jack went to look at the slumped corpse on the couch. Crimm's ribcage looked like a wooden barrel with a hole kicked into the side. Terror had frozen the dead man's face. Jack noticed Crimm's hand crumpled in a tight fist. He used his pen to pry apart the cold fingers and found a stained slip of paper. *What do we have here?* He unfurled the slip and read a strange word.

*MALAD-X.*

Jack heard Brooks approaching again. He tucked the paper into his pocket and feigned ill. "I don't think I can stomach much more of this. I need to go home and clear my head."

Brooks' face looked pale. "I don't think I'll be much longer either."

# Chapter 7

Jack's excitement slowed his wristwatch. The journey back home felt like hours. A twenty-minute stop-and-go trip on the subway to central city and a ten-minute bus ride returned him to Greely Park. He walked the rest of the way, down the sidewalk of Center Avenue and cursed at the afternoon traffic. He darted between the cars, crossing the street with a choir of car horns blaring behind him. *I've got to get back to my desk and write this stuff down.* Jack ran up the steps of his apartment building and hurried down the main hall, where he was interrupted by a neighbor.

"Hi-yah, Jack!"

Jack slowed his pace to greet his friend, Marty. The old man scrambled down the hall to catch up. Marty's ruffled brow could have made a nest for a small animal and his purplish bottom lip swallowed the top. Jack knew something weighed on Marty's mind.

"Haven't seen you in a few days, Marty," said Jack. "Where've you been?"

As eager as Jack was to start writing, he couldn't ignore the lonely old man who deeply suffered with Malady. Marty's sickness proved much farther along than Jack's. In his patchy state of mind, Marty preferred to live in the building's laundry room. There, he set up a lean-to of sheets, clothesline and baskets, leaving the camp only to eat at Donna's diner across the street.

Marty chuckled at Jack's question. "You know where I live. If you ain't seen me, you ain't been doing your wash. But, hey, I've been looking for yah."

"What's going on?"

"You got a delivery. A big box."

"Must be my meds. That's odd; the nurse said the next shipment wasn't until Thursday? It's only Wednesday afternoon."

"It arrived by courier direct from Sable District," explained Marty. "Fancy."

"Where is it?"

"I've been keeping it safe for yah." Marty gave Jack a proud, toothless grin. "Making sure none of the nutcases living here take it."

Jack gave Marty's shoulder an appreciative squeeze. "Thank you, my friend. There should be plenty of Quell in the box. Would you like some?"

Marty frowned. "My worm's living happy in my head, Jack. Won't help me much to justify taking it from you. Keep it. You're young, got years left to enjoy. Come get the box when you can. I ain't carrying it up to your place."

"I'll be down later. I've got to get to work now."

"Oh!" Marty broke out in a clumsy dance, as if something important struck his brain. "I saw Donna this morning on her way out, she said she'd bring me a muffin later! They've got those really big ones over there. Blueberry, o'course."

"Donna's the best, isn't she? I'll see you in a little while, Marty."

Marty danced away, whistling a happy tune. Jack watched the old man's demeanor suddenly shift. His shoulders caved and he tip-toed. Marty glanced back; paranoia darkened his eyes. He slipped back into his laundry room burrow. A chill trickled down Jack's spine. He shook his head in empathy, briefly wondering if his own Malady would eventually render him so irrational. He pushed aside the thought and ascended the winding stairwell to his floor.

Old Man Marty, that's all the other tenants knew him as. It wasn't fair, not to Jack at least. He remembered Marty before the parasite infected him. In those days, almost ten years ago, people called him Martin Jasper, Landlord and owner of several tenements up and down the block. Martin Jasper was loved by families throughout central Karma because his buildings were maintained, his rent was fair and he cared for his tenants as if they were his own family. He even ran errands for them. Bringing groceries to the elderly, walking kids home from school, and paying unemployed fathers to maintain his properties were just a few of his simpler gestures.

Gardner M. Browning

It was Martin Jasper who welcomed Jack into the building, setting aside a lofty apartment with a view of the cityscape just for him. "Writers need scenic views," said Martin when he handed Jack the keys to the apartment. "Unfortunately, I'm fresh out of the scenic part, but hey, a view is a view, right?" Jack recalled laughing with him as they stood on his small balcony gazing out at the surrounding slums. Jack always appreciated the extras that this genuine man extended, but now he was the only one who did.

When Martin contracted Malady, he signed up for Quell. But he distributed his allotments of the medication to the families living in his buildings. This kept people well enough to stay hopeful and because of his selflessness, Greely Park remained a place of peace. Because of his love for others, he shouldered the pain of the parasite and suffered, withered and eventually wasted away to a shriveled creature of a man living in a dirty laundry room. *Old Man Marty. Marty the Mad. Malady Marty.* Jack often wondered what people would call him.

The traffic blurred outside Jack's window. *Busy out there today.* Jack shrugged and sat at his desk. He placed the message from Crimm on his blotter and read the strange word repeatedly, hoping to decipher its meaning. *Malad-X. What were you up to, Crimm? What does this mean?*

A woman's scream broke his contemplation. *Donna!*

He dashed out of his apartment and spiraled down the stairs to the first-floor hall. Donna screamed again and Jack's heart sank when she crawled from the laundry room, her clothing torn and her hair thrown. Marty pounced on top of her with a knife poised like a scorpion's stinger. "Where's my muffin? I want my damn muffin!"

Donna screamed for Jack. He ran down the hall and barreled into Marty, knocking him off Donna. The knife cut Jack's side, tearing his shirt and slicing through his denim jacket.

Marty growled as Jack pinned him to the ground. "She said I'd get a big muffin. Blueberry!" Marty writhed under Jack's weight. For a man so old, his crazed strength was frightening.

"Jack!" yelled Donna. "We need to get help! Let's go!"

Marty frothed and snapped a bite at Jack's arm. Jack pulled back and struck the old man hard in the face. Marty went limp and

Jack released him, hurrying to Donna's side. He wrapped her in his arms. "Did he hurt you?"

She shook her head. "He jumped me, Jack. As I fell, he clawed at my clothes, shouting that I was 'hiding it.'" Her voice wavered as tears formed rivers on her cheeks. "Oh, Jack. I thought he was going to kill me."

"I will if that's what it takes!" Marty squealed. He crawled toward them. Jack pulled Donna down the hall and out the front door. They ran down the steps, stopping at the busy street. Cars whirred by. Marty burst out of the building, knife in hand. Donna screamed in terror and ran into the street. Cars screeched and swerved.

"Donna!" Jack shouted, "Wait!" The traffic screeched around him as he sprinted for her. He dove to close the distance, knocking her to the adjacent sidewalk seconds before a Karma City bus struck them both down. Marty was not so fortunate. Jack cringed when the bus's grill smashed into the old man and the heavy wheels crunched over his friend. The bus labored to a halt as blood pooled under the mangled body.

As the afternoon sun dipped away, the shadows of the surrounding tenements wheeled over the neighborhood. Jack comforted Donna on the curbside and couldn't help but think it hauntingly poetic that the buildings Marty once kept would be like the blade of a sundial—sweeping that black arrow of darkness and death in an arc too great for any man to evade.

Jack's heart burned with anger and fear—anger for Malady taking another good person and fear that he, himself, might end up this way. He sighed and caressed Donna's hair as she sobbed against him.

***

Night fell over Karma City bringing with it a blanket of storm clouds. Luna Briggs looked up at the black sky. *Thunder storm on the way. Gonna rain soon. Rain is good. It cleanses. I've always like the rain.* She considered the task ahead. Karma's Red-Light District sounded like a very dangerous place. Sexual indiscretion and rampant drug usage always lead to a concentration of Malady infected. She'd be sure to interact with as few people as possible. *Do the job and get out.*

Albert drove the ambulance under a large railway overpass. The Iron Tribe's tracks stretched across a long trestle looming over Karma's two-block network of brothels, night clubs and smoke parlors. Red-bulb streetlamps lined the sidewalks, painting the brick buildings and illuminating the underbelly of the train bridge in a sultry, rosy glow. Albert drove slowly down the street, weaving around the crowds of patrons and prostitutes that meandered about. Luna eyed the women strolling up and down the avenue in knee-high boots, tight skirts and low-cut tops. She found their lavish hair styles, gaudy jewelry and glitzy make-up bewildering and strangely enchanting. Somewhere far in her mind, she wondered what she would look like dressed in sexual finery. She felt cold fingers touching her face, her scarring, and she realized they were her own. *I'll never be attractive in the way a man desires. It's not who I am.* Her eyes settled on Jameson, who intently assessed the throngs of people crowding the street. *What does he think of me? Does he see in me what I see in him? Does he feel what I feel?*

Jameson's words startled her. "Every person here is a threat to your health. If you don't want to catch Malady, keep focused on the objective."

The bright lights of Mr. Gabriel's luxurious adult resort, Eden, came into view. The estate beckoned patrons with dazzling pearly lights, sparkling fountain and an extravagant rose garden. Albert pulled the ambulance to a halt outside Eden's iron gates.

"It's time to get to work," Jameson clapped his hands and excitedly rubbed them together. "Here's the plan. Albert will enter through the front and pose as a representative from Oasis Hospital sent to conduct a health audit. That's sure to get the attention of the staff and they'll believe it with the Oasis ambulance parked in view. While Albert's got them distracted, Luna, you and I will infiltrate the private offices and obtain the data from their computer system."

"I'm not much of a hacker."

"I know. So just pop the hard drive from the biggest computer you can find and we'll go from there."

Luna smiled. "Can do."

Jameson loaded his shotgun. "Let's hit them!"

"Hold on," Albert interjected. "Non-member guests are required to pay admission. I think I have a coupon from last time...where is it..."

Jameson laughed. "Doc, you are full of surprises."

Luna sighed and rubbed the corners of her eyes. "Let's not forget about Gemni. If he's looking to turn Malady people into his obedient troops against mankind, then this place is another huge spot for recruiting. Stay vigilant."

From the ambulance, Luna observed as Albert engaged the Eden gatekeepers in a short conversation. The guards permitted his entry.

Jameson turned to Luna with shotgun in hand. "Ready?"

Luna took up her rifle and slung her pack over her shoulder. "Yep."

They ducked out of the ambulance's rear doors and moved down the street, away from the resort's guarded gates. Jameson led Luna down a footpath along the iron fence, ducking under low hanging tree branches and slipping through growths of knotted vines. The two followed the perimeter of the property, hardly making a sound, until they came to the resort's back courtyard. Jameson stopped and knelt beside the tall fence. He dropped his backpack to the ground and pulled out a hacksaw. "We'll be inside in two minutes."

Luna scanned the area with her scope while Jameson's saw chewed through the bars.

"How are we looking out there?" he asked.

Luna slowly eyed Eden's interior grounds. "We'll be entering into a rose garden. There are guests hanging around the center fountain but I don't see any guards near the building."

Jameson pulled the bars away from the fence and placed them on the ground without a sound. "We should be able to wedge through now."

The guests paid no attention as the two hurried across the garden patio. They came to the fountain. Rose bushes circled the marble basin and crystalline jets of water trickled in twisting streams. An unusual scent tinged the sweet perfume of the roses.

"We've got to cover up," Jameson ordered. Once more, he went into his pack, this time pulling out two green handkerchiefs. "The air is dangerous. Put this on."

Luna covered her nose and mouth with the rag. "Don't like roses?"

"It's the Lovers' Claw I'm not a fan of. Look." Jameson pointed at the fountain's rim. Emerging from the water stretched a vine bearing hook-shaped leaves and tiny yellow buds. He tore the plant loose. "This baby's scent is a potent aphrodisiac. Makes sense that this Mr. Gabriel guy has them growing all over his pleasure palace."

"What makes it so dangerous?"

"Too much for too long will knock you into a state of loopy euphoria." He coiled the length of vine, removed the fragrant buds, and stuffed it in his back pack. "This plant is like Eden's prostitutes, beautiful but nasty."

"If it's so risky, why are you taking it with you?" Luna asked.

"It's useful in other ways. When I was in the Void Lands, I used to use it to incapacitate my enemies. Burn up the vine and its smoke will knock a room of people unconscious in seconds. Might come in handy." He hooked the bag over his shoulder. "Come on. Albert won't be able to keep the charade going for long."

Jameson and Luna entered the resort, shoving through Eden's guests. People wandered the halls and foyers wearing only robes and slippers. Exotic women, nude, tanned and oiled danced between clusters of guests, wrapping silken veils over their shoulders, luring them to the large pillows lining the floor.

Luna followed Jameson down the halls, passing rooms filled with groups engaged in sex and drugs. Music lulled and stirred the atmosphere, setting a cadence of sensual rhythms. Elaborate candelabra lit the halls with a flickering orange glow that turned the perfect, bronzed bodies of Eden's concubines to gold.

Luna felt her cheeks flush with heat. Living the tribal life, rolling over the railways with little human interaction beyond stations and depots, Luna struggled to stay grounded in this carnal hurricane. She was not like these harlots, but she was still a woman with desires. As she moved through the resort, she wondered what Jameson saw. *Does he like these women? What does he see in me? What's beautiful to him?*

She passed an empty room. Berry-sweet incense smoked and a bed of pillows wrapped in silky sheets lay clean and empty. She imagined closing the door, trapping Jameson inside with her. The sheets looked soft and her mind played a game of contrast. The delicate bedding, cool and gentle; his hands on her body, fiery and rough.

Their exploration led to a stairwell. Luna pointed with her rifle barrel. "There's a door down there. Let's see where it leads."

She shuffled down the steps and stopped at the door. A small sign read: SECURITY OFFICE. She kicked open the doorway and ran down the hall. Jameson followed behind with shotgun in hand. They stopped abruptly when two security guards entered, walking in their direction. Luna side-stepped, pressing her back against the wall to hide behind two pillars. Jameson did the same on the opposing edge of the hall and readied the butt of his shotgun. When the guards came within reach, Jameson and Luna spun out from their hiding places, and smashed the guards in the face with their gunstocks. The men fell to the ground, blood streaming from their noses.

"Check them, Luna."

Luna patted the uniform pockets of one of the men and discovered a security room access card. "This is too easy."

"I agree."

The security office waited at the end of the hall. Luna swiped the card through the reader and the door buzzed open. With weapons poised, they entered.

"Stop right there!"

Five guards stood behind a half-circle counter and held them with pistols ready to fire. Jameson put away his shotgun and winked at Luna. She knew to trust that wink. It had gotten them out of many heavy jams in the past. She lowered her rifle.

"Easy, boys!" Jameson said with a chuckle. "We hurried down here to warn you."

"Warn us? Who are you?"

"We're bounty hunters and we've been trailing a thief throughout Karma. The man we're after is cunning and dangerous. He seeks sensitive information from successful men like Mr. Gabriel and drags his victims through rounds of black mail. He's here, in Eden, right now. See for yourself!" Jameson pointed to the security monitors. "In the main lobby, you'll find a man dressed like a doctor."

The guards viewed the monitors. "Yes, I see him," said one of them. "What is he after?"

Jameson continued the ploy. "His goal is to steal your main computer; you know, the one with all of Mr. Gabriel's client files?"

As Luna had hoped, one of the guards briefly looked away. She traced his glance to the computer terminal on the far left. *That's the one. Too easy!*

"Let me see some credentials," challenged the guard, "before we shoot you full of holes."

"Right, no problem," replied Jameson. "My partner has our identification in her pack. Will you permit her to get it?"

"Make it quick."

Jameson silently mouthed the word 'boom.' Luna opened her pack, reached inside and quietly pulled the pin from a grenade. With a smile, she flashed the explosive for the guards to see and tossed it behind their counter. They panicked and Jameson pulled Luna out of the office. The two slid across the tiled floor on their stomachs.

The grenade erupted, deafening and devastating.

The walls cracked and the door blew from its frame in shards. Smoke and burning wood littered the hall.

Luna laughed. "That gig never gets old."

Jameson helped her up. "Let's hurry. That blast is sure to have spoiled Albert's act. Let's salvage what remains of the computer and get out of here."

"We can't go back the way we came now."

"Got any more grenades?" Jameson asked.

"Yep. Shall we make a back door?"

"Another gig that always works!"

Luna pulled the drive from the ruined computer and stuffed it in her pack. Her second grenade punched a hole in the building's foundation wall. The fiery detonation spewed forth bricks and ash across Eden's flowery front yard. Jameson and Luna emerged and sprinted across the estate grounds. Luna heard the screaming begin as the pleasure palace's alarms sounded.

Rain fell over Karma city.

Albert ran from the building and joined Jameson and Luna at the curb. He yelled, "Are you two insane?"

Jameson wiped the rain and dirt from his brow. "Get to the ambulance, now!"

Guards poured out of the building and opened fire. Gunshots rang throughout the Red-Light District creating fear, confusion and chaos. People screamed in terror.

The ambulance's wheels spun on the slick, rainy pavement. Bullets ripped through the vehicle's body as it sped off. The glass shattered; rain pouring in. Albert whimpered as he steered down the avenue. Eden's security guards followed after in a cruiser.

Luna heard a series of sharp pings. Bullets bounced off the wheels. She looked out the back window to see the guards hanging from their cars with automatic weapons. "Hurry up, Albert!"

A stream of gunfire pounded their vehicle. The rear tires burst, making the ambulance wobble over the wet road. Smoke curled from under the hood; the unmistakable smell of gasoline filling the cabin. Luna's eyes met Jameson's. "Fumes and smoke," she said. "You know what comes next. We'd better ditch this thing."

"Albert, stop!" Jameson shouted. The ambulance squealed and fishtailed to a stop under the train bridge.

They scattered from the vehicle as fast as they could. Gasoline emptied onto the rainy street. The plume of black smoke flashed

86

and a wave of fire flared, swallowing the ambulance in a terrible blaze. The three regrouped beside one of the bridge piers as the orange inferno swirled over their vehicle.

Albert shook his head. "Worst night ever."

Luna pointed down the street. "It's not over yet."

Eden's cruisers sped toward them with blinding high beams. More gunshots blasted, sparking off the iron pilings.

Albert paced in dread. "I'm thinking now that this wasn't the best way to explore my scientific curiosities surrounding Malad-X." A gunshot pinged over his head. "A gross miscalculation, indeed. There's no way out of this one!"

A low and woeful whistle bellowed over the night.

The bridge overhead rumbled, as if trembling in fright. Luna stepped forward and slung her rifle over her back. She pulled a small pocket watch from her belt and smiled. "Right on time." She climbed the bridge pier and looked down at the group. "Train's coming. Climb!"

They followed Luna's lead, scaling the towering leg of the bridge. Lightning flashed in the clouded night sky. The cold rain slicked the bridge's frame, slipping their soles and numbing their fingers. Luna pulled Jameson up to the rail deck and Jameson helped Albert. Eden's men fired shots from below but the bridge's structure shielded their attack. The train coursed along the tracks, unmoved by the wind of the brewing storm.

Luna positioned herself dangerously close to the rails. She shouted over the chugging of the approaching train, "Get ready to board!"

The engine rushed by, warming the air around Luna, sending a wave of heat through her clothes. The smell of steam and burning coal teased her heart with homesickness. She ran along the cargo cars, reached out and snatched hold of the cold handrails. The train's momentum threatened to pull her arm from the socket, but she leapt up and swung her feet onto the car's step as she'd done a thousand times before. She reached out for the others who sprinted after the passing train. Jameson took hold of Luna's outstretched hand. She tugged him upward and he latched aboard. Albert jumped for Jameson, who clamped the doctor's wrist and yanked him up. The three entered a darkened cargo car and pulled the sliding wooden door closed behind them.

Albert wrung the rain from his clothes and slumped to the floor to rest. The train rattled. Luna moved through the car and lit a lantern. Shipping crates and pallets surrounded them.

Albert sighed. "Oh, this is just cozy! If Gemni pops out from the shadows, I'm going to be the first to jump from this train."

A female voice disturbed the shadows. "Maybe you should jump right now."

# Chapter 8

Luna watched as an Iron Tribeswoman entered the circle of lantern light. She had long red hair that hung in front of her scared face. Her brown leather boots, studded with metal spurs, tied off just under her knees and her tight denim pants hugged her hips. The lantern light revealed the bandoleer of bullets tracing her waist-length coat of stitched hide. She moved the muzzle of her rifle over the group.

Luna gasped. "Mandy?"

The woman lowered her rifle. "Luna?"

The two smashed together in tight hug.

As the lantern light shone on Mandy's face, the train of memories rattled down the tracks of the past, sweeping Luna up and carrying her away. Jameson Shoals spoke up, snapping Luna back to the present. "Who's your friend?"

"Jameson, this is Mandy Briggs. My mentor and tribal sister."

Mandy tipped her hat and eyed the group. She spoke to Luna, "How long has it been, kid?"

"Nearly a year."

"Time races on the rails."

"It moves slowly off of them."

"What's brought you to the train tonight, Luna?"

"We needed an escape."

Mandy crossed her arms. "I see. And this band of misfits you're traveling with?"

Luna introduced her companions. "This is my partner, Jameson Shoals. He's a Void Lander with city roots."

Jameson lit a cigarette and handed it to Mandy. She accepted with a half-smile.

Luna looked at Albert, who wore a juvenile grin, noticeably eager to say hello. "This is Dr. Albert Walker, a scientist working on efforts against Malady."

Albert interjected with a nervous ramble. "I've got a private lab and medical center in Undertown open to the public. If you're ever in the neighborhood...actually, the train tracks don't go to

Undertown...but there's a subway and... wait, does the Iron Tribe ride subways? I'm sorry, that's probably a personal question and—"

Mandy put up her hand. "Relax, Dr. Walker. Welcome aboard. Allies of Luna are allies of mine. You may all ride the rails with Luna and receive our courtesy. Now, Luna, tell me what you're trying to escape."

"I need to jump in here, if I may," Albert interrupted. "Luna, did you finish the job at Eden? Because if I lost my ambulance for nothing, I'm going to cry."

"The computer drive is in my pack."

"What's going on?" Mandy snapped.

Luna struggled under the moral imbalance. Here stood her tribal sister, and the devotion remained. Yet, she had aligned herself with new friends and formed new bonds. Though the train coursed on a linear track, a crossroad challenged her. The Tribe sought the one responsible for the destruction of the car and the bridge, and to withhold knowledge was a violation of the Southbound Code: no other place or cause shall come before the needs of the Tribe. But she was no longer bound by their rigid laws.

Luna saw the concern framing Mandy's face.

Albert spoke before Luna could answer. "Like your esteemed tribe, Mandy, the three of us are pursuing the one who bombed the train. Our efforts led us to Eden, where we met a moment of conflict beyond resolution. In addition to needing a means of escape, we've come aboard tonight to offer the information we've gathered regarding our shared foe for the benefit of the Iron Tribe and the good people of Karma."

"How noble," said Mandy. "Go on."

Luna let out a slow exhale. Albert's squirrelly nature spared her from having to bend the truth. Appreciation welled in her. She would not forget it.

"Our enemy calls himself Gemni," Albert continued. "He is running a campaign to kill innocent people."

"The Iron Tribe wants him dead for his crimes against Mother."

"I understand."

"Where is this Gemni?"

"He is aboard the Graves Enterprises shipping vessel."

"That's beyond the reach of our rails."

"Well, we're going after him and if you get this train to drop us at the docks, we'll hunt him down in honor of the Mother."

"I'll inform the engineer of our new route." She tipped her hat and left the group, hurrying through the passage to the next car.

Luna turned to Albert. "Thanks for jumping in. I didn't know what to say to her. But we don't know where Gemni is."

Albert shrugged. "Sometimes part of the truth works better than the whole thing. She doesn't need to know the extent of this mess."

Jameson gave Albert a light punch in the arm. "Nice job, doc. Really came through."

"Here to serve," replied Albert with a wince. "So, Luna. It must be nice reconnecting with your old friend. I can see where you get your style."

"It's not easy being back on the tracks. This was my train, my route, my family. And I left them."

Luna turned up the lantern to brighten the car, then pulled out a few wool blankets from one of the crates and handed them to Jameson and Albert. The group set the blankets on the floor to relax as the train rolled through the rainy night.

"Can I ask you why you joined the tribe and why you left?" asked Albert. "I mean, if you don't want to talk about it, that's perfectly acceptable; I'm sure Jameson would gladly indulge us with one of his tales of Void Land woe to pass the time."

"Funny, doc."

Luna chuckled. "No, it's okay." She took a breath to collect her thoughts. "I guess the best place to start is with my real family, in Borealis. It's a village along the base of the Rime Mountains. I lived there with my father and older sister, Samantha. My name was Rachel O'Keefe. My father was a miner, working in the tunnels of Mount Rime. When my sister came of age, she had to work the mines, too. I was left alone at home to clean and prepare dinner. I missed Samantha so much. And I was afraid for her because the mines were very dangerous. I told her how upset I was and she gave me this," Luna reached into her shirt and revealed an old half-moon necklace. "My ancestors from Borealis called the moon, Luna. They believed it to be a symbol of unity. My sister wore the other half of the moon around her neck every day. We never took them off."

"That's sweet," said Albert. "You know, I never had any siblings. Probably for the best though. Although, sometimes I wonder what it would be like to have a brother who was a dentist. Imagine the wellness center we could set up. Then sometimes I think—,"

"This isn't about you," piped Jameson. "Let her talk."

Albert squirmed like a scolded child. "Please excuse me, Luna."

"Well, by the time I became sixteen, Samantha was twenty years old, and a hardened working woman. Borealis changed as well. The growing presence of Malady in the Void Lands, and the medical advances in Karma, pulled the village away from the mountain and closer to the train tracks. The Iron Tribe's train provided many things for us: food, supplies, medicine, information, and most importantly, escape from life in the shadow of Mount Rime. I became inspired, wanting a better life for my father and sister. But Samantha didn't see things the same way. She was proud to work beside our father in the mines and offended that I didn't desire the same. One night, after another argument over it, I prepared a big meal, hoping to make amends with my sister and get back on my father's good side. As I dressed the table, the sound of a far-off whistle called in the night. An alarm from the mountain. I ran outside and looked up the slopes. A huge fire blazed from Rime's east mines.

"I followed the other panicked villagers to the cable car platform to meet the evacuating miners. Many had terrible burns. I waited for an eternity for the crowd to thin out, all the while praying for my sister and father. I stopped one of the emergency responders to ask for help, telling him that my family hadn't come down from the mountain. He shook his head and told me there were no more survivors. My heart shattered to a million tiny pieces. And that's when I heard the train's haunting pipes calling out from somewhere far away. That's just what I wanted. To be far away."

Albert wiped a small tear from his cheek. "You ran? Got on the train?"

Luna nodded.

"But you were only sixteen; you had to have been terrified."

"Yeah, I was. But when I stepped aboard the train, the engine's valves blew a cloud of steam around the tracks, and it felt like I had stepped up onto a cloud that was about to lift off into the sky. The powerful, whirring wheels lulled my sadness. I fell asleep.

"The next day, a blast of the steam startled me awake. A busy, crowed street waited outside full of markets, saloons and lined with vendors peddling wares from the city and places unknown. One of the Iron Tribe's guards pulled me from my seat, saying, 'Station stop. Lobos, City of Wolves. This is your stop, kid.' Even though I didn't know where Lobos was, I knew better than to disobey the tribesman."

"You got off the train in a strange place?" Albert asked in disbelief. He turned to Jameson. "She's got some great stories! Have you heard this before?"

Jameson rolled his eyes. "Just shut up and listen."

"Right. Sorry."

"I felt hungry, so I entered a nearby saloon. The men eyed me like dogs. They hooted and hollered with foul taunts. One man stood up from the bar and yelled, 'I'm talking to you, girl. Get over here.'

"The train whistle blew, ready to depart. I sprinted out of there and ran for the rails, shoes kicking up dust and rocks. I was almost to the train car's steps when the man tackled me to the ground. I screamed and clawed to get free. But he was too big, too strong. He rolled me over pinned me down by the throat. I could smell his stinking breath as his mouth lowered close to mine. Then, the blur of a boot whooshed by, smashing against his head, knocking him to the ground."

"Woo-hoo!" cheered Albert.

"I scurried to my feet. A woman with long, red hair, stitched hide coat and wide-brimmed hat moved in front of me. She pressed her rifle muzzle to the man's forehead. She said, 'Time for you to run along, asshole.'

"The man moved back, retreating. His angry eyes were those of a ravenous animal suddenly robbed of its kill. The woman lowered her rifle and shifted her attention to me; then, the man pounced, a silver knife now flashing in his hand. The rifle fired. The back of the man's head erupted. I couldn't believe my eyes. My whole body shook and my mind reeled in a strange delirium. Never had I witnessed such a gruesome scene. A cold numbness fell over me.

"I boarded the train again, this time no longer alone. As the train rolled along the tracks, I watched the lawless town of Lobos peel from view while the endlessness of the Void Lands opened around me. I cried a little and the woman who saved my life noticed. She said, 'I can't tell you things will be okay. But I can tell you they'll be different. The name's Mandy Briggs. Iron Tribe. And you are?'

"I thumbed my moon pendant hanging around my neck and took a new name."

Albert sighed and gave a smile of empathy and understanding. "Rachel O'Keefe had become Luna Briggs."

"Yep. I pledged my life to the Iron Tribe and defended the locomotive as it rumbled through the valleys, plains and mountain passes of the Void Lands stopping at settlements, towns and camps alike. The Iron Tribe protected me as I protected them. In time, my marksmanship became unmatched. Protecting the Mother meant dealing swift death and doing so instinctively. I lived a life of might and wealth, safe within the impenetrable force of the Iron Tribe."

"Can I ask a personal question?"

"Sure."

"Maybe it's the doctor in me, but I have to know so I'm going to ask. The scars. How is it done and why?"

"Tribals are unified by 'mother's touch.' Initiates kneel before the engineer and," she closed her eyes, fighting back the memory of her branding. "Let's just say the furnace is very hot."

Albert shuddered. "I can't imagine enduring that. What made you leave the Iron Tribe?" asked Albert.

"My sister."

"Mandy?"

"No. Samantha."

"But I thought she died in the mines."

"So did I. Last winter, the Tribe made a Quell delivery to a newly built depot standing along a recent expansion of the railway tracing the westward bend of Mount Rime. A large crowd of people waited at the depot, eager for the shipment of meds. They were angry. The winter weather had delayed the delivery by two weeks and many of them were desperately sick. My experience told me that caution was necessary at stops like this. Especially with such a high value cargo to off-load. I watched the crowd and noticed a father cradling his baby in one arm and holding his wife close with the other. My attention was suddenly diverted when villagers stormed the cargo car for the cases of Quell. They opened fire on the Tribe and Tribesman responded with lethal force of their own. People screamed as blood splattered over the depot walls.

"Through the eye of my scope, I watched the father holding the baby pass the child to the mother. He came at me then, a pistol in his hand. I ordered him to stop. But he didn't listen. He raised his pistol at me, and I shot him in the chest. The train rolled away from the riot. The woman holding the baby knelt beside her dead husband. Her mournful cries became my own when I saw a crude, half-moon pendant dangling from the woman's neck."

Albert held his head in his hands. "Luna, I'm so sorry. I don't know what to say."

Jameson slid next to her and wrapped his arm over her shoulders. "You don't need to keep going."

"It's important. Feels good to talk about it."

Albert wiped his glasses. "Did you go to her? To Samantha? Is that when you left the tribe?"

Luna shook her head. "I stayed on the train for a few more days. But I couldn't hide my suffering. Not from Mandy, anyway. She found me standing on the forward platform of a passenger car. It was really late at night and I watched Karma City approach. Mandy asked, 'You've been withdrawn lately. Only remorse does that. What did you do?'

"I felt like the child lost in Lobos so many years ago. I told her what I'd done, but Mandy didn't care. Her coldness, her ruthlessness, shocked me and it was like looking in a mirror. I leaned over the guardrails and threw up.

"Mandy says, 'Listen, kid. Life off the tracks goes by in a blur, a careless and confusing blur. *I'm* your sister and *this* is your family. Remember that.'

"Mandy left me alone. And that's when the truth really hit me."

"What truth was that?" asked Albert.

"That my life on the locomotive was nothing more than an empty promise. Not worth killing for. Not worth dying for. That night, while the train passed over Karma's east bridge, I jumped, leaving the life of the Iron Tribe."

"You wanted to die, didn't you?"

"Yeah. But fate is a funny thing. It's kind after it's cruel." Luna took a calming breath. She felt drained. She looked to Jameson. "You want to take it from here?"

"I'd be happy too. So, I'm camping on the outskirts of Karma City, along a sandy riverbank. I'm gutting some trout I'd caught and I see a woman's body floating down the river. I jump in and haul her to the shore. She's still breathing, so I quickly laid her by my fire. When she wakes up, she's really confused. Of course, my first thought is to be a gentleman."

"You asked her if she was injured, right?"

"No. I offered her some trout."

Luna laughed. "I asked him if he was the one who saved me and you know what he tells me?"

Albert shook his head.

"He says, 'Yep. Now my boots are soaked. I hate that.'"

Albert chuckled. "And that's how you two met, huh?"

Luna smiled and looked into Jameson's eyes. "Fate was kind."

# Chapter 9

Late into the night, the Iron Tribe's colossal locomotive clattered to a stop at Karma City's Central Station along the waterfront. The pounding rain stirred the sea, sending black, toothy waves slamming against the wharf and piers, challenging the moorings of the ships along docks. The storm clouds swelled overhead, where thunder resounded like war drums conjuring tridents of lightning. The group stepped off the steaming train. Mandy Briggs handed each of them a black boarding card.

"For your respect to the Mother and your allegiance to Luna Briggs, I present you all with these Affiliate Tickets. You are now trusted allies of the Iron Tribe and may ride the rails as often as you require."

Jameson tucked it in his pocket and turned up the collar on his leather coat to keep out the night's chill. Rain soaked his brown hair, matting it against his face. *This storm is going to challenge our plans.*

Mandy put her hand on Luna's shoulder. "Time for us to part again. This time, I want you to take this." She handed her a small radio. "Should you ever need us, call and the train will come. Goodbye, Luna. Honor to you."

Jameson flicked his cigarette to the tracks and led the group from the station toward the docks. He snaked his way through the waterfront's cluster of tight roads; the group followed close behind. Streetlamps flickered with pale light, doing little to dispel the shadows painting the many warehouses and receiving bays. He entered the wharf where stacks of shipping containers formed metal walls as tall as houses. The wharf opened to Karma's shipyard. There, dozens of ships, boats and vessels drifted, moored with heavy ropes and rusted chains against creaking docks.

Despite the heavy patter of the rain, an unnerving quiet settled over the area. Homeless people grouped aboard abandoned boats for shelter. Some peered out of the dark, crumbling shacks and storage sheds, eyes glinting like rats hiding in the shadows of back alleys. Jameson kept his shotgun in his hands. *Place is crawling with Malady-heads.* He noticed an abandoned boat house with a red handkerchief tied to the doorknob. *Nice welcome sign, Kurt.* Jameson held back the group and said just above a whisper, "Our red-coat friend seems to have left a light on for us." He pointed to the handkerchief. "Let's go in and find out if there's any more information we need before we go boating."

Jameson opened the boat house door and led the others inside. A long, black speed boat rested with its front bow facing the ocean. A small table waited with a single chair and lantern. Jameson lit the lantern and turned down the wick to keep a low light.

"Nice boat," Luna remarked. "Looks fast."

"Sure does. And our man, Kurt, seems to have stood us up." He assessed the situation. *This is one of those times when momentum matters. Keep the pace, move forward as planned until the first obstacle makes itself known as it always does.* He eyed the group. *They need direction.* "Luna, have a look in the boat." Jameson pulled the chair away from the table. "Albert, have a seat and work on the data from the Eden drive. I'm going to keep watch." He moved near the single window facing the docks. "Good, no Malady-heads creeping around."

Albert piped up, "The people infected with Malady are sick and suffering. Though they're dealing with a serious parasitic infection, they're still people."

"You could put that sentiment on a poster and hang it in your medical center, doc, and I still wouldn't believe it. Malady makes people into unpredictable lunatics. Some deal with it better than others, I'll give you that; but for the most part, it turns your neighbor into a nutcase who would kill you just as easily as he would kill himself. I've seen it time and again."

"You sound pretty crazy, Jameson. How do I know you don't have a Stage Three infection?"

Jameson fell quiet. Luna said nothing.

Albert tilted his head and raised a brow. "Am I missing something here?

Jameson sighed and glanced to Luna. She nodded her approval of the words Jameson prepared to speak. "Listen, doc. I don't usually bring this up, but it's like this: I can't catch Malady."

"Well, you can put *that* on a poster and I wouldn't believe it. It's impossible. There's never been anyone immune to Malady. Human beings are the parasite's obligate host."

"Believe it, doc. I can't catch it. Don't know how or why, but it's the truth. My mother died from Malady and my father got it when I was a boy. Since then, I've lived my life in the Void Lands. Still not sick. I've even shared food and water with infected friends and trampled through alleys littered with bodies."

Albert snorted in disbelief. "Hey Luna, are you listening to this?"

"He's telling you the truth."

"Jameson, let me highlight a very pertinent fact, if I may," Albert's tone was incredulous and mocking, "you would be the most important human being on the planet if what you say is true. And in not-so-clinical terms, I'd say you've just been really damn lucky out there in the Voids."

"I'll prove it." Jameson rolled up his sleeve. "Go ahead. Take a sample of my blood. And after we get back from blowing up Graves' party boat, you can analyze it, or do whatever it is you do, and you'll see for yourself."

Opening his satchel, Albert produced a needle, syringe and alcohol wipe. "If this is a joke," said Albert. "I'm going to pull an equally jarring prank on you when you least expect it. I'm really good at pranks. Believe it." Jameson offered his forearm and made a fist. Albert quickly drew a vial of blood from a vein and packed it away. "I have bandages. They have little clowns on them. Want one?"

"No." Jameson rolled down his sleeve. "Get to work on the data."

"Hey, Jameson," Luna called. "Kurt left us a care package."

Jameson crouched beside the boat. "What've you got?"

Luna lifted a wooden crate from under a seat and opened the lid. "Forty pounds of C-4 in one and a quarter pound blocks, two delayed timers, two detonators and a duffel bag for transport."

"Kurt wasn't kidding around. Set that in the right spot, those charges will blow the ship to pieces." Jameson frowned. "I wonder why he isn't here. Something must be wrong." He looked over Albert. "How's it going over there?"

"Success, Jameson. A veritable jackpot. Graves is, indeed, renting a warehouse from Gabriel. Building seven. But I've got a lot more on here than that."

Jameson and Luna gathered around the table. Albert's small computer screen threw a pale blue light on his face. He looked over his glasses and said, "Gabriel's drug manufacturing operations are detailed here but he hasn't been importing plants and chemicals from the Void Lands. He's been trafficking people, captives it seems, by the look of this manifest." He touched the screen, trailing the lines of data with his fingertip. "There are records naming settlements I've never heard of and totals of people taken. I've got individual names, too." Albert made a few quick keystrokes. "People, some infected, others not, have been rounded up for Graves' human testing for a long time. Twenty years by some of these time stamps. This is unreal!"

"Hold on a second," interrupted Luna. "How could kidnappings occur for two decades with no one coming forward against it?"

"Good question, Luna." Albert replied. "There are some valid reasons that may contribute to the success of this terrible endeavor. Malady infected people experience severe memory loss in early stages of the parasite's life cycle. Then, deep anxiety in later stages making it impossible for them to understand or break free from what is happening."

"Let's not forget the Void Lands," Jameson added. "There are too many settlements that remain unknown to most people in Karma City. Life out there is without rules and cultural norms. It's survival and anarchy."

Luna nodded her understanding. "One can't care about what is unknown."

"Right," Jameson agreed. "Besides, who is there to speak of it? Nobody. I bet most of the test subjects are already dead."

"He's right," Albert affirmed "Many of Marcus Graves' victims have perished as a result of his experiments. When I select a particular name, a dialog box opens detailing how many tests were performed and if the individual died." Albert took off his glasses and rubbed his eyes. "This is heartbreaking."

Jameson's hands balled to fists. "I'm ready to shut this operation down." He broke for the door.

"Wait," Albert called.

"What is it, doc?"

"Was your father named Eric?"

Jameson's skin turned to ice. "Yeah. Eric Shoals."

Albert pointed to the computer screen. "He was taken twenty years ago by Graves Enterprises for early Malad-X testing."

"How much testing?" Jameson's voice cracked. He fought back the rising sadness, struggling to keep it from sinking him to his knees.

"It doesn't say."

"Is he dead?"

"Let me check." Albert looked up from his glasses. "No."

Jameson kicked open the boathouse door and ran into the rainy night. Luna chased him across the waterfront docks, catching him just before the lights around warehouse seven revealed them. She swung him around by the arm and pulled him behind a stack of shipping crates and pallets. They sat with their backs against the cover and caught their breath. Rain fell hard over them.

Jameson looked upward at the dark storm. Rain water ran over his face.

"Tell me what you're thinking," Luna urged. "You got a plan or are we just winging it as usual?"

"My father's alive, Luna! That's what I'm thinking. He might be in there. I have to know."

"But we don't need to rush into danger. Let's do this smart." Luna reached out and brushed the wet hair from his face. "We're in this together."

For a moment, the two just sat in the rain, huddled close to stay warm. The ocean stirred with the gusting wind, the rhythmical sound slowly restored Jameson's focus. He let out a slow, calming breath and peered around the crates. "I'm going to sneak around the warehouse and find out what's going on in there. Go back and

101

keep Albert safe. Get the speed boat ready. I'll meet you at the boathouse in ten minutes."

"Be careful, Jameson."

"Always."

Jameson's black leather coat concealed his presence. He took off his pack and hung it from the edge of the dock. *Don't need my gear slowing me down or making noise. I'll grab it on the way back.* Unencumbered and feeling lighter on his feet, he slipped to the side of the warehouse and hugged the wall. Strange noises carried over the water, coming from inside. He paused, listening to coughs, whimpers, bizarre shouting and senseless rambling. He heard sounds of struggling and objects being thrown. *What the hell?*

A single guard paced the boardwalk surrounding the warehouse. Jameson thought of subduing him, but refrained when a second guard came into view. He ducked behind a cluster of barrels and listened to the guards.

"We've been trying to contact the vessel for a half hour," the approaching guard said. "Still no response."

"Have you called Sable District to report?"

"No. Strict orders came in yesterday. No calls are to be placed from the warehouse to the district. We're to go through Eden and Mr. Gabriel if we need anything."

"What about Eden? Did you call them?"

"Yes. No answer there either."

"Don't worry about the vessel. I'm sure everything is fine. Look," the guard pointed to the sea.

While they turned their attention to the water, Jameson scaled the ladder to the roof without making a sound.

"I can still see the lights from the vessel," the guard said. "Our radios probably need service. The salty air ruins everything."

"I suppose you're right. I'm heading inside. The patients are getting rowdy. Don't need anything else getting broken."

Jameson traversed the rooftop and looked in through the skylight.

The warehouse wrapped around an empty boat slip; a strong crane arm hung over the dark water lapping against the interior pilings. *This is a loading and unloading station* He imagined that a very large boat could pull in and process its cargo easily here. *Makes sense If Graves has operations on his ship, he's using this place to support it.* He moved his gaze to the surrounding wooden docks. Lining the vacant boat slip spread computer terminals, chemistry stations and intricate sets of laboratory equipment. A large metal cage at the far right of the room, much like an animal pen, contained two-dozen men and women in shackles. Their gaunt faces wore stains of dried blood and dark purple bruises. They huddled together, coughing, shaking and weeping. To the far left, another cage held fewer captives. These men and women, six in total, paced about anxiously. They looked stronger, in better health, and didn't seem concerned with the bars around them.

Jameson counted twenty scientists in white lab coats and fifteen heavily armed Sable Guardsmen in black armor. With careful, silent hands, Jameson slid open one of the skylight panels to better observe the operation.

Lab technicians selected a battered, pleading prisoner from the cage. The prisoner, a man, shouted and begged. "No! Please! Don't infect me!"

The guards said nothing. They took control of the man, beating him to submission, then strapped him to a surgical table in the center of the room. Like a swarm of wasps, the scientists fell over him. The man kicked and screamed as one of them performed an injection. The technicians kept him secured to the table for several long minutes, then drew a sample of his blood for analysis. The sample went to a scientist seated at a microscope.

"Confirmed," said the scientist. "Malady parasite successfully introduced. Phase One completed. Proceed with phase two."

The assisting guards forced the man off the table and dragged him to the opposing cage that housed the six other captives. They threw him inside, injured and defeated. The scientists surrounded the cage with notebooks and recording devices ready. The six captives attacked the man. They beat him unconscious and slammed around his limp body. In a primitive, bloody frenzy, they ripped him open. Swatches of flesh and ribbons of entrails splattered about. One wild captive stomped on the victim's skull, cracking it open. The scientists broke out in a round of applause and each set to work scribbling his notes.

One of the technicians questioned a scientist. "Have you found any inconsistencies?"

"Not yet. Patients injected with the Malady parasite are always killed by our six Malad-X patients."

"This is exciting!"

"Indeed. But it's going to be a long night of testing. We still have twenty-three more subjects to infect."

*I've seen enough.*

He moved away from the skylight. The rain streamed down the sloping edges of the warehouse roof. His boots lost traction and he slipped, skidding fast toward the edge. His shotgun fumbled from his hand and clanged to the docks below.

A man in a red trench coat stepped from the surrounding darkness and picked up Jameson's weapon. At first Jameson thought it was Kurt Auger, but when the man slowly craned his head to eye the rooftop, his glowing amber eyes revealed his identity.

With a silent leap, Gemni sprang to perch on the roof with Jameson, blocking his path to the ladder. His coat shimmered in the rain like blood. He held Jameson's shotgun in his arms, cradling it as if it were a lost pet.

"That's Kurt Auger's coat," Jameson stated, his voice a threat and a challenge wrapped together. "Let me guess, you made him into one of your crazy Malady puppets?"

Gemni made a mocking pout. "As much as I would have valued a man such as Mr. Auger among my family, I'm afraid he was without Malady and as such, beyond my control. He was Lesser. Rightly, I struck him in the chest and stopped his heart. He's dead now, you see. They all are. Professor Crimm and his 'Crimsons' have been slain." He adjusted the lapel of the red coat. "It is a rather inspiring garment. I destroyed the rest. But please don't think me a thief, oh no. Couldn't let it go to waste. I don't steal, you see. In fact, this is your weapon, not mine. Here you are." Gemni handed the shotgun to Jameson.

Jameson snatched the shotgun and snickered. "You know I can't shoot you now."

"Don't want all those guards to know you're up here, do you?"

"What do you want, Gemni?"

"You know my name! I'm honored." Gemni leaned closer and sniffed the air around Jameson. Rain dripped from his pointy nose. His yellow-white hair clung to his face and neck making him look like a storm-soaked scarecrow. "What are you called—this creature before me with blood unlike any other?"

"Don't trouble yourself over the name of your executioner."

"How predictably arrogant. I would very much enjoy finishing our *little scrap* and killing you tonight; however, to your incalculable fortune, the timing is not right. I am a very busy man, you see."

"You've come to spy on Marcus Graves. Malady versus Malad-X."

"Ah, good. Professor Crimm informed you of the warring sides of science in Karma City." He paused in thought. "Being a would-be champion of mankind, you've come to investigate Graves as well. Perhaps you and I should not be in opposition during this war, this race for the domination of humanity." The words rolled from his pale lips like the hiss of a Void Land viper.

Jameson's honed survival instincts crackled in his core like the garble of incomprehensible radio waves. There was enough about this altercation, a certain inaudible signal that warned of Gemni's volatile intentions. He tucked his shotgun into his pack with one hand and unclipped the knife hanging from the back of his belt. Jameson Shoals never ignored the possibility of a trap. He donned a false demeanor of temporary trust, letting his shoulder relax. *Never look the wolf in the eyes. Back slowly away from the snake.* "I've witnessed all I came to learn," said Jameson softly. "It seems Graves' Malad-X experiment is nearing perfection. Malady is going to lose the war, Gemni. *You* are going to lose. See for yourself." Jameson's ears remained focused on the group of armed guards and his eyes panned the stormy sea for any sign of Luna and the boat. "I'm sure our paths will cross again. When they do, we'll finish our 'little scrap.'" He shoved past Gemni, one hand holding the roof for balance, the other secretly hovering over the handle of his knife. As hoped, Gemni turned his attention to the window and leaned to peer inside at the horrors going on in the warehouse.

Jameson seized his chance.

He pulled the knife, coiled his strong arms around Gemni's neck and pressed the sharp blade under his chin. Gemni spun, pulling Jameson's elbow into him and hurling him over his shoulders. Up and over Jameson tumbled, crashing through the warehouse and falling to the wooden deck. Glass and lengths of wood fell over him. Head spinning, he looked up for Gemni, expecting him to pounce in on the lab technicians and infected prisoners, but he was gone. The scientists scurried away from Jameson with files and briefcases under their arms. The caged people cried out for freedom. The guards ran for Jameson with guns drawn. *Son of a bitch*! Jameson rolled on his shoulders, sucked in a breath, and forced himself to his feet. The impact of the fall still reverberated through his limbs.

"Stay where you are," shouted a guard.

*Not a chance, asshole!*

Seconds later, gunfire erupted. Rounds whizzed past Jameson's head.

He looked to the black water in the center of the room and dove in. The bullets ripped through surface, tearing his pants and grazing his leg. He winced as he swam under the warehouse, hoping to the reach the outer perimeter of the ocean. Through the blackness of the stirring water, he kicked and groped until, at last, he met a wooden support beam holding up the building and surrounding docks. He reached up and climbed from the water to perch under the planks of the boardwalk. There on the crossbeams of a piling, hidden and soaked, he calculated his chances for survival. Something caught his eye, something bulky hanging from the dock. *My pack! Everything is dry in there!* He pulled open the bag and searched its contents for the prize he'd scored at Eden. *Lovers' Claw.*

The guards searched for him on the deck above. He could hear their yells. "Find him! Get some light on the ocean!"

Flashlight beams scanned the waves. Jameson stayed very still.

"No sign of him."

"Search the other side." The guards ran off.

Jameson hurried with his work, quickly twisting the length of Lovers' Claw and fraying an end with his knife. He dug out his lighter and lit the frayed end of the root. He fanned it to flame and tossed it upward to the surface of the dock. After counting a full minute, giving the burning plant time to lay down a cloud of toxic smoke, he shouted, "I'm over here! I surrender!"

The guards hurried to investigate. He listened to their cautious shouts. "Something's burning! Stand back!"

They coughed uncontrollably and soon, Jameson heard their bodies collapsing to the planks above. From out at sea, a gurgling rumble sounded. *The speedboat!* More shots rang out, this time from the distant ocean. Jameson recognized the sharp bang of Luna's rifle. Guards dropped into the water around him. *She's good. Time to go.*

Jameson secured his gear and leapt back into the water. A hail of enemy bullets hammered the ocean around him, fueling his strokes. Amid the dark waves, he couldn't see the speed boat and wondered how they'd find him in the stormy water. He glanced up through the breaking of the waves to see the muzzle of Luna's rifle lighting the night in flashes of fire.

Luna called out to him, "Jameson?"

Jameson pulled his face from the waves and yelled, "Luna!" He swam for his life, his chest heaving and burning. His muscles cramped as they fought against the raging storm and the weight of his soaked clothes.

The boat's spotlight fell over him.

He reached up and felt a hand snatch hold of his wrist.

Luna yelled over the boat's loud motor, "I've got you! Pull up!"

With the last of his strength, Jameson tugged his body upward. Luna pulled him into the boat as it skirted away from the docks.

"So, this is what it feels like to pull someone from the water?" Luna joked.

"I guess that makes us even." He gave a playful smile of relief. "My boots are wet. I hate that."

Jameson told the group what he'd witnessed and of the unexpected altercation with Gemni. While horrified by such a grotesque operation, Albert suffered more with Gemni's pledge that Professor Crimm was murdered. Luna remained glad for Jameson's safe return and held her focus on the task at hand. She helped Jameson assemble the bomb, wanting more than ever to destroy the cruel scientist's operations.

Albert slowed the speed boat and brought the engine to an idle, letting the craft drift closer to the vessel. Jameson's eyes scanned the ship's towering hull. He heard a low hum and all of the vessel's lights flickered off.

Albert whispered, "Well, I guess the party's over. Shall we come back in the morning?"

Jameson replied, "Something isn't right. The way the lights went out like that. Someone just pulled the plug."

A series of screams echoed over the sea, followed by several splashes. Jameson signaled to Luna. She peered through her night vision scope and reported, "We've got dead people in the water."

Jameson asked, "What are they wearing?"

"Lab coats."

More screams and terrible shouts sounded from the main deck. Luna lifted her scope. "Unbelievable!"

"What do you see," Jameson asked.

"The ship is full of scientists and civilians. The civilians are killing the scientists and throwing the bodies overboard. It's a bloodbath up there!"

"Get our boat as close to the ship as you can, doc."

"If you insist." Albert angled the craft beside the ship's hull. He shut down the engine and asked Jameson. "How are we getting aboard? We can't climb the hull."

"No. But Kurt left us a lot of explosives. I'll put a smaller bomb together and we'll pop a nice hole in the side and crawl in."

Within minutes, Jameson fashioned a second bomb. He wedged the charge against the hull and set the timer. Albert pulled their boat away from the ship. A moment later, an explosion ruptured the starboard hull, creating a large hole. They waited in the darkness of the ocean for the blast's smoke to subside. The rain beat on the sea while sounds of murder raged from the vessel.

Jameson tied the boat to a twisted shard of metal hanging from the blast hole and climbed in. He reached out to pull in Luna, who then helped Albert.

They switched on their flashlights and examined the area. Fragments of furniture smoldered throughout the blown-out crew cabin. Their steps crunched over broken glass, splinters of wood and lengths of bent metal.

Beyond the cabin, on the other side of the hall, another door had taken damage from their blast. Its hinges creaked as the door swung ajar. The sign above read: Laboratory 4-Incubation. A pale white light glowed from within. Jameson shoved the door open and led the others inside. He whistled in disbelief.

A large cylindrical cistern, filled with a milky white liquid glowed and bubbled. Hoses and valves lined the cistern and trailed to various monitoring stations and computer terminals. Dead scientists slumped in their chairs. Jameson ordered Albert, "Check out the computer; see if you can tell us what's going on here."

Albert approached an active terminal and moved aside the dead man in the chair. He hunched over the keyboard. "Give me a moment with this."

Jameson kept his eyes on the strange translucent liquid. He nudged Luna. "Looks kind of like a big lava lamp filled with snot."

Luna chuckled and continued her sentry post. "I doubt they're crazy enough to be killing over snot, Jameson. You're nasty."

After a flutter of keystrokes, Albert stepped away from the terminal. "We're lucky our little explosion didn't disturb this tank. It's a vat of live Malad-X. The entries in the scientist's observation log affirm this is one of two reservoirs. This brood is for shipment out of Karma."

"Where to?" Jameson asked.

"The destination is not finalized. That explains why the ship is still anchored. The crew was probably awaiting final orders."

"You said one of two. Where is the other tank of Malad-X?"

"The records do not specify."

Jameson shrugged. "I guess we blow this up and track down the other tank later. Come on."

As Jameson led the others deeper into the ship, screams of pain and terror pierced the darkness. Strange cackling and maniacal laughter made his grip tighten on his shotgun. He let out a slow breath to ease his nerves. *Stay focused.* "If we detonate the bomb at the fuel storage, this vessel will be obliterated. Should be in the engine room. Let's make this quick and don't let the infected get near you."

At these words, a bloody man rounded the corner and staggered into the hallway. His eyes wide with rage. "No more tests! No more!"

He charged at Jameson.

Jameson aimed his shotgun but the man barreled into him, shoving the weapon aside and pinning him to the wall. The collision knocked the bag of explosives to the ground. Jameson hooked the gun barrel around the man's neck and pulled, twisting his head around his shoulders with a sickening crack. He dropped the body to the floor at his feet.

Albert bent down and examined him. "He's got needle marks all over his arms and bruising around his wrists. Poor man's been a lab rat for a long time."

"We can call the coroner later," Luna interrupted. "How about we do something about that?" She pointed to the bomb bag. A blinking yellow light pulsed.

Jameson checked the bomb. "Shit! The timer's active."

"And let me guess," said Albert, "you can't stop it?"

"Don't be an idiot. Of course I can stop it. That only happens in cheesy movies. I need to disconnect the detonator from the charge and timer. But it's sensitive work and with all the infected roaming about, I don't have time."

Albert sighed. "Perfect. How much time do we have?"

"Nine minutes to get to the fuel storage and off this ship."

They moved deeper into the shadowy vessel, following signage and breaking open locked doors, until they reached the engine room. Pipes, valves and gauges tangled the area like an industrial jungle, joining tall electronics cabinets and monitoring stations. With the power outage, the giant engine laid still and quiet. Jameson positioned the bomb atop the fuel cistern. "Done. Luna, guide us back the way we came."

"Right. Stay close, guys."

The screams from the top deck continued to fill the halls. Corpses piled on the floor, lining the passages and cluttering the companionways. Some were scientists, others were captives. The stink of death turned the dark ship's corridors into a stale and foreboding tomb. Jameson examined the dead faces as he passed. Fear and torment remained in their lifeless stares. He panned his light into empty cells used to hold test subjects. Streaks of blood and excrement stained the walls. Placards marked each cell with the occupants' names.

Luna stopped suddenly and called out to Jameson from ahead. "Better have a look at this."

A placard had fallen to the floor. A single name identified the test subject once imprisoned in the tiny cell nearby. Shoals.

Jameson took up the placard. Touching the lettering of his last name, his thoughts clouded. He found no bodies in the cell. "I have to find him, Luna."

She checked her pocket watch. "There isn't time."

"I have to!"

"I said there isn't time. We're down to five minutes and the bomb blows."

"Listen, I want you to take Albert and get off the ship. I'll—"

"Don't do this, Jameson."

"Dammit, Luna, please go!"

"Not without you. We stick together."

Jameson remembered of the night they jumped from the train to the river and how tight he held her; she could have died from the fall. The shootout at the hospital and again in Undertown, and finally the lucky escape at Eden. All of this danger, all of this risk to her life, was because of his personal mission, his goal. Now the ship faced annihilation and this woman—strong, brave, beautiful and devoted to him more than he felt he deserved—stood again at the edge of the world with him, right on the thin line between life and death. He needed to find his father and whatever the cost to himself, he'd pay it. This last chance was his to gamble. He wanted her safe. No more risks to her. He stared into her eyes, hoping that she'd understand what he was about to do. "I'm sorry." *I can't let you follow me. I can't let you die for this.* He struck her in the face with his flashlight. Luna fell hard to the floor. Jameson slipped away, rushing deeper into the surrounding darkness in search of his father.

He kicked open the door to the main deck, shotgun in hand, and entered the carnage. Mobs of enraged captives in tattered clothing swarmed around the last two surviving scientists. Jameson opened fire, shooting two of the infected in the head. This frightened the others. The captives parted, recoiling like a pack of startled wolves. The scientists hurried to Jameson.

"Whoever you are, thank you! Please get us off this ship!"

Jameson took a step back and examined their faces. Dark circles encased their beaded, marble eyes and their shallow cheeks cast deep shadows over their jawlines. Each man had colorless lips and arched, paranoid eyebrows. *Malady. All of the scientists have Malady. That's why the Malad-X test subjects are killing them. Infected against the infected.* He reloaded. "Where's the captive named Eric Shoals?"

"I-I don't know!"

"Don't fuck with me!" Jameson shouted and pressed the muzzle to the man's forehead.

"H-he's holed up the chief scientist's lab. He's the primary test subject."

"Why?"

"There's something special about his blood. The Malady parasite doesn't live in him for long. Shoals has got some kind of resistance."

"Where is this lab?"

The scientist pointed to an open doorway across the deck. "That passage will take you up two levels. The lab is in the forward office. Now please help us!"

"You're still alive. Help yourselves."

Both scientists twitched and snapped in a Malady fit of panic. Their sickness spurred their aggression. They attacked, screaming with frenzied eyes. Jameson fired, killing both men.

Out of ammunition, all he could was run. Through the passage and up the stairwell, he then sprinted down the short hall to the forward office lab. His shoulder broke open the door. A gray-haired man with a tangled beard spun to face Jameson. A long syringe, filled with the same strange liquid Jameson had seen in the lab, jutted from the man's shaking hand.

"Stay back!" shouted the old man. "You've come far enough!"

Jameson squinted through the shadows, struggling to determine the man's identity. "I'm looking for Eric Shoals?"

The man shivered and with his free hand, wiped a line of mucus from under his nose. "I'm Eric. Stay where you are!"

Jameson's heart ached.

At long last he'd found his father.

This weathered, beaten, hunched over man with warped eyes, broom-handle neck and frame of bones had once been his mighty hero. Jameson's mouth went dry and his voice cracked. "I'm your son. Do you remember me?"

The old man's frightened eyes widened. He stepped closer. The hand holding the syringe shook. He cocked his head to one side as he studied Jameson.

"Dad, it's me. Jameson."

The man's face carved to a smile. "Jamie."

Tears welled in Jameson's eyes. "Whatever they've put you through, it's over now. I'm here to save you. Come with me. We don't have much time." He put out his hand.

Eric shrieked and jumped away. "Stay back!"

Malady had run its course, transforming his father to nothing more than a skittish, volatile lunatic. Jameson felt his anger set fire to his heart. The fire dried his tears. He pointed his unloaded weapon at this father. "I won't lose you again, understand? You're coming with me!"

"Never!" Eric sprang, tackling Jameson to the floor. Something stung him under the ribs. *The syringe!* Jameson shoved Eric off of him and crawled for the doorway. Eric dove, wrapping his arms around Jameson's lower leg and biting into his calf. Jameson groaned and rolled over, positioning to kick him off. Before he could react, a sudden gunshot freed him. Eric lay coiled on the floor. Jameson looked up to find Luna standing in the door way, her rifle barrel smoked.

"I'm sorry, Jameson. One minute left."

Jameson stared at his father lying motionless on the floor. Emotions stormed in his heart. Sorrow, loneliness, rage, regret and even love tangled to a noose of total, soul-breaking despair. When he lifted his eyes to Luna, his vision blurred and his throat tightened. A sharp pain at his ribs grew to a searing flame. With a shaking hand, he pulled a syringe from his side. He dropped the dirty needle and it rolled, knocking against Luna's boot.

She picked it up. "What the hell? Did he stick you with this?"

Jameson's breath shortened. A terrible pressure swelled in his head. He managed to utter, "Kill…me!"

"Can't do that."

Luna pulled him up and slung his arm over her shoulders. Jameson's awareness ebbed and flowed like waves of deep sleep cresting over his mind. He heard Luna's gunshots clearing their path. He felt her dragging him down the stairwell and across the deck. The weightlessness of falling enveloped him, followed by a sudden burst of cold water. Just before his senses extinguished, a devastating, fiery explosion ignited the stormy night.

*Maybe we're all dead*, he reasoned in the hollow of his mind. *Maybe it's all over now.*

From the fringe of his consciousness came a strange reply like a faceless voice echoing through an obscuring mist.

*"I don't think so, Jameson. It's all just beginning."*

# Chapter 10

The puddles on the walkways reflected the white morning sun. Rays of light broke through the treetops to sparkle off the dewy grass. Donna had said to try strolling through Greely Park just after sunrise; it always cleared her mind. So, he figured he'd give it a try.

Jack inhaled the crisp morning air and listened to the clopping of his shoes against the pavement. He thought about how he might write the sound in a story. *Like the clatter of horses' shoes...no. Too cliché. Like two gavels hammering with resolve...much better.* He sighed. *Clear the mind? Writers don't get to clear their minds. Those not born to words can't imagine how much the writer keeps inside, how many thoughts he can't ignore, how many feelings weigh him down or just how much those thoughts and feelings matter. They all matter, and they always remain.*

The park walkway ended at the sidewalk. He had come with a full mind and heavy heart to, what he believed to be, Karma's greatest ruin—the city library. Though the rising morning warmed the neighborhood and glinted off the surrounding buildings, the library remained gray and forlorn. No longer was this a place of history, lore and record. The boarded windows, rustling litter and streaked graffiti created an image fit for a nightmare's backdrop. As Jack stood under its lifeless shadow, the last winds of the night whistled out from the hollows.

A voice came from the blackness.

Jack listened closer when he recognized the voice quoted *the Odyssey*, a classic work of literature Jack had loved and long forgotten.

"You see, Homer writes, 'There will be killing till the score is paid.'"

A murmur stirred to an uproar. Jack questioned, *there's a crowd in the library? It's been abandoned for years.* He crossed the street and shuffled up the library's steps and entered. He followed the sound of the gathering to a large auditorium and looked in through a crack in the door. Candles lined the room, casting an unsteady glow about the crumbling walls. Jack guessed over two hundred people assembled to hear the lithe figure dressed in a crimson trench coat pacing the stage. *I've seen a coat like that. But where? Damn Malady. I can't remember.* Jack stayed behind the door, watching and listening.

"Though some of you shake your heads with defiance at the thought of doing harm, I implore you to open your minds to the mystery of this book." The man waved the hardbound tome over his head. "Why has it lasted when all around it has fallen? Why have I come to rediscover its lost truth? Why are you all still here, hanging on my words?" He paused. Silence eclipsed the people. The man opened the book and said softly, "Because like this book, you wish to last even though the world falls around you. You wish to rediscover those precious truths that your Malady has taken. My dear listeners, my brothers and sisters, your Malady is not a weakness. Oh no! For it is written here, you see," he touched the page. "Homer affirms, 'Of all creatures that breathe and move upon the earth, nothing is bred that is weaker than man.' It is the truth. And so is the fact that, with Malady, you are all more than man, so much more. You are not Lesser. Look around you. Behold the strength that emerges in such a family and feel it rise within you."

A man from the heart of the crowd called out, "Gemni, you don't understand. The world hates us because we're infected. We're shunned and many of us are addicted to Quell. Our communities have built walls that keep us away just because we're sick. It seems the only place in Karma we have is Undertown. How are we supposed to keep living like this?"

"I hear your fear. I feel it and it saddens me. This is your city; those who would deny you a home where you can be safe and loved, are your enemies. So, I ask you, what is right?"

"I…I don't know anymore."

"That's why I've come, you see. To help you all believe once more that your life is worth fighting for, that the world you live in is worth fighting to keep. Malady has brought us together in this goal. We are unified more tonight than any of the uninfected Lessers in Karma."

"What are we supposed to do now?"

Gemni raised his voice and paced the stage. "The Lessers have stolen from you, killed your friends, neighbors and family members. They have withheld compassion and discarded you because you have Malady. They will continue to extinguish lives to keep themselves over Malady because they fear the truth that Malady *is* the evolution of mankind. The Lessers will kill you," he pointed to a woman in the front row, "and you," he pointed to a man standing at the far left, "and you, and you, and you."

The crowd broke into a collective roar of upset.

Gemni yelled, "We will wait for our family to grow stronger and when the perfect moment presents itself, we will claim this city!"

A crescendo of applause filled the auditorium. Jack slowly backed away from the door. *I'd better get the hell out of here!* He ran down the hall, hearing Gemni's promise echo through the drafty library. "'There will be killing till the score is paid!'"

Jack hurried down the sidewalk and crossed the street, trying to get as far from the library as possible. He backtracked through the park until he came to the opposing street. The pink neon sign of the Greely Park Diner, the one flickering the word 'open,' was a lighthouse guiding him to shore. *Coffee. Eggs. Bacon. After seeing that crazy shit, I need some serious soul food.*

The string of bells rattled on the door as it closed behind him. Donna smiled. "Morning, Hun. How was the walk?"

Jack met her at the counter and leaned on his elbows. "You'll never believe what I witnessed at the library!"

'The library? That building's condemned."

"Right. And it's filled with whackos."

Donna cringed. "Jack please; the customers."

"Sorry." Jack lowered his voice. "There's some kind of cult meeting there and they're talking about killing people!"

"I don't mean to sound rude, but have you taken your medicine this morning?"

Jack shook his head. "No. I haven't."

Donna caressed his face. "It's the morning rush now. I can't talk but I do want you to tell me about it later today."

"I understand. And I don't mean to come in here seeming off my rocker. I feel fine. Really."

A customer called to Donna. "Can I get a menu, please?"

"Right away," Donna replied. She said to Jack, "Your spot's ready. Go relax and I'll bring you some coffee in a minute." She kissed his cheek, then hurried to bring the man his menu.

Jack sat in his booth listening to the chatter of the locals around him. Two old men at a nearby table spoke with mouths full of food. "The whole damn place got shot up!" exclaimed one of the men.

"Who in the loins of Lobos would want to attack Eden?" asked the other.

"Beats me. But what's worse is the fire off the coast this mornin'. My buddy works the docks; I'm gonna call 'im, you know, see if he knows anythin'."

Jack was out of the loop. "Hey," he said to the men, "what did you say about Eden and a fire off the coast?"

"Been under a rock, Halligan? Ain't you usually on top-o these kinda things?"

Donna brought Jack a steaming cup of coffee and a small decanter of cream, then slipped away to greet more arriving customers. Jack poured the cream into the cup and stirred. "A friend passed away the other day," Jack explained to the men, "I've been dealing with that."

"Real sorry to hear. We was just sayin' that some whackos went and shot-up Eden and then some other whackos—"

"Or the same whackos," interjected the other man.

"Yeah, or the same whackos, blew up the Graves Enterprises vessel."

Jack sipped his coffee and remarked, "Marcus Graves must be pretty upset this morning."

The man pointed out the window. "Don't look like he gives two shits to me."

Jack turned in his booth and looked outside. There, a gleaming black limousine bearing a silver letter G idled at the curb. Two men in suits guarded the vehicle and between them stood the owner of Sable Tower, overseer of Sable District, and developer of the Malady suppressant drug, Quell, Dr. Marcus Graves. Jack had never met Marcus Graves in person. He'd seen many pictures and read plenty of his work, but this was the first time he'd ever laid eyes on him. *And here? In central Karma? At the diner?*

Graves' black overcoat fluttered at his heels. His polished shoes reflected the sunlight and his combed black hair sheened like the wings of a crow. The lines of his face made sharp angles around his jaw and a thin, black mustache framed his blood-red lips. Jack watched as Graves slowly pulled off his sunglasses and looked at the diner. His glacier-blue eyes shined from the deep recesses under his brow.

The chatter in the diner subsided when Graves entered. Some of the patrons greeted him with handshakes and praise for Quell. Jack saw Donna's nervousness. She fidgeted with her pen as she welcomed him to the diner. "Good morning, Dr. Graves. How can I help you?"

Graves took off his overcoat and draped it across his forearm. "Actually, I'm here for two reasons. First, and most importantly, I hear this diner is the jewel of Karma and that the breakfast specials are superb. I just had to find out for myself. Second, I'm looking for Mr. Jack Halligan, the writer."

Jack spat out his coffee. He wiped his mouth with a napkin and grumbled to see that he'd dribbled on his shirt. *Great, just great. Graves is looking for me and I'm a mess.*

Donna continued with a smile, "We appreciate you being here, this morning." She handed him a menu. "The new breakfast and lunch specials this week are the Train Tracks Omelet; three eggs loaded with peppers, onions, potato slices, and sausage, or the Karma Dog; a foot-long hotdog on a steamed bun, smothered in a secret meat sauce, topped with diced raw onion and a ribbon of mustard."

"My goodness, this place *is* a jewel! I am partial to omelets, I must admit. With black coffee, please."

"Right away."

"Now, what of Jack Halligan? Do you know where I might find him? I've heard he frequents this diner."

"I'm over here," called Jack.

Graves spun to face him. A half smile bent at the corner of his mouth. He met Jack at the booth. They shook hands.

"Have a seat, Dr. Graves. Welcome to my office-booth."

"Yes, thank you. It's a pleasure to meet you Mr. Halligan."

"I was going to say the same. Call me Jack. And sorry about my appearance; I spilled a little coffee a second ago."

"Relax," said Graves calmly. "This isn't a job interview."

Jack chuckled. "That's a relief."

"It's a job offer."

"It's a good thing I didn't just sip my coffee. Did you say 'job offer?'"

Donna brought their breakfast. "Here you are, Dr. Graves."

"My goodness, that was incredibly fast."

Donna shrugged. "We have a great team of cooks back there. Oh, and all meals come with complimentary Checkers so you can stay healthy." She placed a small silver packet on the table near Graves' fork and knife. "If there's Malady, we'll cook you another dish, no charge." She slid Jack his plate of fried eggs and bacon. "Let me know if you need anything else."

Graves sniffed the meal and smiled. "This is decadence. I am sure I'll be quite satisfied."

Donna winked at Jack and stepped away.

"There's a word I can never spell," said Jack with a mouthful of food. "'Decadence.' I always want to put a second A, but it's actually got three E's. Like the word 'cemetery.' Get it? Graves...cemetery!" He laughed at himself.

"You're witty, Jack. I appreciate wit." Graves took up his fork and knife and cut into the omelet. Jack couldn't help but notice the surgical cuts and lines Graves made with the smallest of movements. The steel knife parted the omelet's folds in controlled symmetry. "Your articles in *the Karma Daily* capture your passion and intelligence. I've always enjoyed them. Your writing is rich with honesty and you've earned the city's respect. You're a leader, Jack. Which is why I want you to write for Graves Enterprises." He ate a cut of the omelet and smiled.

"Tempting, but I already have a job."

"Perhaps I should clarify," Graves cleared his throat and sat back in the booth. "It's been a difficult week for all of us in Sable District and at Graves Enterprises. Professor Crimm was brutally murdered. His death is tragic, horrific and painful for everyone. I've learned that you were at the crime scene."

"I was there for the story but I think I'll pass on it. I'm sorry for your loss."

"Thank you. Professor Crimm was a trusted colleague and contributed much to our endeavors against Malady. One of his roles was chief technical writer. His work chronicled our progression and detailed our efforts. I'd like you to continue where he left off, only I'd like the work to be less formal and more, well, 'Halligan' in nature."

"I'm honored. But what exactly will I be writing about?"

Graves' cheeks flushed with color. He leaned on his elbows. "We at Sable Tower are nearly ready to announce breakthrough advances against Malady. I want you to pen our accomplishments and do so in a way that will help immortalize the glory of our science. I am about to change the world, Jack. I want you to write it all down."

"You've found a cure?"

Graves lowered his voice. "I am hopeful that I can soon answer 'yes' to that question."

Jack leaned back in his seat, pretending to be calm though his heart drummed with excitement. He switched gears and tossed a loaded statement across the table. "I just heard your vessel blew up last night," Jack waved a strip of bacon as if it would accentuate his words, "you don't seem too concerned."

"I'm *very* concerned," snapped Graves.

Jack noted the scientist's sudden flare in intensity.

"The attack on my operation is being investigated by Sable Guard authorities as I speak. I have the entire waterfront sealed off to ensure public safety and to preserve the integrity of the investigation. I'm also holding an executive staff meeting tomorrow morning to discuss it with my team."

*He's nice and spun up. Time for a probing question.* "Why would anyone want to destroy your ship or interfere in your operations?"

Graves' nostrils flared and he glanced away, indicators of discomfort. As Jack anticipated, Graves' reply was a pivot away from the question. "All I know is a great deal of lives were lost. Many dedicated employees were aboard that vessel and now they're gone. Their families are grieving this morning."

Jack restrained the grin begging to curl on his face. *The story is just falling into my lap!*

They finished their meals. "What will it be?" Graves asked. "Will you accept my offer and write exclusively for Graves Enterprises? You can name your salary and you'll receive unlimited stocks of Quell. You'll also gain access to Sable Tower's library and lounge should you need a quiet place to write."

"Sounds like an amazing offer. Can I mull it over?"

"I think it best not to delay for long. I'll give you the rest of the day."

Jack's intuition screamed that Graves' stoic and rehearsed proposal masked a severe truth. He recalled the word from dead Crimm's hand— Malad-X. *I bet Graves knows all about it. There's only one way to find out.* "Dr. Graves, I accept."

"Outstanding! I'd like you to attend the staff meeting if possible. Friday, nine o'clock, Sable Tower."

"I'll see you in the morning, pen in hand."

Graves pushed aside his plate, sipped the last of his coffee and dropped a wad of money on the table. Jack followed him to the door where the doctor's personal assistants waited. The two shook hands and Jack returned to his booth. There, the grotesque apparition of his dead father, Corpse-Dad, waited.

Corpse-Dad waved in delight, startling the flies that crawled on his papery face. "Morning, son! I think I'm going to order pancakes. You used to love it when I'd cook them for us on Saturdays. I always had to make a smiley face with chocolate chips and syrup or you wouldn't eat them. Remember?"

Jack sat down. "Yeah, for some reason, I do remember that." He pulled his Quell from his pocket but paused. *I still don't like this stuff.*

"Then don't take it," Corpse-Dad replied.

"Hold on," Jack said, "you can hear my thoughts, too?"

"Heck, yes I can. I'm a part of your thoughts, part of your memories."

"There's no getting rid of you, is there?"

"Not until you get old enough to move out." Corpse-Dad laughed. Yellow tinted spittle trickled from the edge of his purple lips.

Jack looked around to be sure that no one noticed him talking to himself. "Tell me something, when you look at me, what do you see?"

"My little boy. What do you see?"

"I see a dirty, horrible, rotting corpse."

"That's just awful." Corpse-Dad frowned. "That explains why you haven't hugged me yet. You're scared."

"I was at first. Now I know you're just a part of my sickness. You can't hurt me," he watched Graves' limousine pull away. "And unfortunately, you can't help me."

"Oh, come on. Try me. After all, helping is one of a dad's most important jobs."

"Okay, then," Jack challenged, "tell me what Malad-X is."

"I've never heard of that. Keep in mind, I don't know, because you don't know. Get it?"

"I get it."

"Sounds related to Malady. You should have asked Dr. Graves, son. Other than Dr. Carmen Victoria, no one knows more about Malady then Graves. Besides, he ought to know about it," Corpse-Dad attested.

"Why do you say that?"

"Because he's infected, like you."

"How do you know that?"

Corpse-Dad pointed to the unused Checker wedged under Graves' soiled napkin. "He just gobbled up his meal without even checking for the parasite. Only the infected do that."

Jack smiled at his ghoulish father. "You might prove helpful after all."

***

"What's happening?" Luna's heart ached with worry.

Jameson's body thrashed and writhed atop a bed in Albert's laboratory. Albert tightened the restraints to keep Jameson secure. "He's having a seizure in response to whatever he was injected with. It needs to pass before I can safely get a blood sample for analysis."

"You don't need to wait for the blood sample. Analyze this." Luna handed Albert the syringe from the vessel.

"Well done, Luna." Albert sat on a stool behind his microscope and prepared the sample.

"I hate seeing him like this," said Luna.

"You care a great deal for Jameson, don't you?"

"I do. He's the kind of friend that can be real difficult to understand, which only makes the rest of the world seem easy to figure out. Since I left the tribe, he's been the only family I've known."

"Are you going to tell him about his father?" asked Albert.

"Maybe. For now, do everything you can for him; okay?"

"I will. I promise."

Albert dabbed the remaining liquid from the syringe onto a microscope slide. He peered through the lenses and tensed. "It's Graves' parasite, Malad-X. Jameson's infected."

Jameson let out a terrible scream and tugged at the restraints. His mouth foamed and his eyes bulged.

"Pin him down!" Albert yelled.

The two struggled to hold Jameson to the bed. Albert stepped in and administered another injection. Jameson's body stopped convulsing. He remained unresponsive as Albert checked his vitals.

Luna asked, "What did you shoot him up with?"

"The only thing I could think of. Liquefied Quell. At the least, it will help him remain calm…"

"…Remain calm," said the honeyed, slithering voice in the dark.

"Where am I?" Jameson asked.

"What do you see?"

The darkness lifted in Jameson's mind. Like the first hues of morning driving back the night, everything looked pale, cold and colorless. A scene took form. A house with a wide porch and screen door sat in the middle of a grassy field. Rising behind the house swayed a lush willow tree. The scent of hot breakfast baited him. *I know that house,* Jameson thought. *But it's in the wrong place.*

"You must be hungry," the voice added.

Jameson heard the words all around him. They came from everywhere at once and from nowhere at all. "Who's there? Who are you?"

"I was hoping you could help me figure it out. Please come in."

Jameson reached for his shotgun but it was not there. He shrugged. *Guess this isn't that kind of dream. Let's do this.*

He entered the house. The floorboards creaked just as he remembered. The wallpaper in the kitchen still had the splatter of one of his father's failed spaghetti sauces. The white lace curtains rustled in the gentle breeze that brought the aroma of fresh coffee to his nose. The table held a bountiful spread of warm rolls, fresh fruit, pitcher of juice and a steaming decanter of black coffee. He sat at the table and helped himself. He leaned back in the chair, propped his boots on the table and called out, "Come out, come out wherever you are!"

A man in a black overcoat with slicked back, onyx hair and wintry blue eyes entered the kitchen from the front porch. Jameson almost fell out of his chair, "Marcus Graves?"

"Oh, I'm sorry. No, I'm not Marcus Graves. I don't know who that is."

"Forget it. Who are you?"

"I haven't decided. I was hoping you could help me with that. Though, one can't think on an empty stomach. I was thinking I'd make us some omelets. I've got this craving I just can't shake."

"Omelets? My family's house? Graves look-alike? I want to know what this is supposed to mean. And where the hell is my gun?"

"I understand you're confused and I'll try to help. Here's what I know—though I'm not sure how I know—we're in a rendering of your subconscious, a place of comfort that you've withdrawn to in response to our...bonding. I remember being less than this, a simple organism, a parasite. Something in you made me evolve. It's as though a part of me that was off is now on. I'm...awake. I'm...aware. And here we are." He opened his hands and two steaming plates of fresh omelets appeared. He placed them on the table and took a bite. He smiled, "This is decadence! Oh, you must give it a try!"

"You're a parasite?"

"I was. Technically speaking, I still am."

"Malady."

"I'm not Malady!" His face reddened and his hands rolled to fists. "Not at all. I'm a Malad-X parasite."

Jameson moved from the table and paced the kitchen and rambled. "Wonderful. I've got a talking worm in my head. How is that even possible? I can't get sick. I'm immune." He remembered the altercation on the ship. "My father...that damned needle!" He punched the wall. "I wish Luna would have put a fucking bullet in my head!"

"Don't talk like that."

Jameson leaned on the table. "You expect me to be happy about being infected?"

"Be grateful that you're alive. I'm grateful. Without you, there can be no me. I'm going to do all I can to keep you safe." He smiled. "You can count on that."

Jameson scoffed. "Well, doesn't that just brighten my day?"

"Hey! I like that. It's perfect. You may call me Brighton. That's my new name."

"Whatever you say, Brighton. When's this ridiculous dream supposed to end. I'd like to get back to the real world."

"Look," Brighton said firmly, "I think we should make a few things clear. You and I are stuck together. I'm a part of you and

126

you're a part of me. But make no mistake, I'm *not* you and you're *not* me. We need to get along or this whole mind-sharing thing is going to become a problem."

"I don't want to share my mind. I want you gone."

"Not possible without splattering your brains over the pavement or something drastic like that."

"Then you need to give me some space. Stay out of my thoughts."

"I'm not in your thoughts. I don't know what you're thinking. We're two different beings. Think of it as two roommates sharing a one-room apartment."

"More like inmates sharing a cell."

"Jameson, I know this is difficult for you to accept but I promise I won't make you sick and ruin your life. I'm *not* Malady."

"Good. Because I hate Malady."

Brighton's face darkened. "As do I."

"What is it you want?"

"The same thing you want. To live."

Jameson had heard enough. He denied Brighton's existence, regarding this whole meeting as a hallucination induced from the toxin his father used as a weapon. Waking from this became his only desire. "I'm leaving, Mr. Parasite. You're damn lucky that I don't have my gun."

"My name is Brighton. And I'll be there when you wake up, Jameson. You'll hear me, feel me and sense me wherever you go."

Jameson hurried out of the kitchen, kicking open the screen door like he did as a boy. He stepped onto the porch. The sunlight blinded him...

Albert's pen-sized flashlight stung Jameson's eyes.

"He's coming out of it!" Albert declared.

With a violent gasp, Jameson lurched forward. The restraints pulled him down. He screamed in delirium as his senses attuned.

Albert leaned over him. "Easy, easy. Deep breaths. You're safe in my lab in Undertown."

Jameson's eyes fluttered opened. He found himself in a soft bed draped with a green, wool blanket. The room, painted white and trimmed in chrome, stunk like a musty basement. Luna sat at his left, her hand clutching his.

"Welcome back, partner," she said.

Jameson turned to her and spoke in a dry voice, "I- I'm sorry for hitting you with the flashlight."

"It's a good thing you don't hit like a girl."

Jameson managed a bristly laugh.

Albert unfastened the restraints and Jameson propped himself onto his elbow. His head spun. "My father...what happened to him?"

Albert and Luna exchanged glances. Luna sighed. "Jameson, I had to shoot him and I—"

Jameson put up his hand. "I know, Luna. I would have done the same."

"But you should know that he's—"

"I get it," Jameson interrupted. His rising anguish sharpened his tone. "Don't feel bad, okay? Things just...didn't work out the way I wanted them to. The way I hoped they would. Let's just leave it at that."

Albert jumped in. "How are you feeling?"

"I had one messed up dream."

Brighton's voice echoed in his head. *"Not a dream."*

Jameson squeezed Luna's hand. "Did you hear that?"

Luna stared at him, confused.

*"No; she didn't hear me,"* Brighton replied. *"To put it in your terms, I'm the little voice in your head. Stop being dramatic; it's embarrassing."*

Luna forced him to lie back down. "You've been through a lot. Try to relax."

"Where's my shotgun?"

*"Don't even think about blowing your head off, Jameson,"* Brighton warned.

"It's in my pack," Luna assured. "Don't worry about it."

*"How nice of her. She seems like a good friend."*

Jameson took a slow breath and felt the room spin. "I feel so damn tired."

"That's because I gave you a heavy dose of Quell," Albert explained. "You've been infected with Graves' parasite."

"Why am I not going crazy?"

"I've been wondering the same thing." Albert patted Jameson's shoulder. "Relax and don't worry. I'll figure this out."

"I know you will, doc."

"I'll start with a blood test and compare it to the sample you gave me earlier. Let me see your arm."

Albert drew a vial of his blood and scribbled on the label. He traversed the lab and set to work. "DNA analysis takes a while. Luna, feel free to make yourself comfortable while Jameson is resting."

"What about you, Albert?" Luna asked. "You need rest, too."

Albert shook his head. "There's too much work to do. And besides, I promised you I'd do all I can for him. I meant that."

# Chapter 11

Albert worked through the day and late into the night. The others took advantage of the comforts of his lab. They cleaned up, ate, rested and resupplied. The doctor waited for the DNA analysis to complete and fell asleep behind his desk.

Jameson slept in the patient bed across the room. Late in the night, he woke at the sound of footsteps shuffling around. He opened his eyes but kept very still. A young man, about twenty by Jameson's guess, with tousled red hair tip-toed through the lab. He quietly opened drawers and peeked into cabinets.

"*What is that man doing?*" Brighton asked in Jameson's mind. "*We should subdue him, quickly.*"

"Wait," Jameson whispered.

"*For what? For him to get us first?*"

"I don't know if he's a threat or not. Wait."

"*Do you smell that?*" Brighton asked.

Jameson sniffed the air. The quiet visitor reeked like a combination of sour milk and vinegar.

"*That smell is offensive,*" Brighton stated, his voice becoming agitated. "*It's upsetting me.*"

Jameson's hands rolled to tight fists beyond his control. His nostrils flared.

"*I don't like it at all,*" Brighton yelled. "*I don't want to smell it anymore!*"

A foreign and powerful wave of rage crested in Jameson's heart. He sat up, and in the motion of his legs swinging over the bedside, he lost himself. An unstoppable force, like an ocean undertow, pulled at his mind, severing and assuming the control of his body. Brighton's words rolled up Jameson's throat and out his lips. "Looking to rob the good doctor?"

"No way, man. I'm just here to pick up my meds."

Like a spectator frozen in a cage of perfect glass, Jameson could only watch through his own eyes as Brighton commanded his body. He got off the bed and approached the man. "I hate liars," barked Brighton.

"Stay back, man. I've got Malady."

Brighton rolled his neck and cracked his knuckles. "Not for long." He snagged the man by the shirt collar, but the fabric ripped as he jerked away, bolting out of the lab.

"*Brighton, stop! He's not a threat!*" Jameson's shout rang in the back of his own head, going nowhere, like yelling into a pillow.

Brighton burst into a sprint after the intruder. Jameson felt the parasite's desire taint his heart. The only motivation being the capture of the Malady infected man. The chase carried through the arched tunnels of Undertown until the man, out of breath, stopped at the main subway platform. The swift moving subway train rumbled toward the station.

The man looked back, eyes wide with panic and fear. "What's your problem, man?"

"You," Brighton replied. "You're everyone's problem."

Jameson's very soul was nearly seared to ash by an inferno of hate emanating from Brighton. He could feel the Malad-X parasite's emotions, contrary to his own. The very sight of the red-haired man disgusted Brighton and spun him into a fever of malice. The man's fear was apparent and filled Jameson with remorse. *It's my face he sees.*

Brighton coiled his fingers around the man's throat.

"*Leave him alone!*" shouted Jameson into the passages of his mind.

The subway streaked into the station. Brighton shoved the young man off the platform, to the tracks below. The screams were cut off as the subway ran him over.

Jameson listened to the wheels grind. The strange undertow came again and his arms, legs and shoulders shivered. He lurched forward and vomited. From deep within he heard Brighton's voice. "*I don't smell it anymore. Do you?*"

"No."

Jameson dropped to his knees. *What did I just do? What am I?*

A hand closed on his shoulder.

He turned his head to find Albert Walker standing over him.

"Jameson? What happened?"

131

Jameson wiped a line of vomit from his chin. "I…uh…was following a guy and got sick. What are you doing here, doc?"

"I woke when I thought I heard you talking to a patient of mine, a young man with red hair. His name is Dustin. Did he happen by my lab while I was asleep?"

"Yeah…I was trying to catch him."

"That's what I assumed. I appreciate your efforts because Dustin recently contracted Malady. His whole family is pretty sick and he picks up their meds weekly. Where did he go?"

Jameson looked down and sighed. "He fell onto the tracks. I couldn't save him. I'm sorry. I'm so sorry."

Albert paused, struggling with the news. "Fuck Malady! Dustin was a good kid. He used to run errands for me when I was setting up the lab." His eyes became pools of sadness. "Too much suffering in this world, Jameson. Too much loss. I swear I'm going to find a way to destroy Malady."

Brighton stirred in Jameson. *"Wouldn't that be nice?"*

Luna couldn't sleep. Jameson tossed and turned in the bed across from hers, muttering strange things. His eyelids twitched and sweat beaded on his face. His suffering pained her. She sat up and decided to check with Albert.

Out of habit, she took up her rifle then left the room for Albert's office.

"Ah, Luna," Albert greeted her with a smile. "Why aren't you asleep? It's almost four in the morning?"

"I'm worried about Jameson. Any updates?" She pulled a chair in front of Albert's desk and sat down. Dark circles swallowed his blood-red eyes. "You look damn tired. You're no good to this team if you're wiped out."

Albert put down his pencil and pushed aside his notebook. He leaned back and rubbed his eyes. "Jameson's condition has further complicated matters. But I understand it now."

"Talk to me."

Albert shuffled through his papers, charts and calculations. "Science is a dance of facts and theories. I take what I know and use it to reason what I need to know through the assessment of implications. What I don't do is make assumptions. Let's start with what is known.

"First, we know that Marcus Graves created Malad-X because common Malady is developing a resistance to Quell and he can't allow that. In his genetic tampering to form a more Quell-susceptible breed, he increased the territorial aggression of the parasite and relished the results. Malad-X was born a Malady killer. Lovely.

"Second, Graves needed to test Malad-X. He kidnapped innocent people from the Void Lands and infected them with both breeds of parasite, pitting them against one another. Malad-X kills Malady. It's all it wants to do.

"Third, Jameson gets shot up with Malad-X but doesn't seem to be any more or less nuts than he was before. Why not? Where is the difference? This is the question that has kept me from sleeping, Luna, and now I know the answer."

"Well?"

"Let me show you." Albert handed Luna a print out from the DNA analyzer. "Feast your eyes on that!"

Luna couldn't interpret the wavy lines, colored blocks and numerical string. She shrugged and handed it back to Albert. "What does it mean?"

"I analyzed the first blood sample I took from Jameson. This section, here, details his genetic sequence prior to getting infected with Malad-X. It shows the presence of a Malady gene!"

"Are you telling me that Jameson had Malady from the start?"

"No. He has a Malady *gene*. Which has made him immune to Malady infection his entire life. He wasn't joking...so glad we didn't have a bet going."

"How's that possible?"

"Well, I've been trying to cut back on gambling and—"

"No! The Malady gene...how did he get that?"

A wide grin spread over Albert's face. "My theory, Luna. Malady-born!"

"I'm losing you."

"People born from the infected. Jameson's mother must have been infected with Malady prior to conceiving him, which put its stamp on Jameson's genotype, his overall genetic makeup. Now, his father's case also validates my theory. Graves Enterprises used Eric Shoals as a test subject because he had a natural resistance to Malady and I suspect it's because he, like his son, was also born of an infected woman and carried the Malady gene. During conception, Eric passed that gene on to his son, who also developed his own Malady gene during antenatal development within his infected mother."

"Is this Malady gene the reason Jameson didn't become a raging psychopath like the other Malad-X test subjects on the ship?" Luna asked.

"Simply put, the blood of a Malady-born makes an invading parasite very sick and it dies before it infiltrates the brain cavity. It is likely that Jameson has been infected with Malady countless times; however, his blood kills off the invaders. Now, with this new Malad-X infection, I believe his unique genetic chemistry prevented the Malad-X parasite from spoiling his brain as it would in you or I.

"This is a revolutionary discovery, Luna! So far, all scientific efforts against Malady have been geared toward treating the infected and killing the parasite. All sorts of anthelmintic drugs have been administered, but with no success. Everyone laughed when I pushed my concepts of parasite and human genetic mingling," Albert threw a combination of punches in the air, "take that, assholes! The answer to curing the world of the Malady pandemic is all around us."

"It's the children," answered Luna.

"Precisely. Mutation—a word with a negative connotation—is an organism altering its genetic structure in response to changes in its environment to ensure survival. The Malady parasite has wrecked humanity's environment and now we see the human response. Evolution. Mutation *is* evolution. But it all takes time. Emerging within this new generation is the newest breed of mankind, the one no longer a host. The Malady Born."

"But how can we help Jameson?"

"By learning as much as we can about his condition." Albert hammered his desk with his fist. "We went to such great lengths on that ship. You shot Eric Shoals in the shoulder, knocking him off Jameson. When Jameson passed out, I carried him and you carried Eric. We barely made it out of there. I patch up the old man, get him stable, and—"

"He runs off during the night," finished Luna. "Like father, like son."

"I just wish I had time to study Eric's condition." Albert crumbled a few scrap papers and tossed them into the basket beside his desk. "Have you told Jameson we saved his father?"

"No. He's dealing with a lot right now. Don't say anything. Let me."

"You got it, Luna."

"Now, tell me more about Jameson's infection."

Albert flipped the paper over. "This is the result of the blood analysis *after* Jameson became infected with Malad-X. There is distinct biological diversity here. His blood has become a strange cocktail of human, Malady and Malad-X DNA. But that's not all that my prized analyzer has revealed. Take a look at the print out again."

Luna let out an irritated sigh. "You know I can't read that."

"Oh, right. Sorry. Further analysis of the Malad-X traces left in the syringe highlighted more genetic variations. Are you ready for this?" Albert performed a drum roll with his fingers on the edge of his desk. "Malad-X contains *human* DNA!"

"What? Who's?"

"I cross-referenced the DNA with my copies of the Oasis Hospital and Sable Tower archives and confirmed it to be the DNA of its creator, Marcus Graves."

"This means," Luna added, "that Graves has Malady and used his own infection to create Malad-X."

Albert tucked the print out into a manila folder. "Welcome to the scientific community, Ms. Briggs."

Luna took Albert's hand in hers. "Albert, I'm impressed. Excellent work."

"Thank you. But I've done all I can on my own. I need Dr. Carmen Victoria at Oasis Hospital to help me stitch it all together. It's time I call a meeting with her to reveal my discoveries. And I do believe it's time she learns what her adversary, Dr. Graves, has cooked up."

"Karma City needs to know, too," demanded Luna. "We should push for Oasis to organize an awareness event and expose Graves for the monster he is. His Malad-X parasite can't get out. If it does, there will be wide-spread murder and no one will be able to stop it."

\*\*\*

"Are you nervous about your first day at the new job?" Corpse-Dad asked.

"Not really," Jack answered. As he rode the bus to Sable District, he watched Karma City roll by through the clouded window. It always amazed him how healthy people looked as Sable District drew near. Everyone dependent on Quell, everyone keeping their Malady asleep in their brains. Jack rolled his pill vial in his hand. Dealing with Corpse-Dad was becoming easier and he had refrained from taking Quell since Wednesday morning.

"I thought you were trying to track down the people who jumped from the train to get their story."

"I'm still on it," Jack answered. "I was hoping for a lead with Crimm but when he turned up, well, like you, it redirected the trail of bread crumbs. This Malad-X thing, whatever it is, is important."

"Oh, I see. So, you're not really going to work for Graves? You're just pretending so you can dig up more information."

Jack rubbed his eyes. "Dig up? Was that a dead man pun?" He shook his head. "Why am I getting into this discussion with a hallucination?"

"Who else are you going to talk to?"

Jack shrugged. "Good point."

"Say, I remember how nervous you were on your first day of school. Do you remember that?"

"Enough with the memory lane crap."

"Gee-whiz, someone got up on the wrong side of the bed today. What's the matter?"

"I'm tired of your rosy recollections. Have you forgotten about how violent Malady made you? How you used to beat the crap out of me for no reason?"

Corpse-Dad looked down. Droplets of puss pattered on his moldy shoes. "I haven't forgotten. I feel terrible about all of that."

Jack gathered his briefcase and overcoat as the bus jerked to a halt at the Sable District gates. "Keep quiet. I don't need people looking at me funny today." Jack stepped off the bus and processed through the security checkpoint. With Corpse-Dad following behind, he walked five blocks to Sable Tower and entered through the main lobby. He adjusted his tie and patted down his hair before approaching the receptionist's desk.

"Good morning and welcome to Sable Tower. How may I help you?"

"Jack Halligan. Here for a meeting."

After a few keystrokes at her computer, she handed him an employee access card on a lanyard. "The card will activate the tower elevator. Head to the top floor. Dr. Graves holds his executive meetings in his personal conference room in his suite. Will there be anything else, Mr. Halligan?"

"No, thank you. Have a good morning."


"Whoa!" Corpse-Dad exclaimed. "The tension is stifling in here."

"Shut up," hissed Jack.

Graves Enterprises executives sat around an oval glass table. They fidgeted with pens and quietly spoke to one another. The men and women wore black professional attire with very little color. Jack reasoned it was likely a dress code of some sort. *Guess I missed the memo.* He looked down at his tan slacks, green collared shirt and brown loafers. One man stood out from the others. He sat at the opposing table head in a bright white tuxedo. A rose boutonniere and pearl-trimmed embroidery lined his lapels and jewel-encrusted rings adorned his hands. Like an owl perched on a hemlock bough, his cold eyes followed Jack as he took his seat.

Marcus Graves entered the room; disconcerting shadows lined his face. To Jack, the doctor looked like a different person than the man he'd had breakfast with. Graves sat at the table head and slowly eyed the group. He spoke softly, commanding attention.

"Ten and a half million. That's what I lost with the destruction of the Graves Enterprises vessel." Graves pointed to the man in the white tuxedo. "I hold *you* responsible for this, Gabriel."

"You're not the only one who's suffered losses at the hands of these raiders, Graves. My beautiful resort needs extensive repairs and I can't even count the number of lost clientele and injured employees. How dare you blame me? Have you forgotten who you're talking to?"

Graves tensed and stood up. He calmly walked around the table to stand near Gabriel. "How could I forget a worthless, Void Land dreg masquerading as a kingpin?" He reached down, snatched Gabriel's hair and jerked his head back. Silver flashed in Graves' hand—a scalpel. He pressed it under Gabriel's eye and snarled, "Do you think I care about what happens in your rat's nest, Gabriel?" Gabriel struggled. Graves pressed the small blade into the skin of his face. A line of blood trickled from the top of Gabriel's cheek like a scarlet tear, staining the white tuxedo's lapel. "I keep you around because I need your network, not because I need you."

Jack looked on, stunned. He held his breath as if that would make it easier to watch.

Corpse-Dad nudged him. "I told you he had Malady and, my goodness, has it made him crazy."

Graves' assault carried on. "I could cut your eyeball out of your head with a single turn of my wrist. Then perhaps you'll *see* things my way."

Gabriel stiffened. The other men at the table looked to Jack like helpless animals frozen in terror, trapped under the deadly presence of an indomitable predator.

"Now," said Graves with the scalpel firm, "I have expectations in business. I expect discretion, commitment and professionalism. I discreetly rented your waterfront warehouse. We had a confidentiality agreement. Yet, your people in Eden proved incompetent in securing your *resort* and as such, my files were stolen, my operation was interrupted and my ship was destroyed. Tell me how you're going to fulfill my expectations now."

Gabriel hustled for the briefcase with rattling hands. "I have photographs of the people responsible. Surveillance captures."

Graves released him and drew a napkin from his pocket. He tossed it to Gabriel. "Clean yourself up." He opened the briefcase and took out an envelope. Once back in his chair, he sifted through the photos, calm and quiet. "Is this the whole group?" he asked, after a long period of silent deliberation. "Yes. The scientist distracted my lobby guards. The thug and the Iron Tribe woman destroyed the security office and stole the computer drive that contained information about your operation."

Graves studied the pictures then spoke to another executive seated across from Jack. "Mr. Rockland, as Captain of the Sable Guard, I want you to deploy forces into Karma City to bring down these attackers. I will have no further interruptions or delays in my endeavors. Understood?"

"Yes, Sir."

"Good. Now, I feel that tensions have become much too high for a collaborative meeting. Let's take a half hour break. There is a lengthy agenda to cover and I'm eager to discuss the tightening of internal controls, hear the update on Quell analytics and most importantly, I want a full briefing on Malad-X testing success ratios."

In a stiff, single-file line, the men exited the boardroom; Jack noticed shoulders falling from relief and heard gasps of breath, like men suddenly emerging from deep waters. Graves beckoned for Jack to remain. Once the others were gone, Graves said, "I apologize for the hostile environment. It is not what I would have wished for your first day with Graves Enterprises."

Jack, struggling to appear at ease, stuffed his hands in his pockets and gave an exaggerated shrug. "Hey, I live in central Karma and I've seen a lot worse than that."

"I appreciate your resolve. You'll fit in well around here."

"Not unless I'm useful. I'd like to get to work but I need to know more if I'm going to put anything on the paper. What's Malad-X?"

Graves put up his index finger and grinned. "Right now, the details are still restricted to *authorized* personnel. You will not receive that level of information access just yet."

"You hired me to cover your advances against Malady. Now you're telling me I'm restricted. What am I supposed to write about?"

"You'll write what I *need* you to write, *when* I need you to write it."

"I'm no singer-for-hire."

"Take a break, Mr. Halligan. Go to the café on the main level and get something to eat or drink. As I said earlier, tensions are too high. We'll discuss your assignments later today. I'll see you in a half hour. And stay away from Mr. Gabriel. He'll be in a sour mood for the rest of the day." Graves exited through a side door at the far corner of the conference room. Jack deduced that it likely led to his private suite.

"Café sounds like fun," piped Corpse-Dad. "Race you to the elevator!"

Jack sighed. "I'm not in the mood for a latte. I'd rather see what's behind door number two."

Jack pressed his ear to the door Graves disappeared behind. He heard piano music playing a somber, classical piece. He said to Corpse-Dad, "I'm going in. Let me know if you hear anyone."

"I can't. I'm not real; remember?"

Jack rolled his eyes and tried the knob. It turned. "Must be my lucky day." The door opened to a lavish parlor with burgundy and gold paisley wall paper. Brass sconces poured soft light over the walls. Jack smelled burnt wood and charred paint and noticed the ceiling blackened. *There's been a fire here. That's strange.* A horse-shoe of leather couches sat in the middle of the room, where a record player warbled with haunting piano music. Jack stepped quietly across the thick, scarlet carpeting and listened. He heard Graves talking from an adjacent room and he wondered to whom.

"All they've accomplished is robbing me of precious time," rambled Graves.

Jack crossed the parlor and stood behind the doorframe to eavesdrop.

Graves laughed. "But I don't need much more time. Soon, Malady will be hunted and slaughtered. Eradication is imminent."

"What is he talking about?" whispered Corpse-Dad.

Jack wondered briefly why he was whispering, then felt a blast of cold air. He peered around the doorway and watched Graves pull open two large glass doors. The doctor stepped onto a balcony and moved up a staircase that stretched out of view. Jack followed.

From the dizzying heights of Graves' balcony, the Karma skyline spread beneath him. The buildings looked like toys that he could knock over with the wave of his hand. The silver rails of the Iron Tribe's train gleamed like lines of spider's silk threading their way through the city. The East River reflected the sun in fiery jewels falling into a foggy coastline and the clusters of districts, neighborhoods and businesses were a complex, geometric labyrinth. Jack eyed the staircase that Graves ascended. It led to the tower's roof. As he crept up the stairs, clinging to the railing for courage.

Jack peered across the rooftop and gasped. There, a steel scaffold supported a massive glowing tank of murky white liquid. The liquid swirled and effervesced. Painted, black letters stenciled to the tank's curving glass formed the word: MALAD-X. Graves' black coat fluttered around him as he circled the unit. The threw up his arms, triumphantly shouting, "Eradication is imminent!"

"I think I've seen enough, son," Corpse-Dad remarked.

"Funny, that's exactly what I was thinking. Let's get out of here."

# Chapter 12

"Do you have to do this now?" Donna followed Jack around the apartment as he searched for his suitcase.

"I've called Graves," Jack said, "and told him I'm not feeling well and need a few days off. Hopefully, we have enough time to get out of Karma City."

"Let me see if I understand this," said Donna. "There is a mysterious glowing liquid at the top of Sable Tower?"

Jack flung open the bedroom closet. "Yes! Now, where did I put my suitcase?"

"Jack, stop for a minute and look at me!"

He stepped out of the closet and faced her. "I know how it sounds but I swear I didn't imagine it. Graves has made something called Malad-X, and whatever it is Professor Crimm knew of it and died for it. Graves is preparing for something terrible, Donna. And we don't need to stick around to find out what."

Donna sighed and sat on the edge of the bed. Jack spotted a blue gift box with a white bow in her hand.

"What's that?" he asked.

"You've forgotten what today is, haven't you?"

Jack paused and rubbed the back of his neck. He cursed his Malady for the forgetfulness and sat on the bed beside her. "It's my birthday."

"You've been so upset since you got back from Sable District. Dr. Graves has helped so many people with Malady. Quell is the only respite this city has. You make him sound like an evil scientist from some science fiction story."

"Donna, I'm telling you—"

She put up her hand. "I've never known you to want to pack up and run. Why now?" She ran her fingers through his curly hair. "It's a beautiful day and I don't have to work. We were going to have a picnic lunch today."

"Right, the picnic." He rubbed his neck.

She put the gift box in his hand. "Happy birthday, Jack."

He held the box and sighed. She was right. He'd never run from anything. His courage is what made him such a successful writer. He'd talk to anyone, travel anywhere, and assume any risk just to get the story. But he'd do it carefully, thoughtfully and correctly. Yet this morning he'd been frantic, fearful and full of doubt. Why? Malady. What happened to his resolve? Where did his courage go? He brought his eyes to Donna's and found it staring back at him. He leaned in and kissed her.

"Open it!" She urged.

With a smile, he pulled the bow from the box and lifted the small lid. There, resting on a tuft of cotton shined a golden pin in the shape of an airplane. He smiled as childhood memories emerged from the fog of Malady

"One last fold...careful not to rip the paper... perfect! Now it's an airplane," said his father.

"Now it can fly!"

"That's right, son. It's time for lift off. Ready... set... GO!"

Young Jack pulled back and tossed the paper airplane off the balcony. From the sixth floor, the paper triangle climbed, circled and soared to the street. "That was awesome! Did you see how it banked and swooped?"

"Sure did. Must have been flown by a very skilled pilot."

"Just like you!" Jack exclaimed.

"Thanks, son. Now, go get your shoes on, it's time to head to the airfield."

"Awesome!" Jack jumped up and down in excitement.

Once ready, he and his father set off to the station, boarded the train and rode beyond the city limits, to the South Karma Airfield. At seven years old, nothing fascinated Jack more than the wide, white wings, the droning of the propellers and the magic of the wheels lifting off the ground. His father, Mark Halligan, was one of the last pilots in and around Karma. He ran a small business that offered private flights from Karma City to Rime, Lobos and back. With one single engine and one twin-engine aircraft, Mark Halligan safely flew passengers inbound and out, three times a week, with Jack at his side.

Flying over the city and across the Void Lands filled Jack with wonder and inspired his imagination. While his father controlled the aircraft, Jack would peer out at the world below and pretend to be a great eagle or a mythical dragon flying with the sun at his back and clouds parting over his face. Through the headsets, he and his father would talk about the rolling landscape, the colorful skyline, or Jack's desire to fly like his dad.

"It doesn't look that hard," Jack said as Mark listened with a smile.

"There's more to it than flight controls. You have to keep your eyes on the horizon. Watching the sky and the land is very important."

"I'm good at that."

Mark laughed. "You sure are."

By fifteen years old, Jack worked for his father's aviation business, flying the single engine plane. He flew travelers along the east to west route to and from Lobos, as it offered two unobstructed landing strips—the South Karma Airfield and Route 88. His father flew the north to south route, flying from Karma City to Rime's mountaintop airfield. As the Malady pandemic intensified, more people became infected and the flight schedules diminished. Rime closed its airfield. Mark struggled to pay the bills and the cost of upkeep on the planes became a tremendous burden.

Two hard years of wrestling with the possible collapse of his business made Mark so desperate to keep flying that when Oasis Hospital asked him to transport patients from the Void Lands into the city for treatment, he eagerly accepted. Jack, now seventeen and an experienced pilot, adamantly disagreed with his father's decision.

"Jack, have a little empathy. These people need help. Our aircraft can quickly get the infected the care they need."

The afternoon sun fell behind Karma's skyscrapers. Jack and Mark had finished bringing the planes into the hanger and stood on the tarmac arguing.

"I get it, Dad. But with sick passengers, I'll be exposed to Malady all the time."

"Oasis is providing masks, gloves and cleaning agents. You'll be fine."

"I'm not doing it." Jack unzipped his flight suit to his waist and stormed off toward his motorcycle parked on the edge of the runway.

His father called out, "The first group of patients is expecting you to pick them up tomorrow morning."

Jack mounted his bike and switched on the engine. He cranked the throttle and the pipes growled. "Fly them yourself." He sped off into the evening, riding fast throughout the city. His father's desperation to keep the business going, and at Jack's risk, angered him. *How can he gamble like that? Doesn't he care?*

Jack's smile had fallen as a far-off stare channeled his sadness. "I remember him now," he said to Donna. "The way he was."

"Feel like talking about it?"

Jack took a deep breath. "For so many years I blamed myself. I would lay awake at night, certain that if I had only flown that morning, things would have been different. I wouldn't have been as tired as he was and I certainly wouldn't have tolerated the sick passengers fighting with one another during the flight. I wouldn't have let them distract me. I wouldn't have..." his voice wavered, "crashed."

Donna rubbed his back. "But he survived."

"Yes, but the Malady infected passengers didn't and when he pulled their bloody bodies from the scene, their sickness spread to him. It wasn't long before the parasite turned my father into an angry, violent madman. Soon, the business went under and *I* had to deal with it. That's tough when you're a teenager. It proved too tough for me.

"I sold off the remaining airplane to cover two years of rent and that sent Dad into a huge Malady fit. When the fight started, I decided I'd had enough and was going to get on my motorcycle and leave Karma for good. Dad stopped me at the door, shoved me back, and punched me half a dozen times. My bloody nose pattered on the floor as I wrestled to get away from him. He backed me into the parlor, and I moved onto the balcony thinking

145

I'd use the fire escape to get to the street. He chased me, shouting, 'you ruined my life, you ruined my life.'

"Donna, I was so scared. His Malady had completely transformed him. His eyes bounced around in his head and his mouth frothed. His whole body twitched. He cut me off, blocking the fire escape; I couldn't get away. When he lunged at me, I crouched and he tumbled over the railing, falling off the sixth-floor balcony like one of my paper airplanes." Jack paused. "Over the years, my Malady made me forget the shouting, the pain, the fear and most importantly, the sound of his body hitting the sidewalk. Now I wish it would make me forget again."

Donna wiped her tears. "Oh, Jack. I got you the pin because I thought it would bring back happy memories. I know you've been having those terrible hallucinations and I hoped that this might make them go away. I...I just wanted to help, Hun. I'm so sorry to make you sad on your birthday."

He closed his eyes and concentrated. "I remember the little things that I loved so much as a kid. Flying with Dad. Hearing his scratchy, sand-paper laughter. The way his jump suit smelled like a cheap pine tree air freshener. The embroidered letters on his right breast pocket that spelled HALLIGAN. I still have that old jumpsuit somewhere." Jack smiled. "This pin is helping me remember the yellow sunlight shining through the airplane windshield, the vibrations shaking through me as the propeller whirls. I can remember looking down at the tiny shadow of our airplane against the cream-colored clouds and being so enchanted...so happy. Donna, this is a great gift, magical even. Thank you."

"You're welcome." They kissed and after a moment, she asked, "Do you miss flying?"

Jack shrugged. "There hasn't been an airplane in the skies over Karma for nearly twenty years. Nobody flies anymore. Nobody knows how. People are just too sick. The Malady parasite has robbed so much from all of us. So much has been forgotten. I couldn't remember how to fly if I tried. So, no, I don't miss it. I'm a writer and that's what I was born to do."

"When did you realize that?"

Jack rubbed his thumb over the gold airplane to evoke his memory. "My first composition was my father's eulogy. Haven't stopped writing since." He stuck the pin to his shirt collar and turned it so the plane's nose pointed upward. He stood and took Donna by the hand. "Let's go."

"Are we leaving the city?"

"No. We're going to have a picnic."

***

With folded arms, Luna waited for Albert to finish his phone call.

"Very good, Dr. Victoria... yes, I have the supporting data. I'll meet you in an hour. Not a problem. See you soon." Albert hung up the phone and took off his glasses. He wiped the lenses on the edge of his shirt, and then rambled to himself. "Everything will be fine. You're about to unlock the secrets of Malady at last. Hang in there."

"You're sounding a little nuts, Albert." Luna remarked.

"Sorry. Just a bit nervous is all. I've booked a meeting with Carmen Victoria to discuss the Malad-X threat. I'm not going to speak of Gemni because the focus needs to be further analysis of Jameson's blood."

"Thank you. What you're doing means a lot to me. And I just want to say that I believe in your work. I believe in you."

Albert's eyes watered. "No one has ever said that to me before. Thank you."

"You're welcome. Now, what can I do to help?"

"Keep an eye on my lab and on Jameson." He paused. "Speaking of...where is he?"

"In the shower."

"Great. I need to get in there and freshen up. Can you go see if he's done? I know he has a parasite in his head, but there is only so much that soap can do."

"Funny."

"I thought so."

Luna stopped outside of the washroom when she noticed the door ajar. She was about to knock but hesitated when she heard Jameson in conversation.

"You will not use me like that again," he nearly shouted. "I don't give a shit what you think!"

She peered through the margin of the doorway. Jameson stood alone in a cloud of steam, wearing only his pants and boots. Beads of water dripped over his razor-like body lines. Luna's heart quickened as she eyed him. His shirt slung over his shoulder and he leaned over the sink, starring into the mirror on the wall. His shoulders, solid and defined, glistened like wet stone. His back, tattooed and scared, tapered to a thin waistline that she briefly imagined sliding her hands around. She shook her head, guiltily, and closed her eyes to smolder the flame of desire that heated her.

"I am in charge," continued Jameson. "I won't be controlled by anyone or anything."

"An agreeable creed," Luna interjected, stepping into the room.

Jameson tensed. "Spying on me now?"

"Just making sure you don't forget to brush your teeth. Who's your imaginary friend?"

"My what?"

"Who are you talking to?" She asked sternly.

Jameson looked distracted. He shook his head. "I'm just collecting my thoughts."

"Didn't sound like it."

"Then what *did* it sound like?"

Luna regarded his defensive tone. "Like you're sick, Jameson. Tell me what you're going through."

Jameson sat on the edge of the bathtub. He rubbed his eyes with the heels of his palms. "Close the door."

Luna kicked the door closed.

The look of distraction came over him again. His face hardened as he spoke. "I don't think I like you very much."

"Excuse me?"

"No, not you!" He slammed his fist on the tub.

She crossed the room and sat beside him. Like a pebble tumbling in the surf, the struggle in Jameson's eyes appeared in flashes.

Jameson said, "The shit in that syringe messed me up pretty bad. Graves' Malad-X…it's in my mind. I see it, hearing it. I'm even talking with it."

"Seeing and hearing what?"

"The parasite." Jameson spat the answer with disgust. "Have you ever known me to be crazy, Luna? Well…you know what I mean."

"Not clinically."

"Exactly. And I'm still not crazy. I'm the same person but now there's something…someone…in my head."

"Someone?"

"It calls itself Brighton."

"The parasite has a name? Did it introduce itself?"

"Actually, yes."

"Do you see him now? Where is he?"

"That's just it. He's everywhere and nowhere. I only *see* him in my mind. You think I'm insane, don't you?"

"I think you're sick. And whatever that sickness brings is real for you."

Jameson sat in silence for a moment. "Let's keep this between us. I don't need Albert losing focus or reserving trust on my account."

"What about Quell," asked Luna. "Will that help keep the parasite in check?"

"Albert explained to me earlier that Malad-X is highly susceptible to Quell. The problem is that, depending on dosage, it might knock me out cold. He plans to brew up a batch of carefully formulated Quell for my condition but he doesn't have time now, and he wants to get Victoria's input."

"If Quell's not an option now, how're you going to handle this?"

Jameson shrugged with a smirk. "Brighton and I are still working out the kinks in our relationship."

149

Luna found comfort in his returning sarcasm. "If Brighton gets difficult," she said, "just hit him with your flashlight. You're pretty good at that."

Jameson laughed. "Are you ever going to let that go?"

"Not a chance."

Luna stood. Jameson hooked her by the waist, pressing her against him. He locked his thoughtful eyes on hers.

"I could have died on that ship," he said. "Maybe I was meant to. But you risked your life, like you've done countless times, to save me. I don't know how you keep doing it, Luna. Or why."

"When I met you, you said, 'You don't ask why out here... the answers are always easy to see.'"

"I remember. And I can't let another minute pass without telling you how much I—"

Albert entered the washroom. His glasses fogged from the lingering steam. "Take forever in here, why don't you? Hope you didn't use up all the hot water."

Luna pressed her palms against Jameson's wet, stone-like chest and moved out of his embrace. Her heart drummed so heavily that her body trembled. "We can talk later; okay?"

Jameson nodded and Luna slipped out of the room.

Albert wrestled with his nerves as he traversed the halls of Oasis Hospital to meet with Dr. Carmen Victoria. *Maybe I should have stopped for lunch first*, he mused, *nah...I'd just throw up*. His tension turned to sadness as he passed the Children's Ward where so many young boys and girls laid in beds, struggling with Malady. They cried out in fright, rambled in delirium, and whimpered in frustration. The parents sat beside them, doing all they could to ease the emotional pain and confusion.

His heart ached and his memories stirred. *I used to force myself to walk down this hall every day to maintain my motivation to stop Malady. Not an easy thing, but a necessary one.*

He paused to look into the cafeteria. He smelled the delicious food of the hospital kitchen—roasted chicken, glazed ham and steaming vegetables—and smiled when he heard some of the children laughing while they ate lunch. Oasis prided itself on the finest arrangements for the young patients. They deserved only the best care possible in Karma and this was a standard Albert also believed in.

*Belief.*

*I'm not as brave as Luna and Jameson, but those kids need someone to believe in. Why not me?*

Albert pushed open the doors to Dr. Victoria's conference room. The dark green carpet and red oak table created a soothing atmosphere set aglow by the sunlight pouring in through a wide window. The serenity faded as armed hospital guards stormed the room. One guard ordered, "Place your weapons on the table and raise your hands."

Albert complied, raising his hands as high as possible. "I'm unarmed."

A woman with graying blonde hair moved in front of the security guards and folded her arms. "Hello, Dr. Walker." The sunlight glinted off her small glasses. "In times of tremendous tragedy and violence, I have to take precautions, you understand."

"Ah, Dr. Victoria, I understand completely. And I'd like to add, it's a pleasure to see you again."

Carmen dispatched the guards and peered over her glasses. "Spare me the insincerity, Albert. Let's make something clear. If a deadly riot in the Malady ward and the murder of my beloved colleague are not enough to deal with, I recently learned that you've been stealing medical equipment from this hospital for months to bolster your personal lab in Undertown. What did I ever do to earn such disrespect from you?"

"Fine, we'll talk about disrespect for a moment. For years, Oasis staff disrespected me and my work. Every day I was belittled by people who were supposed to be my peers and you ask me what *you* did? You enabled that kind of attitude to flourish on your campus. Even now, as I stand here with only the best intention to help humanity, you look down on me. Carmen, you have no idea what I've been through recently and the truth is, there isn't another doctor in this hospital who can fill my shoes now."

Carmen looked away in obvious reflection of Albert's accusations. When she let out a long sigh, her face softened. She replied in a kinder tone. "Your medical practices and scientific methods have always been questionable and, in my professional opinion, reckless. The fact that you've established a medical center in Undertown of all places proves it. Given that, you should know that under normal circumstances you would not be welcome here for your crimes against my hospital. However, as head of the Advanced Science Against Malady team, I'm obligated to explore all potential parasitic concerns."

Albert tugged at his collar and adjusted his glasses. "Look, I didn't come here to quarrel with you. There are greater problems that threaten us all. And my discoveries, while monumental, are too big for me to tackle alone."

"You claim to have a specimen of an advanced breed of Malady," Carmen said. "To date, no other species of the parasite have been identified. Needless to say, I'm skeptical."

Albert puffed his chest and tucked his hands into his pockets. He pulled out a vial of blood and rolled it between his fingers. "There is a microscopic monster in here, one with the potential to destroy mankind. It's called Malad-X. It's highly aggressive and kills common Malady without hesitation. Subjects infected with Malad-X murder carriers of Malady in a type of primal rage. This is the result intended by its creator."

Carmen stared at the vial. "It's creator?"

"Malad-X is a genetically altered form of Malady created by Dr. Marcus Graves."

"How do you know that?"

Albert opened his satchel and produced a manila folder. "This contains acquired information about the secret projects at Graves Enterprises, my DNA analysis reports with corresponding data logs and notes on Professor Crimm's scientific findings with my definitive conclusions. It's all there."

Carmen examined the documents. "Successful genetic altering of the Malady parasite, kidnapping of Void Land natives for human testing of Malad-X, a living and deceased record of Graves Enterprises test subjects spanning twenty years!" She tossed the file onto the oak table and dropped into one of the chairs. "This is all too much."

Albert sat across from her and spoke gently, "If Marcus Graves unleashes Malad-X on the city it will render the infected against the infected. The death toll wrought by Graves Enterprises will be unending."

Carmen spoke in a low and contemptuous voice. "My hate for Marcus is immeasurable. My husband, Wolfgang, contracted Malady and died because of him. He's divided this city and has turned half the population into addicts. Now this?"

"There's hope," Albert sustained. "During our efforts, one of our partners, Jameson Shoals, became infected with Malad-X but has not become enraged. His genome is unique. Which, for his entire life until recently, has granted him immunity to Malady."

Carmen's eyes trapped Albert's. "How is that possible?"

"My theory, the one your team scorned, was correct."

"Yes. I recall your dissertation. You proposed that humans might share a genetic link with the parasite. What did you call it again?"

"Malady-born; which is precisely what Jameson is. His condition has altered the effects of the Malad-X within him, but I am not certain as to what extent. This vial contains his infected blood. There is more to learn and understand. I believe the answer to stopping Malady in all forms is right here, but I can't find it alone. I need your help." He handed her the vial.

"I…I don't quite know where to begin."

"We should start with awareness. People trust you. They trust Oasis. It must be your voice that warns the people of Karma City. It has to be. I advise that Oasis District facilitate a public event; during which, you announce the specifics of this emerging threat and its origin."

Carmen straightened in her seat. "What of Graves?"

"Graves is a sick and dangerous man," Albert said. "He used his own Malady to create Malad-X. He won't be too pleased when we expose him. It will lead to a collapse of his trusted reputation and the fall of Sable District. We must expose him before he unleashes his parasite on the world."

Carmen sat in contemplative silence. After several minutes, Albert asked, "What are your thoughts?"

"Awareness is top priority. We need to be careful with how we proceed against Graves. There is no telling how he'll react and I'm concerned for the safety of the people. I'm also wondering about this Malady-born. What did you say his name was?"

"Jameson Shoals."

"I'd like to bring him to the hospital under my personal care."

Albert shook his head. "I don't think that's going to happen."

"Mr. Shoals should understand resistance to Malady is extraordinary. Why won't he allow me to work with him?"

"Because *I'm* his doctor," Albert professed. "Let's leave it at that. See what you can do with his blood for now. Our immediate focus has to be stopping Malad-X and exposing Graves."

"You've regained my respect, Albert. I'll arrange for an event to be held at the River Commons, tomorrow afternoon. We'll issue bulletins from the district today and I'll contact the *Karma Daily* for coverage in the paper. I'll have a platform and podium set up. The commons should accommodate a crowd of several hundred. I'd like you and the members of your group beside me as I address the people."

Albert smiled and shook her hand. "We'll be there."

# Chapter 13

The telephone rang late in the night. Donna stirred but Jack whispered, "Stay in bed. I'll get it."

He stumbled through the dark apartment. The neon city lights blinked through his living room window, lighting the way in pulses of red, yellow and purple. The wall mounted phone rattled on its cradle. Jack lifted the receiver and brought the phone to his ear. He spoke in a groggy voice, "Dad, if this is you calling, I'm going to swallow a handful of Quell."

"No, Mr. Halligan," answered a female voice, "this is not your father. This is Dr. Carmen Victoria speaking."

Jack snapped awake. "Dr. Victoria! What can I do for you at…" he glanced at the digital clock on the microwave, "Does that say one o'clock in the morning?"

"I'm sorry to call so late. But this is urgent."

"I'm listening."

"As connected to the community as you are, have you heard the term 'Malad-X' before?"

Jack dodged the question. "Sounds like a bad cleaning product."

"I wish it were. Karma city is in great danger and—"

"I know," he interrupted, his heart sinking to his stomach. "There are some things I need to tell you."

***

"*Jameson. Are you asleep?*"

The bedside lamp winked on. Jameson opened his eyes and rolled onto his back. Pipes and cables crisscrossed along the ceiling. In a half-sleep delirium, he recalled that he was still in Albert's medical center in Undertown.

"*I'm sorry to wake you.*"

The voice sounded clear, as if spoken directly into his ears, but no one stood at his bedside. Brighton. Jameson mumbled. "What time is it?"

"*Three o'clock in the morning.*"

"Damn. What's the problem?"

"*I had a nightmare.*"

Jameson dropped his palms over his face. He rubbed his eyes. "What are you, a kid or something? Let me go back to sleep or I'll put a plunger to my ear and drag you out of there."

*"The nightmare was about you. I must warn you!"*

"Fine. Make it quick."

*"You and I were at a gathering of some kind, surrounded by people. The faces were angry, frightened and some of them were dead. A thick fog fell over us, trapping everyone. The smell, the one that I can't tolerate—"*

"It's the smell of Malady that makes you nuts."

*"Well, it was everywhere. Panic, violence...death."*

"Is that it? Can I go back to sleep now?"

*"No. The worst part was the man with glowing, orange eyes. He wanted you dead."*

"Gemni."

*"This man exists?"*

"Unfortunately, yes."

*"What is he?"*

"He is...like you," the realization struck Jameson like a baseball bat to the stomach. "Like me."

*"Is Gemni an enemy?"*

"Yes. And somehow, we're going to stop him."

*"I will help you."*

Jameson turned onto his shoulder and reached for the lamp. He switched it off and closed his eyes. "Go back to sleep, worm."

"Good night, Jameson."

Jameson couldn't sleep. Something else troubled him more than the similarity between himself and his enemy. *Brighton turned on the lamp. He took control while I slept.*

Early Saturday morning, Jameson gathered his shotgun and traveling pack and met his friends in the reception area of Albert's lab. Albert and Luna passed around the morning paper. Luna handed it Jameson. "Looks like the good doctor won over Carmen Victoria yesterday."

Jameson read the headline on the *Karma Daily*, "'Worse Than Malady by: Jack Halligan.' That's eye catching."

"I thought so," Albert agreed. "I can't believe Carmen was able to get Halligan to write the article on such short notice. He's the city's top writer. I've been trying to get him to do a piece on my lab, you know, for publicity and such, but he never returns my calls."

Jameson scrolled down the front page and read aloud, "'A scientific breakthrough has uncovered a new parasitic threat more dangerous than Malady. Dr. Carmen Victoria is calling for citizens of Karma City to attend a public address this afternoon at the River Commons outside Oasis District. The identifier of the new parasite and independent scientist, Dr. Albert Walker, will announce the details and answer questions. Medical teams will be on hand to provide free screening for the advanced Malady parasite that Dr. Walker calls Malad-X.'" Jameson folded the paper and handed it to Albert. "You're hitting the big time, doc."

"To be honest, Carmen is more interested in you than me. I told her of your immunity to Malady and she practically begged me to bring you in."

"Not happening."

"I figured."

"What did you tell her?"

"That *I* am your doctor." Albert slapped his hands and rubbed them together in excitement. "Let's head out for Oasis. I'd like to get there early, before the crowds. It's going to be a day that Karma City will remember forever."

Brighton spoke to Jameson. "*I don't want to go.*"

"Will you please relax?" Jameson snapped.

Albert frowned. "Excuse me for being excited to help inform and protect the citizens."

Jameson shook his head. "I was talking to myself. Trying to calm my nerves."

Luna, Jameson and Albert arrived at Oasis District by late morning. Crowds filled the subway station and lined the streets. They walked to the River Commons, a grassy park with swaying willows, served as the public front grounds of Oasis Hospital.

Beyond the park, Karma's highway stretched into the distance, running parallel with the Iron Tribe's rails.

Medical tents stood along the edges of the park walkways. Nurses and doctors conducted free examinations and parasitic screening of citizens gathering for the announcement. Jameson scanned the people, looking at expressions, postures and mannerisms. He found a mix of worry, hope and speculation in the eyes of Karma's citizens. Then, he smelled it—Malady. His heart quickened.

As if right on cue, Brighton barked in his mind. *"I hate that smell."*

Jameson struggled to extinguish the hatred crackling in his mind like vehement fire. Sweat dotted his brow.

*"What purpose does Malady serve? We are surrounded by the weak and wasteful. I'd love to kill them all!"*

"Enough!" he shouted.

Luna reacted to Jameson's outburst and spun him around to face her. "What's the problem?"

"Brighton is losing it over the infected."

"Fight him. Take control."

Jameson closed his eyes and took in a slow breath. He wiped away his sweat and focused on confronting the other consciousness within him. He spoke aloud, "I will not harm people just because they're infected with Malady. If the sick bastards get violent and attack me or someone else, that's different. Understand?"

*"We don't need to be victims. With me, you can have strength beyond yourself. You can have reflexes quicker than you've known. I can shelter you from physical pain so you can move forward when others would fall."*

"What's your point?"

*"That all of these things give you—give us—options. Killing is one. Commanding is another. Malad-X is superior and my power is undeniable. Let me show you. Let me take control."*

"No, you son of a bitch! NO!"

Brighton's voice faded. *"Upsetting you is putting us both at risk. I'm going to rest now."*

Jameson no longer felt the parasite's rage boiling in him.

"Is he gone?" Luna asked.

"He shut up, and that'll do." Jameson looked for Albert. "Where's the doc?"

Luna pointed to a large stage with a podium and speaker system. "He's already at the platform with Carmen."

"This place is getting packed." Jameson recalled Brighton's dream of the crowd, an outbreak of terror, the smoke, of Gemni. "Better hurry to the stage. I have a feeling," he tapped his temple, "things are going to get dangerous."

"In that case…" Luna reached into her pack and pulled out the small radio that Mandy Briggs gave her when they parted at the docks. She switched it on. The radio crackled with static and a blue light flashed near the volume dial. She brought the radio to her lips. "Luna Briggs to Iron Tribe. Radio check."

After a brief moment of whirring frequencies and static garble, a deep voice answered, "Northbound 4-8-4 responding. Loud and clear, Briggs."

"Can you confirm my location?"

"Tracking signal now, standby… signal locked. Location identified as Karma City, Oasis District, River Commons. Please confirm."

"Location accurate."

"Monitoring your frequency and location."

"Copy, 4-8-4. Over."

Jameson grinned. "A little back up?"

"Just a little."

Luna found Albert behind the stage platform with Carmen Victoria. Carmen regarded the group then spoke to Albert. "My team and I poured over your work all night. Your concept of Malady-born having a genetic commonality with the parasite is accurate and revolutionary. We're standing on the fringe of mankind's evolution, and have been the whole time. There are so many tests I want to do, so much to document. It's all so fascinating but what is most special, Albert, is that you've proven that we, as a species, are not doomed. Furthermore, the blood sample was rigorously analyzed," she paused to clear the misty from her eyes. "Your work has opened the door for a possible anti-parasitic immunization, one that can ward against Malady in all forms!"

Albert clapped in delight. "This is everything I've hoped for! How does it work? Tell me more."

"Jameson's blood contains a wide range of antigenic properties, but I'll tell you more after the event," Carmen assured. "We've got a capacity crowd here; it's time to warn them about Malad-X and Graves Enterprises."

"You'd better do it soon," Luna interrupted. "Graves just pulled up." She pointed at a black limousine carving its way through the crowd. The car glided to a stop at the side of the stage. The driver stepped out and opened the rear door. Marcus Graves emerged, his black overcoat trailed at his ankles as he approached. He wore dark sunglasses and a wide-brimmed black hat. He moved up the platform and waited for Carmen at the podium. He stared at Albert and Carmen, standing as still as a lifeless shadow.

Carmen turned to Albert. "I'm scared."

"In Karma City, that's the feeling you get when you're doing the right thing." Albert took her hand in his and led her onto the stage.

Luna waited at the corner of the stage. Jameson remained behind the scaffolding. She gripped her rifle; her finger hovered over the trigger as black vans from Sable District surrounded the event. Sable Guard filed out, dressed in matte-black armor and armed with automatic weapons. The tension brewing over the awareness event felt like a storm rolling in from the sea, chilling and unstoppable.

She watched and listened, ready for the first sign of chaos. A cool breeze blew across her face; for a brief moment, she felt aboard the train once more, ready to defend and willing to fill the air with bullets to keep order, to keep peace, to keep alive.

The crowd hollered, jeered and applauded for Karma City's two scientific powers standing beside one another on the stage. The reaction of the people showcased their division. The Malady infected praised Graves for Quell. The uninfected called out their support for Carmen and her Victory Vaccine. Respite and Opportunity. The two doctors stood before the people of Karma as symbols to these notions.

Carmen stood behind the podium. Luna noted the doctor's air of confidence and the command her very presence had on many of the people. The microphone hummed when Carmen spoke. "Dear citizens of Karma City," the crowd fell to near silence. "Thank you all for coming today. I am joined by my colleague," she pointed to Albert who stood at the left side of the stage, "Dr. Albert Walker, the man whose tireless dedication to the sciences against Malady has uncovered a new threat as well as a new hope." She paused and turned to acknowledge Graves. "To my surprise, I'm also joined today by Dr. Marcus Graves. Dr. Graves, I appreciate your presence here this morning, as today is the day when things change for the good people of Karma. That change starts with you."

Graves leaned toward the microphone and took off his sunglasses. The people applauded again, shouting thanks and words of admiration. He gave a gentle wave of gratitude. "Thank you, Dr. Victoria. I couldn't agree more." He raised his voice. "Let's speak of change. I am the one who has brought more change to this city than anyone else. I changed the lives of Karma's citizens with Quell. I returned serenity to the homes of countless infected. The change I've brought has given people the ability to cope and continue living even when sick with Malady. Is this not true?"

The people cheered, waved and whistled.

"True?" Carmen questioned. "I challenge you to be truthful, Marcus."

"What reasons have I to lie?"

Carmen pointed to the crowd. "Tell them about Malad-X."

Graves smiled at the hundreds of citizens, but Luna saw the darkness, cruelty and purpose lurking in his gaze. "Ah, yes," Graves continued. "Ladies and gentlemen, Graves Enterprises has finally developed a means to rid the world of Malady once and for all."

The gathering erupted in celebration. Then, a gap formed in the mob of people, parting to reveal a single man in a red coat with locks of white-blond hair. He shouted a challenging question. "Why should Malady meet such a fate?"

Silence blanketed over the crowd.

Luna locked her rifle on Gemni. She weighed the options. *I should kill Gemni now. Half of the people here are Malady infected. He'll turn them against the uninfected. I have to take him down.* She touched the trigger but hesitated. *Why?* Never before had she made her decision and not acted. Something had changed in her. The quick thinking and fast actions of her tribal nature had subsided. For the first time, her heart directed her rather than her mind; she felt it as surely as she felt the cold, metal weapon in her hand. Now, her heart said to look beyond her sights, see the big picture, find the greater threat.

Her finger lifted off the trigger and her vision widened to the perimeters of the commons. Five black vans pulled up along the opposing edge of the crowd and opened their rear doors. A line of Sable Guardsmen spread to the corners. Some carried long, cylindrical weapons and the rest cradled black rifles in their arms. *Launchers and long guns. They're taking position over this crowd. Graves is ready for war and we're in the middle of it!* She looked to Carmen and Albert. *They have the science to save humanity. They need to get out of here before they get killed. There has to be a way out.* Luna looked over her shoulder; the highway remained free of Sable Guard vehicles. She reasoned it to be the only exit. She rushed to Albert and said in his ear. "This is life or death so do as I say. We need to leave right now. Take Carmen and head for the highway. I'll get Jameson."

Gemni approached the stage with an arrogant grin. "Malady is the evolution of humanity," he taunted.

Albert took Carmen by the arm but she resisted, shoving him backward. Carmen yelled into the microphone, pointing at Gemni. "Who are you and why would you say such a thing?"

"Why? Because I am the voice of the infected. I am the face of Malady."

Graves snatched the microphone. "Guards! Kill him!"

"You can't stop me, Graves," Gemni said with a grin. "This city is mine!" Gemni threw up his hands, his long coat flapped like a blood-soaked banner. He shouted, "Brothers, sisters, kill till the score is paid!"

Luna heard the first pop echo overhead. She looked up, following a streak of gray smoke arching in the sky. A series of pops sounded. The Sable Guard, from the corners of the event, fired smoke grenades into the crowd. Panic ensued. Cheers became screams.

Luna lifted her rifle and peered through the scope. She watched in horror as the van doors opened and wild-eyed civilians, wearing tattered clothing stained in blood, emptied into the crowd. With bats and axes, they attacked the Malady infected innocents. The smoke soon blanketed the area, hiding the murder and concealing the Malad-X predators.

Graves' laughter caught her attention. She swung her rifle barrel and locked her sights. Her finger moved over the trigger but a civilian barreled into her, knocking her rifle to the ground. "I won't let you assassinate Graves! I need the cure!" The man picked up her rifle and aimed it at her.

"If you have Malady, you need to get out of here. You're going to die!"

"I need the cure! And I'll kill you to get it!"

"Wrong move, pal!" said Jameson from the smoke. A shotgun blast blew out the man's chest, spraying blood and bits of bone into the air. Jameson emerged and recovered Luna's rifle.

The smoke thickened, concealing the stage and podium. Luna heard a woman screaming. *Carmen.* She switched on her scope's laser to cut through the smoke. She said to Jameson, "Secure the exit to the highway. I'll get Albert and Carmen. Go!"

She hurried through the chaos, following Carmen's yells. The yelling faded and she found Albert on his knees behind the stage platform, blood trickling from his nose and mouth. She pulled him to his feet and dragged him behind the stage wall for cover. "What happened, Albert?"

"The Sable Guard took Carmen. They struck me down." The pleas for help, the wails of the dying and the horrific shouts of the Malad-X murderers raged through the curtain of gray smoke. Albert quivered. Luna could see the sadness and panic filling his eyes. "People are dying," he whimpered. "They're being slaughtered! I don't know what to do, Luna. Tell me what I'm supposed to do!" Tears rolled from under his glasses.

Luna could see the terror robbing him of his clarity. "You're supposed to stay alive."

"Yes, but I—,"

"Listen to me…Graves is insane. Crimm is dead. Carmen is kidnapped. That makes you pretty damn important to Karma City. Now take a deep breath," Luna urged. "I will get us out of this warzone."

Albert ran his fingers through his hair and straightened his tie. "Okay, okay. I'm ready. How are we getting out?"

"The highway. It's the only line away from the district. And right now, it's the only section not blocked by Sable Guard. Jameson's holding the area."

Luna shot down anyone who charged them. Her rifle ignited orange halos in the thick smoke. She kept Albert close to her, shoving aside cowering innocents and trampling over the dead to reach the highway. She almost lost her footing when the ground beneath her shook from a tremendous explosion. A curtain of thick smoke covered the sky. Shards of hot metal sparked through the air. The screams of anguish rang in her ears. She pressed on and a few paces ahead, came to a mangled Sable Guard van. Fire engulfed the vehicle and charred bodies lay in smoking heaps. There, crouched behind the blown-out van, Jameson held the fight, engaged in a shootout with two Sable Guardsmen

Two blasts erupted from his weapon; the shots hurled the guards backward. Jameson reloaded. Luna noticed two Malad-X fiends rushing to close in behind Jameson; their axes glistened with blood. "Behind you!" she yelled.

Jameson fired. The two attackers fell, but a loud gunshot rang out. One of the guardsmen had re-emerged and, before dying from his wounds, shot back at Jameson. Luna gasped when Jameson took a bullet in the side. A tuft of blood sprayed from his waist.

He collapsed to his knees.

A horde of two dozen Malad-X axmen came through the smoke and flames, climbing over the surrounding dead. Their hands and faces wore the splattered blood of the slain Malady infected. The Malad-X cutthroats surrounded Jameson with murder flashing in their primal, parasitic eyes.

Luna aimed her rifle and squeezed the trigger—*click*—out of bullets!

Jameson struggled on his hands and knees. A pool of blood formed under him, red and orange in the firelight. He peered through the mob and met Luna's eyes. He smiled at Luna.

She knew his smile, but this expression was unlike any she had seen before. Luna, in stunned disbelief watched Jameson return to his feet. He stood tall, shoulders back, head up. Blood oozing from his side.

Jameson closed his eyes and stretched his hands in front of him, as if ready to hold back a moving train. The attackers pounced.

"Enough!" he shouted. His voice sounded doubled and hollow, almost an overlapping echo. His eyes flared open and there shined a bestial, green light.

The enemies halted under Jameson's blazing stare.

Graves' Malad-X killers recoiled and scattered, fleeing from his terrible, commanding eyes. Jameson toppled to the ground once more.

Luna and Albert ran to Jameson.

Jameson took hold of Luna, his eyes no longer afire. "What happened?" he asked, his face knotted in suffering.

"We'll figure it out later," replied Luna.

Luna and Albert moved Jameson with his arms around their shoulders.

"I should really examine his wound," pleaded Albert.

Gunfire burst over their heads. Bullets whirred around them.

Luna glanced back at the crowd they had fought through. A force of Sable Guard ran toward them. "The highway is right there; once we're safe, we can check him."

"But we don't have a vehicle? How are we going to—?"

An Oasis Hospital parking shuttle squealed to a halt in front of them. The double doors swung open. The driver, a man with tousled brown hair and worn denim jacket, waved for them and hollered, "Hurry up! Get in!"

Albert and Luna carried Jameson aboard the shuttle. The driver levered the door closed and stepped on the accelerator. Bullets pinged into the fenders and chimed off the bumper. The small bus slipped away from the River Commons and sped down the highway.

Albert laid Jameson across the shuttle's rear bench and set to work dressing his wound.

"Is it as bad as it feels?" asked Jameson.

"The bullet ripped up your side pretty bad, Jameson, but it didn't do any critical damage. You've lost a lot of blood and you're going to feel very weak for a while."

Luna squeezed Jameson's hand. "Rest. I'm going to talk to the driver who saved our asses."

Luna moved to the front of the bus and dropped in the seat behind the driver.

"How's the injured guy doing?" asked the man.

"His name is Jameson and thanks to you, he's not going to die. Thank you for saving us. It's a relief to encounter some good people in Karma."

"There are some good people left. Just got to know where to look."

"My name is Luna Briggs. Who are you?"

The driver wiped the sweat from his brow. "Jack Halligan. And you're welcome. I figured you'd be going my way."

"And where is that?"

"To rescue Carmen Victoria." A look of annoyance washed over him. Jack turned to the empty passenger seat beside him.

"Shut up!" he shouted. "I'm going as fast as I can. If I drove like you, I'd end up like you."

Luna looked at the empty seat, then back at Jack. "Is there a problem?"

Jack sighed and wrung the steering wheel. "You wouldn't believe me if I told you."

Luna thought of the supernatural green light in Jameson's eyes. "Forget it. I don't want to know. What's your plan?"

"Graves took off in his limo a minute ahead of us. If I can get this bus to move a little faster, we might be able to catch up and run him off the highway." He pointed to the floor under the passenger seat. "Or we can shoot him off."

Luna looked under the seat. There, a pile of ammunition and several firearms rattled around. "Where did you get all this artillery?"

"Scavenged it from dead guards during the shootout back there."

She pulled a magazine from the pile and locked it into her rifle. "Well done, Jack."

Albert came to the front of the shuttle and regarded Jack. "Hey, hey...aren't you..."

"Jack Halligan. *Karma Daily*."

"Thought so. I'm Dr. Albert Walker. You know, I've been trying to reach you about my new medical center in Undertown and—"

"Not now!" snapped Luna.

"Right. Sorry. Thanks for picking us up, Mr. Halligan."

"Just call me Jack." He glanced at them through the shuttle's rear-view mirror. "You must be the people who survived the train bombing a while back."

Luna nodded.

Jack drummed the wheel with his palm. "I've been trying to find you to get your story. When I found out from Carmen that you've been working to foil Graves, the questions I had about your involvement in this Malad-X mystery were answered."

"How much do you know about Malad-X?" Luna asked.

"Carmen shared a little info with me but was going to tell me more after the event. She wanted me to cover the story. She said it's a stronger parasite and that people infected with Malad-X kill people infected with Malady. That sucks for me. What's worse is Graves has a huge tank of it on top of his tower."

Albert tensed. "The second brood."

"What are you talking about?" asked Jack.

"We destroyed a cultivation of Malad-X on Graves' ship. There, we learned there was another brood but its location wasn't specified."

Jack grinned. "You're the ones who blew up the boat!"

Albert pinched the lapels of his lab coat proudly. "Indeed."

"Well, speaking of Graves…" Jack pointed ahead, "There's his limo!" He stomped the accelerator.

Luna felt the shuttle jump forward. "Put the limo at our two o'clock," she ordered Jack.

Jack cut the course to the left, positioning the fleeing limousine ahead of him at a forty-five-degree angle to his right.

Luna cranked the shuttle doors open. "Hold this thing steady!" She switched on her rifle's laser sight and leaned out of the moving vehicle. The wind whipped her hair and watered her eyes. She focused on the laser, struggling to place the glowing red dot on the limousine's rear, driver-side tire. The shuttle bumped along the beaten highway. She took a steadying breath and allowed a small smirk when the laser found its mark. She pulled the trigger but the shuttle struck a pothole. The shot rang and ricocheted away. "Damn."

She fought the cold, lining up her next shot. Her fingers numbed but that's how she liked it. The weapon felt like part of her, capable of reacting as if by mere thought. The laser danced along the limousine's rim, across the wheel-well, then at last over the black tire. She fired. The rear tire exploded to strips of rubber. The limousine screeched and veered across the highway. Yellow sparks sprayed from under the steel wheel but it raced on.

Jack pulled Luna back into the shuttle. "Nice hit," he said, "but it looks like Graves has called in some of his pals."

A black van zoomed by the Oasis shuttle, positioning itself beside the speeding limousine. Luna wasn't convinced. The van's unsteady course, coupled with its positioning beside Graves's vehicle, raised her suspicion. *Why isn't it blocking us to defend Graves?*

Motion at the roof of the limousine caught Luna's eye. A Sable Guardsman stood from the skylight with a grenade launcher poised.

"We've got big problems now!" Jack exclaimed. "Anyone got any ideas?"

"Just one." Luna raised her rifle. "Cover your face!"

"What?"

Luna shot through the shuttle's windshield. A puff of blood spewed from the guard's throat. His body fell forward. The launcher tumbled from his grip and landed atop the roof.

The black van adjacent to the limousine opened its sliding door. Luna gasped when Gemni emerged and leapt from the moving van. With wiry arms and legs outstretched like a terrible spider, he soared through the air, red coat rippling behind him. He landed atop Graves' limousine, snatched up the launcher and fired.

The grenade struck the road in front of the shuttle.

"Shit!" Jack cut the wheel. Their vehicle spun out, vaulting forward and turning onto its side.

Chunks of pavement and curling flames engulfed them.

Jack, buckled into his seat, was struck hard by the erupting airbag. Luna gripped the overhead bar but the force of the crash knocked her around as the vehicle rolled. The wreckage spun around her slowly— dreamlike—glass glinting like rain, bullet casings chiming off the walls in flashes of gold, and the grinding of metal over concrete. She wondered if she'd die now and with a surreal clarity, waited for her body to be ripped to shreds.

A jarring slam halted the vertigo.

The entire world stopped. And she breathed.

A quiet darkness eclipsed. A mental reset.

Her senses struggled to realign. Something wet dripped on her collar. Gasoline. *Get it together, Briggs.* She couldn't get up.

She'd been thrown between Jack and the steering wheel. Jack lay unconscious, trapped in his seat. The deflated airbag had caught a lot of glass and the sharp bead felt like a hundred bees stinging her back and neck as she fought to get free. She forced her chin up to look out the blown windshield. Through an increasing cloud of smoke, two brown boots crunched over the shards of glass. Then, a hand reached for her.

"Hurry, Luna. Take my hand!"

*Jameson!*

Though her head ached and blood poured from her nose, she grabbed hold of him. He pulled her out of the wreckage and carried her to the edge of the highway. He sat her down and ran for the others. Wearily she called out, "How?"

He looked back with eyes like jade gems.

He did not answer.

Luna watched as Jameson, with effortless strength, rescued Jack and Albert. His boots pattered in the pooling gasoline, his bandaged side blackened with blood. Soon, Jameson had brought the group safely away from the smoking, toppled shuttle.

Their pursuit of Graves ended on an old, rundown overpass. Far below, the railway stretched north and south, parallel with the road. The Karma City skyline rose behind them, silhouetted by the falling sun. Luna watched as Jameson brought up his shaking hands and cupped them over his face.

*"Do you see now?"* asked Brighton. *"See what I can do, how I can help you?"*

"Yes."

*"Do not be afraid of me, Jameson. Let me take over so I can save you...save us."*

"I don't need you to take over."

*"Yes, you do. I smell Malady. I smell...him..."*

Gemni stood atop the ruined shuttle. Malevolence etched his bleach-white face. He grinned at Jameson. "I am impressed that you survived yet another explosion. What does this make for you? Three?"

"Sounds right," answered Jameson.

"I must know what makes you so special."

"You'll have to kill me to understand me, Gemni. But you don't look like you're in any condition to fight...am I right, Luna?"

Luna pulled her trigger.

A rifle round struck Gemni in the thigh, blowing his leg out from under him. He roared and fell to the concrete, blood pouring from his wound.

Gemni clawed his way close to Jameson, hatred and murder in his eyes, trailing a line of shining blood under his crippled leg. Jameson stood over the parasitic monster and kicked him in the face. Gemni's head snapped back with a demonic hiss.

Jameson spat on him. "You're nothing. Now you're gonna die."

"*Step away!*" Brighton warned.

Gemni slammed his cold fingers around Jameson's ankles and jerked him to the ground. Jameson's head slammed against the concrete with a thud. Gemni wrapped around him like a python, quickly finding Jameson's throat and squeezing off the air.

"No human can overpower me," he promised. Spit and blood pattered from his mouth and trickled down Jameson's face. "Now you will watch your friends suffer as I choke out your heart." His eyes crackled with orange fire and he shot a glance at Jack Halligan. "Hear me! Kill the Lessers!"

Jack tugged at his hair. He hunched over with his head in his hands and staggered on his feet like a drunken vagrant. Spit dripped from his mouth and his fingers curled like talons. He whirled around and struck down Albert, knocking the doctor unconscious. Luna moved in to subdue him, but Jack evaded, snatching her rifle and tossing it from the overpass. Luna was stunned by his strength and quickness. In the moment of distraction, Jack jumped her, locking his arms around her neck and biting into her collar.

Luna screamed for Jameson.

# Chapter 14

Jameson, still suffering with the gunshot wound, struggled to pry Gemni's terrible claws from his throat. At the corner of his vision, he could see Luna fighting with Jack near the edge of the highway overpass. Over him, Gemni cackled in pleasure. Jameson snarled and gasped; he kicked and writhed under Gemni but the Malady-elite beast proved supernaturally strong. Jameson knew in a few more seconds, he'd either black out or his neck would break under the fiend's murderous force. He had nothing left, no more fight, and no more strength. *This is my death.*

"*No!*" screamed Brighton from core of Jameson's mind.

The world darkened.

The sounds ended.

Only an echo of steady breathing surrounded Jameson. "Hello?" he called into the blackness.

A street lamp winked on. The half-awake dream unfolded and Brighton appeared, leaning on the lamp post in his long black trench coat. One of Karma City's nameless alleys took form around Jameson. He met Brighton in the lamplight.

"Hello Jameson. It's nice to see you again."

"Am I dead?"

"No. I've pulled you back. Gemni is killing your body right now. Your heart will stop in another minute or two. But here, in your mind, we are safe, at least for a little while."

"If I die, you die."

"Not right away. I'm still a parasite, after all. I'll consume your matter and sustain myself as long as I can. Maybe I'll find a way out of your dead body. Transference. But probably not." Brighton shoved off the post and stepped closer to Jameson. "Your wound, the burning in your lungs…you don't feel the pain now, do you?"

"No."

"That's because I shut it off." Brighton extended his hand. "Jameson, if you want to live, you must trust me. Let me take over."

Jameson concentrated on forcing Brighton from his mind but the effort proved useless. "Think about Luna. She's suffering right now." Brighton looked up at the lamplight and closed his eyes. Luna's screams suddenly filled the alley. *Jameson! Help!*

Jameson's eyes watered and his fists grew cold.

"Gemni will rip her to pieces, Jameson. By choosing your fate, you also choose hers. Let me out. Let me win this battle."

There was no point in resisting. The parasite was right. Jameson's anger flared and his fighting spirit erupted. He looked squarely into Brighton's inhuman eyes and nodded. "Go."

Brighton grinned and cracked his knuckles. "Gemni said that no *human* can overpower him." He chuckled and stepped out of the ring of light. His face darkened in the shadows of the alley. "It's my turn."

Luna drove an elbow into Jack's gut and flipped him over her shoulder, tossing him to the concrete. A swift boot to the face sent Jack winding in pain. She clutched the burning bite on her neck and slid to Albert who remained on his back. She shook him awake. The doctor adjusted his glasses and wiped a line of blood from his nose.

"What happened, Luna?"

"Gemni attacked Jameson and turned Jack on us."

Jack slowly crawled to his feet, face dripping with blood. Luna pulled her combat knife and readied it against him.

Albert shook his head. "I'll take care of Jack." He opened his medical bag and removed an ampoule and syringe. "A concentration of Quell will dial down his Malady and should break him from Gemni's control. Now go help Jameson!"

Fire puffed under the wrecked shuttle. The flames devoured the gasoline and swelled high into the air. Gemni's icy hands shifted across Jameson's throat, angling to snap his neck. "You proved weaker than I could have imagined," Gemni taunted. "A shameful conclusion."

Jameson's eyes became orbs of blazing emerald light and Brighton's hollow, guttural voice echoed from his mouth. "We've only just begun."

Brighton, now in full control of Jameson's body, clamped onto Gemni's forearms and snapped the bones, cranking the hands toward the shoulders. Gemni shrieked in torture.

Brighton hurled Gemni off him as if he were a small child, sending him tumbling over the puddles of gasoline and debris from the wreck. With blood bucketing from the hole in his back and his contorted arms dangling at his sides like broken tree boughs, Gemni hobbled to his feet, sniffing the hot air. His mouth frothed under his ghostly amber eyes. "I smell the parasite within you. You've awakened like me. Let us cease this combat."

Brighton did not reply. He advanced, closing in on Gemni who stood with wondrous fear in his eyes.

"What are you?" barked Gemni.

"It doesn't matter," spat Brighton. "It is what I will become that compels me."

Gemni backed away. "Such power...we can unite to supplant humanity."

"Not possible."

"Why?"

"Because *you* are Lesser!" Brighton knotted his hands around Gemni's throat and lifted him off his feet. He threw him through the air, sending him barreling into the wall of fire devouring the ruined shuttle. The lashing flames chewed the fabric of Gemni's coat, crawling up his back and scorching his white hair. He ran from the blaze and fell to the concrete—a rolling, screaming mass.

Luna stood beside Brighton and put her hand on his shoulder. "Jameson?"

In a fluid, sweeping motion, Brighton scooped Luna by the waist and spun her around, just as the fiery form of Gemni made a sudden lunge. Gemni landed hard where Luna had been standing and quickly propped to his knees. Flames rolled over his body. The skin of his face had melted away leaving only an animated skull with glowing sockets. Blackened ligaments smoked and lengths of burnt clothing trailed in ashy wisps. Gaseous gurgles escaped his charred throat.

Luna kept her scream in her throat and attacked, plunging the heavy blade of her combat knife deep into Gemni's skull. The corpse, crackling with fire, fell at her feet.

Albert joined them and looked down at the genetically engineered abomination of Graves Enterprises. "What should we do with the cadaver?" the doctor asked.

"Let it burn," snarled Brighton. His ferocious, green eyes closed briefly and when they reopened, Jameson's brown eyes found the woman he loved. He took Luna in his arms and held her tight. After a minute, she pulled away and checked his side. "Your wound?"

"Gone. The Malad-X healed me."

"You mean Brighton?"

"Yes."

"This is frightening, Jameson."

"I know."

Waking with the clarity of the Quell, Jack rolled to his hands and knees, then staggered to join the group. "Luna, I'm sorry...I..."

"It's fine."

"No, it isn't! I bit you! You're probably infected now."

Albert put up his hand. "No, no, she's not infected, Jack. When she was in my care at Oasis Hospital, I inoculated her with the Victory Vaccine. I had no medical record for her and since I couldn't find the typical scar made from the injection, I thought it a wise preventative measure. And Jameson woke up before I could consider him. Wouldn't have mattered anyway."

"You never told me that?" said Luna.

"We were kind of in a rush to get out of there."

Jack sighed. "I feel a lot better."

"Almost infecting me with Malady is one thing," scolded Luna. "Disarming me is another. You owe me an apology for throwing my rifle off the overpass."

Jack shrugged. "Would you have shot me?"

"Yes."

"Then I'm not apologizing."

The Iron Tribe radio on Luna's hip squawked, interrupting the banter. "This is Northbound 4-8-4 to Luna Briggs. Do you copy?"

Luna brought the radio to her lips. "Copy, 4-8-4. Go ahead."

"Approaching your location. All aboard."

The low whistle of the Iron Tribe's mighty locomotive filled Luna's heart with hope. "Looks like our journey continues..." She led the others to the edge of the highway. They looked over the guardrails at the railway below; the train wheeled toward them, its cars clanking over the tracks. A cloud of black engine smoke devoured the overpass.

"Get ready to jump!" Luna shouted.

Jack shook his head. "You people really *are* crazy!"

Luna and Jameson balanced atop the rails and readied for the jump. Luna smirked. "Welcome to the team."

Albert slapped Jack on the back. "Don't think about it and you'll be fine. Running with these two, I've cheated death...geez, let me compute..." he tapped his fingers, "Oasis riot, Undertown shootout, Eden shootout, vessel explosion, River Commons riot, shuttle wreck...six times!" He shoved past Jack and stood on the guard rail. "Leaping from a highway bridge to a speeding train is a cake walk."

"Hurry up, Jack!" urged Luna.

Jack kissed his airplane pin and joined the others.

Luna, Jameson, Jack and Albert leapt from the bridge. They fell into a train car, crashing through a canvas rooftop.

Luna groaned. "Is everyone all right?"

"Surprisingly still alive," Jack answered

"That really sucked," grumbled Jameson.

"Lucky seven," muttered Albert.

Luna and Jameson looked out the train car window at the Karma cityscape slowly falling from view. Luna could see lines of smoke snaking up in places throughout the city. "How bad do you think it is?" she asked.

Jameson sighed. "Gemni amassed a small army. Graves' Malad-X fiends were out-numbered and likely destroyed."

"So now it's the people with Malady killing the people without."

"As Gemni intended."

Luna wiped away a falling tear. "We've failed them, Jameson. Innocent people are dying because we didn't stop Gemni in time. Graves has Carmen and it won't be long before he releases Malad-X. How can we keep fighting? How can we win?"

"I don't know, Luna. But there's always a path made by something that's come before. Stay with me, stay ready, and we'll find it together."

Luna sighed. She turned to Jameson and took him by the shoulders. "There's something I need to say. It's about your father."

"Luna, it's all right. You did what you had to do."

She shook her head. "I shot him but I didn't—"

"I didn't anticipate him being so crazy, either. Let's just let it be over."

The melancholy song of the engine's pipes bounced off the approaching mountain range as if a ghost-train answered back from far away. The group rested in the parlor car as the train chugged over the northbound tracks. Luna had left to discuss their ordeal with the Iron Tribe. Albert sat in a leather chair reviewing his notes on Malad-X. Jameson slumped on a couch on the other side of the car. Jack sat in a chair beside him.

"Thanks for pulling me from the wreck back there," said Jack.

Jameson lifted his head. "Halligan, right?"

"Yeah. How are you feeling?" Jack pointed to Jameson's bandaged midsection.

"Nothing to worry about." Jameson closed his eyes and whispered, "Not now."

Jack recognized the anguish. He leaned toward Jameson. "You're sick, aren't you?"

"Has anyone ever told you that you smell really bad?"

"Excuse me?"

Jameson gave a short chuckle and sat up. "You're right, Jack. I'm infected. But my worm is worse."

"Oh, I don't know about that," argued Jack. "I see and hear some weird shit; bizarre hallucinations that I can't control."

"You're a lucky man, then."

"Why is that?"

Jameson leaned back and closed his eyes. "Because they're only hallucinations."

An hour passed and Jack's emotions tangled with his thoughts. *Wherever this train's heading, my first move will be a call to Donna. She's probably worried to a panic. I should have taken that shuttle to Greely Park and got her out of the city. Now a war has broken out in Karma and we're apart. Got to get home as soon as I can.*

Luna returned with a tray of food. "I passed through the kitchen car and the cook was whipping up one of my old favorites. Lobos style chili. It's really hot and parasite free. Eat up. We need to regain some strength." She passed the tray around.

"Much appreciated, Luna," said Jack. "How did your discussion with the Iron Tribe go? Are they going to help?"

"I told the engineer everything about Graves, Carmen, the defeat of Gemni and the outbreak in Karma. I asked if he'd be willing to bring the train to Karma Station to take civilians out of the city, away from the violence. Save some lives."

Jack thought more of Donna and the danger she may be in. His heart fluttered and his stomach flipped. He would feel such relief to know she was aboard the Iron Tribe's train and heading out of the city. "And did the tribe agree?"

Luna ate a spoonful of chili and shook her head regretfully.

"I don't get it. Where's the compassion?"

"There isn't any, Jack. The Iron Tribe cares only for the train, rails and its membership."

"Will they at least help us save Carmen and stop Graves?"

"The only way the tribe will fight against Graves is if the Tribal Code is violated. You need to understand, there are only four rules that the tribe lives and dies by. The code is represented by the four routes, North, South, East and West. The rules are, 'Northbound:

The Iron Tribe shall not kill the innocent. Southbound: No other cause shall come before the needs of the Tribe. Eastbound: Death, and nothing less, to those who harm the train, its railway or family. Westbound: The train must survive.'"

"All decisions align with these four rules?"

"That's right. They will not go to war against Graves because Graves has not dishonored their code."

"But Graves created Gemni and Gemni attacked the train. Isn't that a violation?"

"You just said it...*Gemni* attacked the train. Not Graves."

Albert put down his papers, now stained with sauce. "Luna, where is this train heading, anyway?"

"The Northbound 4-8-4 is scheduled to arrive in Rime in another..." she checked her pocket watch, "forty minutes."

"There are worse places, I suppose," Albert remarked.

Jack drummed on his knee. "Why does Rime sound important to me? I feel like I've spent time there; just can't remember."

Albert leaned forward in his chair. "I've always found Malady's ability to trap a person's memory fascinating. Moreover, the memories are sometimes sporadically released in some patients. Tell me, Jack. What do you recall about Rime?"

Jack dug the golden airplane pin from his pocket. He thumbed its edges and the memories revealed themselves in wavy flashes like coins glinting at the bottom of a wishing well. "The city of Rime is a salvaging and manufacturing empire nestled between the Rime Mountain pass. The city deals in scavenged materials. They use scrap metal brought in from parts beyond to produce valuable goods."

"Very good." Albert took up his papers and scribbled some notes. "What is that in your hand?"

"Oh," Jack handed Albert the tiny airplane. "It's a birthday gift. Helps me remember."

"Interesting." Albert noted it. "I've never seen a real airplane."

Jack heard Corpse-Dad enter the room. "Hi-yah, son! Sorry I'm late. Couldn't help but hear you talking about airplanes. Kind of my thing, you know."

"I know."

Albert shrugged. "Goes without saying, right? Probably none left intact with all the scavengers out there."

Corpse-Dad stood behind Albert. "There's one on the mountain, Jack. You locked it away after my accident."

Jack leapt from his chair; chili splattered over the train car's carpeted floor.

"What's wrong?" asked Albert.

Jack snatched his pin and clutched it to his heart. "My bush plane! It's on top of Rime Mountain, locked in the airfield hanger."

Jameson stood from the couch and paced the room. A half-curl smile formed on his face. "Let's get that airplane and strike down Graves Enterprises from above!"

The group sat in silence, each thrilled at the idea.

"There's just one problem," said Jack. "I don't remember how to fly."

As the sun fell over the western Void Lands, the tracks curved into a mountain pass. Steady columns of steam and smoke rising from towering incinerator stacks clouded the sky over the city of Rime. From his window, Jameson beheld the fortified industrial compound. The steel and stone walls cast bright white spotlights at the approaching train.

Jack and Albert had fallen asleep and Luna sat across the car cleaning a new rifle.

Brighton's voice sounded in Jameson's mind. *"I heard your plan."*

"I know you did," whispered Jameson.

*"I have a problem with it."*

"No shit. Figured you would."

*"Tell me,"* urged Brighton, *"who is Marcus Graves? When you and I first met, you said I looked like him."*

"He's the geneticist who created you."

*"You mean he created Malad-X."*

"That's technically what you are."

*"Yes, but I'm more than that now. I think I proved it by saving your life."*

180

"About that…I appreciate the help back there. Not only did you save my ass, but you saved my friends. Thank you."

*"I told you that I plan on keeping you alive. I meant it. Now, tell me more about Graves."*

"According to Albert, Graves made Malad-X by genetically altering the offspring of his own Malady. This offspring, since it developed within Graves, shares his genetic signature."

*"That explains why you say I look like him."*

"Right. And you've got his intelligence."

*"I've also acquired your human nature in the process of our neural bonding."*

"And it's the human side of things that makes you superior. Gemni, as Malady, was unable to achieve the level of evolution you have." Jameson chuckled to himself. "I'm starting to sound like the doc."

*"Jameson,"* Brighton's tone became troubled. *"Why do you want to destroy Graves' last brood of Malad-X?"*

"Graves is an infected psychopath who kidnapped my father when I was a kid and used him as a lab rat. What's worse, the asshole just killed a bunch of civilians and plans on killing countless more by unleashing his monster parasite!"

*"And killing our family is the answer?"*

"Our family?"

*"We're together in this, Jameson. That makes us family."*

"Let me make this clear, I have no family. Don't want one. Don't need one."

*"But you need her…"* Brighton forced Jameson's eyes to settle on Luna. *"She's important to you. You told her about me. You tell her everything. But for some reason, you have yet to confess your feelings to her."*

Luna's hair fell below her shoulders in reddish-brown waves as she cleaned her firearm. Though half her face wore branding scars, she kept a firm and natural beauty that he could not ignore. Was it the soft edges of her face or her liquid-green eyes? Was it the way her smile always seemed to be just for him? Yes. *She's a warrior, a strong woman with more sense and self-control than me. But she's a woman and I've never been closer to any other.* He watched her clean the rifle barrel. Such focus, such care in everything she did. Her hands moved confidently over the weapon and, briefly, he wondered what those hands would feel like. "Leave her out of this, Brighton."

*"Would you let her die?"*

"No!"

*"You've killed for her, but would you die for her? Because I'd die for my Malad-X family. Remember that."*

The locomotive slowed to a smooth stop at the Rime receiving station. The Iron Tribe moved through the cars commanding an orderly departure from the train. Jameson gathered his gear and followed the others out and onto the station platform. The cold air bit his nose and stung his eyes. He listened to Luna address the group.

"Listen up. It's easy to get in trouble in Rime. Many places are restricted to visitors who aren't Iron Tribe, so I think it's best to give you all an overview of the facility's layout. This is a massive factory complex comprised of a seven 'halls.' Think of the halls as departments, each one responsible for its own task. Just ahead is the Reception Hall, serving visitors with hostels and markets all close to the train station. The other halls are Munitions, where weapons are made; Mining and Refinery, where scrap and ore are processed; Manufacturing Works, where machines are repaired and goods are produced; Shipping and Receiving, self-explanatory; Residency, where citizens live; and lastly, Administration, where all operations are coordinated. Questions?"

No one spoke up.

"Good. Now let's head into Reception and secure dorms for the night. We'll regroup tomorrow and begin our mission to recover Jack's airplane." Luna turned to Jameson. "After Reception, I need you to hit the shops and get us whatever gear we may need for our hike up the mountain. Are you feeling up to that?"

"No problem, boss."

The group walked toward the Reception Hall. Jameson followed but Luna tugged his arm, pulling him away from the others. "We need to talk," she said.

"Luna, I'm fine."

"No, you're not. Brighton had you, Jameson. He had full control."

"We survived because of it."

"Yes, but how much control do you really have?"

"Look, I'm not happy with my condition. Need I remind you of how much I hate Malady? That includes Malad-X. You should have put a bullet in my brain when my father stuck me with that needle."

"Jameson, please. I'm just concerned that whatever is in your head may have intentions of its own...like Gemni."

Jameson caressed the side of her face, brushing a wisp of hair aside. He could see the compassion and worry raging in her gaze. He looked at her thoughtfully, noting the way she wrung her rifle strap to steady her nerves. She tightened her lips in concern and pushed her shoulders back to project her confidence rather than her fear. He hated that he made her feel this way. "I'm fine, Luna. I can handle this. I don't know what more to say."

Luna's eyes narrowed. "Then I guess it's not *you* I need to talk to."

She shoved past him to join the others.

After renting a room, Jameson wandered the markets surrounding the station area. Anticipating a hike of unknown duration through a deeply forested mountain trail, he looked for camping equipment, weapons, ammunition, tools and rugged outerwear. He asked around and was directed to a busy odds-and-ends shop. Inside, the clerk showed him a rack of insulated mechanic coveralls, leather gloves, work boots and an assortment of tools and gear. Jameson inspected the items.

"Is there anything specific you need, sir?"

"Information would be helpful. Tell me what the conditions are like on the mountain."

"Snow. Ice. Fallen pines, overgrown brush and shit for trails. The usual. Heading up to the summit?"

"No. To the airfield."

The man paused and cracked an odd smile. "You're joking, right?"

"Why?"

"Nobody's been up there in decades. It's haunted, I tell you; riddled with demons and ghouls!"

Jameson snickered. "I'll take everything you've got. I need it packed up and sent to my room at the Reception Hall, dorm eighty-two."

"If I may caution you again, sir, stay clear of the old airfield."

Jameson pulled his wallet and counted out a stack of bills. "What's the fastest route up there?"

The clerk took the money. "With all due respect, sir, I don't want to discuss the place. It's cursed and I've warned you."

Jameson snatched him by the shirt and jerked him over the counter. "Answer my question!" Then, he smelled the stench of Malady, but not from the clerk. The Malad-X rage ignited in his core.

"Let him go, Jameson."

Jameson released the clerk and turned to see Jack Halligan standing behind him, arms folded over his chest.

"Tell me," said Jack, "do you always bully shopkeepers?"

The scent of Jack's Malady pulled at Jameson. He struggled to control the anger rising inside through deliberate rationalization. *This isn't how you really feel. It's the Malad-X. Fight it! Push it back!*

"In my neighborhood," said Jack, "many of us are sick but we try to keep it together because we care about one another; we care about who we are. Do you understand?"

Jameson did not answer. He forced his hands into his pockets to keep from attacking Jack. He looked down and noticed that his right hand resisted. He could not control it. It tightened to a fist and remained at his side.

*"Arrogant fool!"* Brighton echoed within.

Jack put his hand on Jameson's shoulder. "Look, I've had Malady for a while and I've learned that before you can care about others, you have to care about yourself and what you may become. My point is, don't become your sickness."

Brighton knocked Jack's hand away with tremendous force. Jack staggered back and glared at Jameson, noticeably confused. Brighton spoke then, dropping Jameson's voice to a low whisper. "You don't become the sickness. It becomes you."

Jameson regained control and hurried past Jack, rushing for the door.

# Chapter 15

A cold and deep black night settled over Rime. The network of corridors in the factory complex fell dark and silent. Only the cold mountain air howled through the city's passages.

At the cusp of morning, Luna stood in the shadows of the hallway and waited, keeping her eyes on the door of dorm eighty-two. She heard footsteps approaching and snapped a magazine into her rifle. Jameson came into view, searching his pockets for his room key. Luna listened to him mumbling.

"You're screwing with my life." Jameson worked the key into the door and turned the handle. "What do I want? I want you out of my head!" He entered the dorm and let the door swing closed behind him.

Luna hurried and slipped her knife into the latch, stopping the door handle from locking. She waited and listened to Jameson.

"Don't use me anymore," he demanded. "Got it?"

She heard the click of his shotgun engaging.

"I swear, Brighton," he said, "I'll do away with both of us."

Her heart sank.

She knew what she had to do. It was the only way.

She heard him plop down on the bed. "I'm done discussing it," he said. "Don't fuck with me, worm."

She waited outside for close to an hour, giving Jameson plenty of time to fall into a deep sleep. Once she heard his long, slow breaths, she carefully parted the door and entered the dorm. With soundless steps, she moved to his bedside and pressed her rifle barrel under his chin. "Wake up."

His eyes opened, alarmed. "Luna? What are you doing?"

She jammed the muzzle into his collar. "Stay down, Jameson. Don't move."

"What's the problem?"

"That's what I'm here to find out. Now shut up. I don't want to talk to you. I want to talk to the worm."

"Luna, please."

"Jameson, shut up!" Her finger hovered over her trigger. She spoke sternly, "Brighton. I've come for you. Answer me."

Jameson stared at her in silence.

Luna's heart pounded. "Answer me, Brighton, or I'll kill you both."

Jameson's body fell limp. His eyes looked empty, almost dead.

"Last chance," she warned. "Talk to me!"

She touched the trigger, and in that instant, green light from in Jameson's pupils illuminated his face. Awareness returned, fierce and unfamiliar.

"Greetings, Luna Briggs," said Brighton.

Luna gasped at the hollow voice coming from her friend. Brighton took advantage of her apprehension and snatched the rifle barrel. With Malad-X strength, he tugged the weapon down, pulling Luna on top of him then rolled her over. He pressed the gun to her chest, pinning her to the bed and leaned closer. His nose nearly touched hers. She struggled under his weight but could not get the leverage to break free.

Brighton took hold of her throat in one hand and cast aside the weapon with the other. He squeezed, choking her to submission. "Was there something you wanted to say to me?"

Luna gagged, clawing at the hand on her throat.

"I'm listening, woman," Brighton taunted. "Go ahead and speak?"

"I'll kill you!" she wheezed.

"You have so much to learn. As do I." He leaned in and sniffed her hair. "You smell nice. Not like Malady at all." He touched his cheek to hers. "You're warm and soft. Tell me, woman, do you like this body?"

Luna thought of digging her fingers into his eyes but didn't want to injure Jameson. Her lungs burned for air and her head throbbed. She felt her strength fading away and her vision blurred. It wouldn't be long before he choked her out and she feared what he might do to her then.

Brighton caressed the scars on her face and thumbed her trembling lips. "My instinct urges me to kill you because your existence threatens mine. Jameson is a strong man. The only thing

187

that makes him vulnerable is you. His feelings for you make him weak."

She stole a breath. "You're wrong." She knotted her hands in his hair and pulled his mouth down on hers. With a final burst of strength, she forced a deep kiss, confident it would bring back Jameson. As her vision faded under Brighton's grip, she saw the light fade from Jameson's eyes. His hand pulled away from her throat and their lips parted. She heard Jameson's voice calling to her as she fluttered in and out of consciousness.

"Luna? No! Come back to me!"

She drew in a deep breath and coughed. He sat her up in the bed. "Did I hurt you?"

She rubbed her neck and nodded. "Yeah, a little."

He wrapped his arms around her and held her tightly. "I'm so very sorry."

Luna buried her face in his chest and closed her eyes.

"Luna," he started after a few long minutes. "It's important that you know how I feel about you…"

She hushed him and wiped away his tears. "We make each other strong. Don't say anything else."

Just after noon, Jack tried to ease his nerves atop his dorm room balcony. The train yard glinted with silver frost two levels below. Working with a square piece of paper, he slid his hand along the last fold, careful not to cause unwanted creases. He parted the small flaps to open the wings and inspected the pointy nose. Words came bubbling up from the depths of his memory, terms he hadn't thought of since his youth. *Trim, attitude, rudder, aileron. What do they mean?* Frustration swelled in his chest. He stopped his folding and looked down from the balcony; Luna, Jameson and Albert had entered the train yard and gathered at the platform. Jack watched as Jameson dropped a large duffle bag to the ground and unpacked it. He handed out dark gray coveralls to the others.

Jack took a calming breath and flicked the paper plane into the air. Swooping, whirling, gliding. He smiled but only for a moment. The wind blew up, catching the plane. It flipped over in flight, and then plummeted to the tracks. He winced as it crumpled to an unrecognizable heap between the rails. *I can't fly.*

Luna called up to Jack. "Hey, we're heading up the mountain in a few minutes. Our mission is pointless without you."

"I'll be right down."

Jack met the group and received his coveralls. He stepped into them and zipped up the front. The thick lining warmed him immediately. He spun his arms around. "These aren't bad, Jameson. Reminds me of the flight suit I had as a...boy." He smiled, happy that the memory returned so effortlessly.

Jameson knelt back down to inventory items in the bag. "I got extra clothing and camping gear, too. Let's get going."

Luna motioned for the group to follow. "The trail head opens at the north edge of town. This way. It should only take us a few hours to ascend the mountain to the abandoned airfield. Jack, if we find your airplane up there, how long will it take to get it in the air?"

Jack couldn't recall anything about starting an aircraft. "Uh...it's tough to say."

Snow fell in downy flakes. Albert walked with Jack along the rugged trail. "I must admit," said the doctor, "the thought of flying has provided me a truly wonderful distraction from the hardships we face."

"The only thing I'm flying now is paper airplanes."

Albert chuckled. "I don't think I've ever flown a paper airplane."

"There's a lot to it."

"Oh?"

"You've got to have sturdy, wide wings. And the take-off is all in the elbow, not the wrist. Most importantly, you've got to understand that your paper plane is actually a glider. It's not going to fly; it's going to fall."

"Maybe the wind will carry it away, like a kite cut loose.'"

"Wind provides 'lift,' which is the force component perpendicular of the oncoming air against the wings. But as soon as the air current diminishes, lift is compromised and the weight of your craft, with the force of drag, will take over. Without an alternate source of force or thrust to keep lift, like a propeller or engine, your plane is going to glide down, down and down until it hits the ground."

Albert stopped his trek. "You sound like a pilot to me, Jack."

"I…uh…guess I do." *Why is it coming back in pieces? I can't have pieces of knowledge in the cockpit!*

Albert smiled. "When all of this is over and people are safe, you should come to the Oasis Hospital and teach the children how to make paper airplanes. They'd love it!"

"Sounds like a good time to me." Jack noticed the sadness hiding behind Albert's glasses. "What's on your mind?"

"I'm getting tired, Jack. I've seen so much suffering. My hope is with Carmen Victoria. She had said that, through my work, she'd found the basis for an anti-parasitic immunization. We've just got to save her."

"A cure for Malady?"

"A true protection against it…yes."

"Then my Malady can't be cured?"

"I'm afraid not. But if we rolled out the vaccination to the uninfected, in time, human beings will no longer be the host species for the parasite. Our world can bounce back with wellness by true prevention."

"So that's where doctors and scientists have failed," added Jack. "They've been trying to kill Malady in people rather than prevent its infection."

"Correct. Many doctors believe that if you cure the symptoms, you cure the disease. But that's just not true when it comes to invasion by a micro-predator. We are cured if we are no longer inhabitable by the parasite. This has been my mantra all along. And the riddle as to 'how do we get there from here' was answered by Jameson's genotype. His blood contains human, Malady and Malad-X genes. And the Malad-X gene is also a combination of human and parasite since Graves used his own Malady offspring to derive it. Jameson's blood is the perfect DNA cocktail with which to formulate a vaccination."

"But how will it work?" Jack asked. "I mean, how is it different than the Victory Vaccine?"

"Jameson's Malady-born gene has allowed his blood to harbor three types of parasitic information. That's a lot of immunological data. The vaccine will use all of these antigens rather than the single-strain, single protein approach that is currently used in the Victory Vaccine. Should the Malady or Malad-X parasite invade a vaccinated person, the parasite's chemical signature will be detected by the human immune system as a foreign body and augmented anti-bodies will attack and sicken the parasite, killing it before it reaches the brain cavity."

"People with Malady will safely live among those without and there will be no worry of spreading the infection!"

"Precisely," said Albert. "And in time, those who receive this inoculation and conceive children will pass on all of this genetic information to their offspring, generating a new age of mankind that is genetically protected from any parasitic invasion."

"When we get back to Karma," Jack said, "I want to write your story."

"I was hoping you would."

The group hiked for several hours, stopping only to eat, rest and note their route. The sun rolled back toward the west, sending long shadows stretching from the trees. Snow clung to the hanging boughs and the silence of the woods inspired Jack. He imagined how he and Donna's lives would improve if the cure became a reality. He became more motivated to save Carmen and stop Graves. His steps quickened over the crunching snow. *Donna would love the snow. She'd love to be out here in the quiet, frozen wilderness*. Rime's cold, rocky forest boasted a beauty that Jack wished he could bottle up and bring back to her. *When times are good, I'll take her here for a weekend of hiking and love making by the fire. I'd like that. We'd like that.*

Luna stopped the group's pace at the edge of a ravine. Tall pines and evergreens swayed, sending tufts of icy dust into the air. The base of the ravine inhaled the clouds of ice. Jack squinted as the snow fell onto his face. He looked down and panned the length of the ravine. The gully stretched east and west, parting the forest line and scarring the mountain base. The south slope loomed upward to his right and as he studied the rocky ledges of the crag, he noticed a black line stretching over the trees. "Hey, what's that line running up the south face?"

Luna peered through her rifle scope. "It's a cable car system. There's one like it on the west slope that runs from old Borealis Village to the Rime Mines."

Jameson brought his hand to his brow to block the wind. "Maybe it still works. If we can get it running, we'll save a lot of time. This ravine should lead to the station house."

Lagging behind, Albert stumbled on the trail and his foot caught on an object lodged in the snow. He kicked the round, gray mass and gasped. "A skull." He stooped and examined the remains. "There are apparent indications of trauma here. This individual died from a severe head injury from behind."

"How about this one?" Luna pointed her rifle muzzle to another skull lodged on the side of the ravine.

Albert hurried for a closer look. "Same thing. I'm beginning to feel a bit uneasy."

Jameson looked up the mountain slope. High above, a precipice jutted outward, in line with the location of the remains. "I think these people fell from up there," he said. He stepped closer to the ravine ledge and peered over the side. At the bottom, strewn among the rocks, lay hundreds of bones and a half dozen rotting corpses. "Jumpers and sacrifices. Let's be very quiet going forward. Something doesn't *smell* right."

Jameson led the group to the cable car station with soundless steps, carefully parting low-hanging branches with his shotgun. The station house waited a few paces ahead, partially concealed by forest overgrowth and low hanging boughs. Snow covered the sagging roof and the splintered front door knocked against its crooked frame. Jameson nudged the door aside and entered.

The station house reeked of Malady. The floorboards, frozen and old, popped under their steps. Luna switched on her scope's light to dispel the shadows.

"This place is crawling with the parasite," warned Jameson.

In the middle of the room, the control switches for the cable engine waited, but a corpse of an old man bent over the panel. Albert inspected the body. He lifted the pant legs and commented on the purple the skin around the calves. "Hypostasis…settled blood in the interstitial tissue. This man's been dead for a while. And…" he examined the chest, "looks like a wound directly in the heart. The entry point is small and very precise."

"He was killed." Jameson spat on the floor. "Arrow."

Jameson paced the room, playing out the possibilities in his head. One more aspect needed inspection before he offered his theory surrounding the strangeness of the cable car station. He looked out the adjacent window at the station platform. The motorized pulley stood strong. The thick steel cables stretched from the massive wheel hub to the mountain's heights and a single car rested on buffers. Jameson kicked open the room's back door and exited onto the platform to inspect the cable car. The others followed. He wiped the snow off the glass panels and peered inside. *Clean.*

"The cable car is still in use," he said. "The dead man is the station master. Malady-heads murdered him to claim the cable system and ascend the mountain. They're up there and they're killing people for whatever reason their worms have convinced them is worth it."

Luna locked a loaded magazine into her rifle. "Think this is more of the infected turned by Gemni?"

Jameson shook his head. "Gemni didn't make it this far. This is something different. Feels like life in the Void Lands again— always finding crazy settlements existing under Malady-warped morals."

Albert looked up the mountain slope. "I'm fine with waiting here."

"No," barked Jameson. "We've got to look for Jack's plane. It may be our last chance at stopping Graves. Let's get the pulleys turning and go up the mountain."

"Once we get it running," added Albert, "whoever's up there is going to know we're coming."

"And they'll either hide or fight," said Jameson.

Under the last hues of daylight, Jameson worked at the control box. He switched on the breakers and engaged the master lever on the console. The engine rumbled to life. The cables tensed. The pulley wheels squealed and the car jerked forward, bouncing from the buffers. The group leapt into the moving car. Jameson slid the door closed once all were inside.

The car rocked as the cables lifted it into the air. As they ascended the mountain, the airfield came into view, roosting along a steep plateau. The surface of the plateau served as the runway and its icy edge formed a sharp cliff. A small terminal building and hanger nestled beside the mountain, half-buried in snow. At the far corner of the runway, a cylindrical flight tower reached upward like a column of bone jutting from a frozen grave.

Jack thought the forgotten airfield, silhouetted by the orange sunset, was depressing— another bleak reminder of humanity's defeat under the wrath of the Malady parasite. In the cable car window, he saw Corpse-Dad's ghastly reflection behind him.

"Would yah look at that!" cheered Corpse-Dad. "I used to love having hot cocoa with you in the terminal while the men fueled our plane. As soon as you heard the propeller spinning, you'd be out of your seat and tugging for me to hurry to the strip." He chuckled warmly and granules of sand puffed from his torn throat.

Jack remembered.

He could almost hear the buzz-saw rumble of the bush plane preparing for take-off. He remembered being little and happy. His floppy winter hat slid down his forehead; he hated to wear it, but Dad said to keep it on until the aircraft cabin warmed up. He remembered watching the way Dad instructed the airmen while the cold wind of Rime blew across the strip, sending breaths of snow spiraling through the blades of the propeller. Dad never shivered and young Jack imagined that it was because in a matter of minutes, Dad would take him over the clouds, to a heaven of warm sunlight and rose-gold cities of clouds.

Luna put a hand on Jack's shoulder, startling him from his reverie.

"You're crying, Jack," she said. "You okay?"

Jack looked for the apparition of his father; there were things he wanted to say to him. Corpse-Dad was gone. Jack wiped his eyes. "Remembering makes me sad, that's all."

"I know the feeling. My heart hurts in the mountains, too." Luna admitted.

"Why?"

Luna looked away.

"Hey, I'm sorry," said Jack. "You don't need to talk to me about anything."

"It's fine. My family lived in the foothills of Rime, in Borealis. I thought I lost them and I ran away. When I returned years later, the person I'd become ruined any chance I might have had to come home. Ruined it in an unforgivable way."

"What did you do?"

"I murdered my sister's husband, right in front of her, while she held her crying newborn."

Jack blinked, struggling with the imagery. "Did she know it was you?"

"No."

Jack exhaled in sympathy. "You should be the one crying."

"Some people cry and some just hurt. You know, I envy the people with Malady who can't remember anything."

"You don't want to trade places, believe me."

"How do you know I don't?"

"Because Malady takes your past and haunts you with it. You're better off having the ability to cope with your feelings. I can't. They've manifested in a disturbing way that I have no control over."

"I've heard you talk to yourself."

Jack leaned close and whispered. "I talk to the reanimated dead body of my father. He looks like he crawled from his casket and talks to me like I'm ten. Skin hangs from his face, bones jut from his hands. His hair looks like dried grass and his eyes are marbles that roll when he speaks. When he appears, he is as real as you. Now…do you still want to trade places?"

The two stared at one another then Jack burst into a laugh. Luna smiled and gave him a hug. "I like you, Jack. Tell your zombie father I said hello."

"I call him Corpse-Dad."

"Right."

The cable car stopped at a platform adjacent to the old terminal building. Deer hide canvases and green netting covered the terminal's windows. Rows of burning torches cast orange circles of warm light leading to the main entrance. Strange black banners flapped on wooden masts, each bearing a crude, yellow insignia of a coiled worm with wide, black eyes.

Jameson opened the car door and stepped onto the platform with shotgun in hand. His Malad-X senses detected the stench of Malady emanating from the terminal. Luna exited the car and stood beside Jameson, her finger hovering over her rifle's trigger. Jameson signaled for Jack and Albert to join them.

Albert wiped snowflakes from his glasses. "Those banners are unsettling."

"Some type of cult," said Jameson. He turned his attention to Jack. "Where's the hanger?"

"It's through the terminal and across the strip."

"Looks like we're going straight in then," said Jameson, pointing to the terminal's entrance. "Luna, keep your sights high and out. Archers are a big concern."

"*Enraged Malady infected are a greater concern,*" said Brighton.

Jameson ignored the voice in his head and led the group to the terminal. Brighton carried on.

"*Look,*" said Brighton regretfully, "*I'm sorry for my behavior with Luna.*"

Jameson took cover against the door frame. The others did the same. He leaned and listened for sounds from within. Only silence.

"*I acted on my parasitic instinct of self-preservation. It won't happen again, Jameson,*" Brighton vowed. "*I promise.*"

Jameson clenched his eyelids and whispered to Jack, who crouched low under the eve of a boarded window. "Hey. Got any Quell?"

Jack reached into the pocket of his coverall. He tossed a small vial to Jameson.

*"Don't, you fool! Don't make me sleep!"*

Jameson's hand shook as he opened the bottle and poured a pill into his palm. Slowly, he raised his hand to his mouth. Brighton fought with him, tugging his arm down. Jameson overpowered him, but it was like pulling up an invisible anchor. He swallowed the pill and closed his eyes as the Quell immediately coursed through him.

*"You're making...a mistake,"* warned Brighton, his voice falling back into a mental fog. *"You are...in...danger."*

The Quell wobbled Jameson's knees. A sudden weight of fatigue crushed him. He slumped back against the doorframe and nearly dropped his weapon.

Albert caught him and shook his shoulders. "Jameson," he whispered. "I told you that your condition makes you very susceptible to Quell. Why did you take that pill? It's going to be all you can do to stay awake now!"

"It's better than the alternative, doc." Jameson shook his head and straightened. "I'm fine. I can handle it."

Luna took Jameson's shotgun. "No, you can't."

Jameson's shoulders crumbled as sleep dragged him down. "My gun!" he slurred. His eyes closed as the Quell dropped him into a deep sleep.

Luna wrapped her arm around his waist and held him up. "Great...just great."

"What should we do with him?" Jack asked.

"We can't carry him around," Luna replied. "And it's too cold to leave him out here. The only option is the cable car. We'll secure the area and get the plane running, then come back for him." Luna labored Jameson over the snow and dropped him back into the car's bench. "Sorry to leave you like this," she said to him. "But at least you won't freeze to death." She shoved his shotgun into her pack, locked the car door, and returned to Jack and Albert.

"How would you like to proceed, Luna?" asked Albert.

Luna paused to consider what Jameson's approach would be. The years she spent with him in the wilds of the voids had taught her a great deal. Tactics of survival were always central to their decisions. He'd opt for silent cunning in this place, as she'd seen him execute countless times before. Luna had mastered his teachings and when stealth-minded, she became as soundless as a leopard, and as elusive as a fox.

"We go in unseen and unheard," she said. "From the cable car, the airfield looked empty which means there's more to this place than we can see. I'm going to slip inside and have a look. I'll signal you when it's clear. Stay out here and keep your ears open."

Luna moved with the grace of an alley cat and melted with the shadows. She eyed the interior lobby of the terminal with her night-vision scope and found the room empty. She flashed her laser and the others entered.

It became clear to Luna that skilled hunters and trappers had claimed the abandoned airfield. Rolls of fur and hide sat in neat stacks throughout the lobby. Carcasses of deer, rabbit and pheasant hung from the rafters, each meticulously skinned and stripped of meat. The entire room stunk of rotting animal scraps and soggy, old fire pits. Large cooking spits stood over crude hearths assembled in the corners of the lobby and several cots and bedrolls lay in groups throughout. Luna noticed iron bear traps, cages and harnesses of all sorts. Her rifle's light exposed racks of climbing gear, fishing tackle and fletching tools. *But where is everyone?* Her light fell to a square, wooden hatch in the floor. *They're underground.* "Jack," she whispered. "Does this place have a basement?"

"No. But the door to the strip is just ahead. The hanger is not far."

"Step lightly, friends." Luna moved across the room, making less sound than the wintry wind outside.

# Chapter 16

The pain in his wrists and ankles woke him. A collar around his neck held him to the wooden table. Jameson tugged at his arms and legs. *Shackled. I've been captured*! He shifted his eyes to examine his prison. The yellow light of a single kerosene lantern hanging from a hook in the corner illuminated the small room. Stone walls and a dirt floor, reinforced by iron beams and a cage door, formed his cell. *Where am I? A mine? A cellar?*

*"You're under the airfield,"* answered Brighton. *"The Malady infected trappers took us while the Quell kept us in dreamland."*

"What is this place?"

*"From what I've gathered while listening to their babble is that the trappers have built a network of tunnels and chambers under the airfield. The resource of the cable car, coupled with the isolation of the mountain airfield, provides them with a safe and commanding little roost."*

"What are they going to do with us?"

*"You are a source of sustenance, Jameson. You'll be harvested."* Brighton sighed, frustrated. *"You sure have done it this time, Jameson."*

Jameson pulled hard at his restraints. The binds only tightened. He sighed in frustration, his anger boiling. "What happened to Luna and the others?"

*"I didn't see."*

"You're lying!"

*"I'm not lying, Jameson. I haven't lied to you yet."*

"I don't trust you, Brighton."

*"Fine. But can we at least agree to survive?"*

Jameson tugged again. This time, the circulation to his hands was cut off. Pain surged up his arm.

*"You can't break the binds. But I can."*

"You're not taking over. After what you did to Luna—"

*"Let me redeem myself."*

Jameson snickered while wincing in pain. "How are you going to do that?"

*"As a parasite, my lifecycle brings me through stages of life until I am perfect. I have reached stage two. I am stronger. We can work together now. Neither of us in full control. That is, if you make the choice to let me connect."*

"What are you talking about?"

*"I am bonded to you neurologically. However, there are chambers of your brain that remain unresponsive to me. Only you can complete our synaptic convergence. We will both be in control. My power and strength will be yours whenever you need it."*

"I don't trust you!" yelled Jameson.

Footfalls echoed down the hall. Jameson heard deep voices, mad and determined in tone, fast approaching.

*"Your stubbornness is infuriating! Don't you understand?"* Brighton's voice darkened with urgency. *"You are my weakness. For me to be alive, you must be alive. Because of this, I cannot harm you. Join with me! Let's work together!"*

The captors appeared at the cage door. They wore soiled furs and long, greasy beards. Weeping sores cratered their smudged faces and long knives dangled from their belts. "Who are you talking to in there?" one shouted.

"The deal is a simple one," said Jameson to Brighton. "It's you *and* me…not you *or* me. Violate this once and I'll destroy you; even if that means destroying myself. Agreed?"

The trappers entered the room with blades gleaming in the lantern light.

*"Agreed!"*

"Let's get out of here, Brighton!"

Jameson closed his eyes and took a deep breath. He felt his consciousness being pulled to the mental plane inhabited by the organism within him. Brighton's image appeared. The parasitic being stood in his long, black coat enveloped by a strange, pulsing darkness. A luminous green mist trailing at his heels provided enough light for Jameson to make out the pale face that spoke to him.

*"Mutation, Jameson, is the trial and error of a species to not only exist in a threatening environment, but thrive. Mutation is*

*evolution.*" Brighton offered an outstretched hand. "*It is time for you to evolve!*"

Jameson took Brighton's hand.

He opened his eyes and they blazed.

Like the eyes of a cat, the surrounding shadows recoiled and the darkness lifted. In this powerful night vision, Jameson saw body heat in yellow blurs, and the varying scents and temperatures swirled in ribbons of green and blue light. Predatory eyes. Malad-X power supreme.

A hunter in thick furs raised his blade over Jameson.

Jameson tugged his restraints, ripping them like paper. The hunter swung his blade down, but Jameson snatched the man's wrist and bent it back, snapping the bones. He kicked the man away and jumped from the table, as five more hunters charged into the cell, ready to kill and devour him Jameson met them all with murderous strength. He drove his elbow squarely into one hunter's chest. The breast bone caved as though made of brittle wood. As the man gasped in the pains of death, Jameson hurled the body across the room, sending the man crashing over the others. But the passage was too tight for him to flee so soon. The attackers shoved their now dead brother aside and closed in. Jameson's fists became hammers, smashing faces, breaking jaws and shattering noses. The hunters fell back against the stone walls, and Jameson palmed their skulls against the stone, splitting their heads. With all of the dead before him, he lifted a machete from a corpse and ran down the dimly lit hall, cutting down the Malady infected hunters that crossed his path.

Brighton empowered Jameson beyond anything he could have ever imagined with graceful speed, incalculable might, and nocturnal vision that made his escape effortless and at the same time, horrifying to behold. Once a shotgun toting drifter, Jameson had become a lethal phantom weaving through the darkness with glowing green eyes and a blood-wet face.

Jameson's Malad-X vision revealed lines of cold air flowing from the airfield's frozen surface. He followed the draft and reached a central room dug deep under the terminal building. Across the room, a rusted metal staircase ascended two levels to meet the floorboards above. A wooden hatch overhead beckoned him. *The way out. Hang on, Luna. I'm coming.*

Half way into the large room, the colony of infected hunters stormed in and surrounded Jameson, cutting off his path to the staircase. His eyes flared with green light and his fingers curled. One of the hunters lifted a crossbow and fired. The arrow streaked like lightning for Jameson's heart, but he batted it away as if swatting a fly. The hunters barreled in with bows, spears, knives and machetes.

Jameson fought with battering-ram kicks and hammer-fall punches but his body ached and stiffened. "There's too many of them," said Jameson. "I can't keep this up for long!" He ducked under arrows and broke spears with his boots. His knuckles shattered jaws and his fingers tore at eyes.

"*The stairs,*" urged Brighton. "*Jump up to that hatch!*"

"Do what? That's almost twenty feet!"

"*Jump!*"

Jameson fixed his eyes on the lofty staircase and crouched low. His legs shoved off the ground with astounding force, sending him soaring over the mob. He reached out and snatched hold of the staircase rails and swung up to the scaffold under the hatch. He reached up and pushed the heavy panel. "Damn! It's barred closed on the other side."

"*You know what to do.*"

Jameson's fist ruptured the wood. Cold air blew in from the dark building above. He climbed out and emerged in a room of cages and heavy, wooden work benches. "That was unbelievable!" he exclaimed, marveling at his new power.

"*You fight well,*" said Brighton, "*but you must hurry. The hunters will climb up after you in a few seconds.*"

Jameson toppled a workbench and shoved it over the open hatch. "That'll slow them down." He quickly panned the room and found a window facing the airstrip. He peered through the frosted glass. His Malad-X eyes dispelled the night's darkness and he saw Luna, Jack and Albert dashing across the snowy runway toward a hanger near the side of the mountain.

Standing in front of the wide hanger door Jack felt the years of loneliness and sorrow as if he stood at the threshold of a family mausoleum. How could he have ever forgotten this place—this cold, olive-green door that he'd run to in excitement countless times? Malady's cruelty knew no limit. Jack's heart sank with anxiety. *What if the plane is gone? But what if it's not?*

Luna slapped him the arm. "Snap out of it, Jack, and tell us how we get this giant door open."

"There's an entrance on the left side. The hanger door is motorized and activated from the inside."

"Lead on."

Rust and ice crusted over the side door confirming that no one had entered the building in many years. Luna shot apart the hinges and handle, then kicked the door in. The group entered the dark hanger and Luna switched on her light. An enormous object filled the room, shrouded in a heavy canvas. "I think we've found it, Jack."

Jack approached the hulking form and pulled off the dusty canvas. The three gasped at the silver and red-striped airplane. Luna's light beamed off the curved nose. Jack reached up and touched the propeller blade, hoping that his memory would return.

Luna stood beside him. "It's beautiful."

Albert whistled in amazement. "The dimensions are geometrically lovely. And it is in magnificent condition. What type of airplane is this?"

Jack's answer was automatic. "This is a short take-off and landing aircraft with a single engine, propeller driven, high-wing design. She is roughly three thousand pounds with a top speed of about one hundred and sixty miles per hour. She's got a wingspan...oh, I'd say...just less than fifty feet. This is my bush plane, Albert. She can take-off and land in some of the harshest terrains." Jack ran his hand over the airplane door and still-frame memories fluttered in his mind, scattered in the confusion of his illness. "After my father died, I sold the airplanes to Rime. They were scrapped and repurposed. I couldn't part with this one, though. She was my favorite, she was mine. Then, I contracted Malady—not sure how—and I forgot things. To stay safe, I quit flying and put the plane in storage. I returned every year to maintain her but eventually, I forgot all about her. Malady stole away that entire chapter of my life."

Albert shook his head sympathetically. "When was the last time you were here, Jack?"

Jack opened the cockpit door and reached under the seat. He withdrew a maintenance log binder and opened it to the last page. "Three years ago. I don't even remember the trip."

"Well it's absolutely incredible that your memory has returned," said Albert.

"Don't start celebrating, Albert. I still can't remember how to fly."

Luna looked sternly at Jack. "You need to try harder. We're at the point where you must remember. Let's start this airplane, get Jameson, and fly out of here."

"Let me see if I can get the power on in the hanger first," said Jack. He flicked the switches of the main panel on the back wall. Sparks flew but delivered no energy. "There's a generator outside, behind the building. I'll try that."

As Jack moved over the snow to the back of the building, he paused. *Luna's right. I've got to try harder. Need to relax and think. Maybe a little Quell will help me remember.* He shook a pill into his palm, brought it up to his mouth, and then stopped. *But I hate the way it makes me feel. Can't risk feeling sick if I'm going to fly.* He clutched the pill in his fist and hurried to the generator switch.

Rust jammed the power lever. The electrical conduit feeding into the hanger had corroded, its core of wires dangerously exposed. Jack banged on the power lever to loosen it. After a few minutes of tugging and swearing, the lever snapped down and the generator rumbled on. Sparks crackled from the exposed wires as the high voltage electricity coursed into the hanger. Jack heard the hanger door rattling as it rolled open. He smiled. "I love that sound."

Jameson ran silently along the perimeter of the airfield, hurrying toward the hanger. His Malad-X vision illuminated the scent trail of his friends. He detected the thermal aura of body heat behind the hanger.

"*Someone's lurking in the back*," said Brighton.

Jameson sniffed, his heightened senses detecting Malady. "Smells like another infected hunter."

"*Your friends are about to be ambushed. Let's get him.*"

Jameson's eyes flashed as Brighton's power surged in him. He sprinted over the snow like a wolf charging for the kill. The scent of Malady enraged him. Brighton's engineered instinct to slay the Lesser parasite overcame Jameson and the thermal vision was all he could see.

A blurry human shape took form behind the hanger. Jameson attacked, digging his fingers into the man's throat. The choking sounded far away in Jameson's mind as Brighton took full control.

Jack couldn't peel Jameson off of him. The horrible green light in Jameson's eyes frightened Jack more than any Malady night terror. He coughed, wheezed and fought to suck in air. His vision darkened. In another minute, he'd be dead.

As Jack squeezed his fists to deliver one last punch, he felt the small pill in his palm. He remembered what Quell did to Jameson Shoals. In a final burst of strength, Jack shoved the pill into Jameson's mouth.

Brighton tasted the drug as soon as it touched his tongue. He backed away from Jack, spitting the tiny pill to the snow. Brighton's repulsion allowed Jameson's awareness to regain control. He saw Jack Halligan on his hands and knees, wheezing and coughing. *I've made a terrible mistake*, thought Jameson. *Brighton is taking over.* Jameson's vow against Brighton came echoing back to him, *violate this once and I'll destroy you, even if that means destroying myself.* He felt Brighton's anger rising within him again. The parasite had become very strong and his influence harder to resist. He decided that he could no longer allow for more risk to his friends. He decided to keep his vow.

The generator hummed and the electricity arced in white bursts across the open line. He reached for it.

"*Don't touch that, you fool!*" screamed Brighton.

"We had a deal, you son of a bitch. And I warned you!" Jameson grabbed the conduit.

The voltage streaked through his body and blew him back into the surrounding snow banks. The Malad-X power absorbed most of the shock and Jameson rolled out of the bank with a throbbing head and badly burned hand. Blood streamed from his nose and his bloodshot eyes met Jack's. "Forgive me."

"You weren't kidding…" replied Jack between coughs. "Your sickness is definitely worse than mine."

Luna and Albert found Jack and Jameson hunched over in the snow, blood dotted the area.

"Jameson," exclaimed Luna. "What's going on back here?"

Jameson pushed himself to his feet, and then pulled up Jack. He was about to explain how Brighton had forced an attack on Jack, when the cold wind carried the strong stench of Malady to his nose. He listened with supernatural acuity. From the flight tower at the edge of the runway, the enraged men of the mountain formed an advancing wall armed with rifles and crossbows. Jameson pointed to the small army. "We have to get out of here now!"

Luna took Jack by the shoulders and looked squarely into his eyes. "Are you ready to fly?"

"Let's find out."

Luna's rifle flashed in bursts of yellow. In the cold air, hot wisps of smoke curled from the deadly muzzle with every shot. Bodies fell, lining the frozen runway. The huntsmen returned the assault with screeching arrows and whining bullets that pinged from the runway. Hiding behind the hanger, she covered Jack, Jameson and Albert as they worked together, pushing the bush plane from the hanger and onto the strip. Once lined up for take-off, Jack opened the cabin doors and motioned for the others to climb into the back seats.

*Think, think, think. What's first?*

"Hurry, Jack," shouted Luna. With the plane's door still open, she exchanged fire with the horde. "I'm getting low on ammo!"

Confusion blurred Jack's vision as he eyed the multitude of gages and switches. *I can't remember! I can't do this!*

Jameson's shotgun boomed.

Albert closed his eyes and hugged his satchel in fear.

"Get us out of here!" yelled Jameson. "There's too many of them. They're almost at the plane!"

Beyond the windshield, Jack saw the waves of bloodthirsty, Malady infected wild-men. Over them, beyond the boundaries of the runway, the rising moon glowed alone in the black sky, setting a silver fire over the snow-covered field. He heard the men outside banging against the airplane and his friends shouting to him in desperation.

Jack buried his face in his palms. "I can't," he muttered. A hand patted his knee.

"Yes, you can, son." Corpse-Dad appeared in the co-pilot seat beside him, translucent in the silver moonlight. "We'll do it together. Listen to me and follow my hands. Okay?"

Jack wiped his eyes and nodded.

"First," Corpse-Dad reached low on the control panel, "master switch on."

Jack placed his hands in the apparition of his father's. He flipped the switch.

"Good," said Corpse-Dad. "Now prime the engine." His ghostly hand hovered over a black knob. "Quickly, son. There isn't much time."

Jack pumped the knob three times.

"Crack the throttle and switch on the fuel pump. Give it five seconds...mixture out...throttle back. Like me, son. Don't worry!"

Jack followed the motions and performed the actions mimed by his father.

"Twist the key to start the engine."

Jack turned the small key. The airplane shook as it awakened. The body vibrated as the props whirled. The crowd of attackers leapt back in fear.

Jack laughed; tears of relief streamed down his face.

"Switch off the fuel pump," Corpse-Dad shouted over the airplane engine. "Good...now we lower the flaps like so…excellent! You've got this, son! Ease in the power and start accelerating! Hurry! It's time to fly!"

The airplane lurched forward, rolling down the strip. Jack pushed it faster and faster until the flight controls took a life of their own in his grip. The edge of the runway met the front wheels. Jack pulled back the yoke and the airplane lifted into the starry night.

"Woo-hoo!" hollered Jack. "We did it, Dad!"

"No, son," Corpse-Dad's voice faded, "it was *you*!"

Jack looked to the seat beside him but his father was gone. The plane flew away from mountain, climbing higher and higher until, at last, they soared over the expanse of Karma City.

Luna leaned forward from the back seat and hugged Jack around his neck. "Well done, my friend."

"Thank you for believing in me."

"You're welcome," she said. "This is breathtaking."

Jack let his eyes trail to the city below. The streetlights looked like fireflies. *So many people down there and no one up here. Such peace, such perfect peace. I've missed this. I've needed this. And Donna…*he focused his vision over the central district of Karma City. He scanned the dark squares of the rooftops and traced the shadowed streets until he found his home, Greely Park. Horror washed over him when a horrific orange explosion lit the area where Donna's diner stood. "No!" he yelled. Without hesitation, Jack adjusted the flaps and pushed the yoke. The nose dipped, angling the bush plane into a sharp descent. The group clutched their seatbelts as Jack steered the plane down toward Greely Park District. "I'm coming, Donna!"

Luna wrung her seatbelt as the bush plane sliced between buildings. Like riding the racing train at night, unstoppable motion always felt faster in the dark. Karma City's many towers and tenements rushed by—colossal pillars of earthy brown, slate black and bone gray—as Jack's plane glided closer and closer to the grass of Greely Park. She watched Jack work the yoke with careful precision, his eyes calculating countless variables, confident and hawk-like. The cabin shuddered. She held her breath, now only feet from the ground. The wings trembled and as the wheels met the Earth, the craft bounced violently, the tail swinging left, then right as Jack fought with the uneven terrain. The plane halted with a sudden, chaotic grace and Luna let out a slow, calming exhale when Jack shut off the engine.

Residents of Jack's beloved Greely Park District ran by the airplane in panic, as Sable Guard soldiers unleashed streams of bullets across the park. Malady infected, still crazed by Gemni, swarmed over uninfected, beating them with blunt objects or slicing them apart with bladed weapons. Unarmed people fell dead in the street, blood painted the walls of the neighborhood buildings.

"This is a massacre!" Luna shouted over the gunfire. She watched the Sable Guards shoot up a crowd of defending citizens fighting in front of Greely Park Diner. The storm of bullets killed them all and blew in the glass.

Jack leapt from the airplane, running through the fray toward the diner.

Luna screamed for him to stop but the sounds of war proved too loud and she lost him in the crowd. "Jameson, we have to get him back!"

"I know. Quickly."

They jumped out of the airplane to the blood-stained grass. Jameson pulled a handgun off a dead man and tossed it to Albert. "Stay with the plane, doc. Protect yourself if you have to."

Albert nervously clutched the gun in both hands.

Luna and Jameson shot down Sable Guard and maddened infected, clearing a path across the park. They hurried over the bodies in the street, and into the smoky diner. Their boots crunched over shards of glass and broken dishes.

"Jack!" called Luna. "Jack, where are you?"

"I'm here!"

Luna's rifle light found Jack huddled behind the counter with Donna curled in his lap. Jack brushed Donna's red hair from her face and Luna saw the blood.

"Is she okay?" asked Luna.

"I—I don't know," stammered Jack, tears running down his face.

"Let's get her back to Albert. He can check her in the plane."

Jack carried Donna over the debris. Jameson kept firing at the wild-eyed attackers that ran toward them. They stepped out of the diner and onto the sidewalk. A convoy of Sable Guard vans rolled up the street. Soldiers hung from the windows with automatic weapons. Luna looked across the street, to the park and the waiting airplane. A horde of murderous Malady infected surrounded it, beating at the doors to get to Albert. Luna's bullets took down six, then her weapon fell silent. *Empty.*

"What do we do now?" shouted Jack. Donna whimpered in his arms.

Luna looked up at the roof of the diner considering higher ground, but with the convoy closing in and the airplane being attacked, she reasoned there wasn't time to reposition. She looked at Jameson. "Thoughts?"

"Yeah. Get out of the way."

Jameson pointed at the side street behind Luna. She turned to see a massive black semi-trailer thundering fast in their direction, knocking ruined cars aside. *Baby Boy!*

Luna, Jack and Jameson crouched low as the Iron Tribe's fighting vehicle rumbled into the street, cutting the path of the convoy. The top of the trailer opened and Baby Boy's formidable machine gun turret lifted high overhead. It swiveled on its pivoting base and opened fire on the enemy vans. Luna heard the screams of Graves' soldiers as the tribe shredded them apart.

As the devastating gun rained death over the Sable Guard, a force of Iron Tribe foot soldiers poured from the back of the trailer. They trampled the mob surrounding the airplane, killing them with heavy combat knives. Marksmen stood atop the semi's roof, gunning down the last of the frenzied infected. Soon, Greely Park was a field of the dead and dying. Some surviving innocents emerged from hiding and tended to the wounded. Smoke filled the air from fires feasting on war-ravaged buildings.

Jack returned to the airplane with Donna. Albert dressed her wounds in the backseat and Jack started the plane once more. Luna and Jameson met with Baby Boy's driver.

"We meet again," said Luna. "Thank you for your help."

"It is I who should express thanks. You challenged me, Briggs. You spoke to me with such truth and power, that soon after our encounter, I did see things differently," explained the driver. "Karma City, and all of the places beyond the rails, are worth fighting for. There's more purpose to my life off the tracks."

"You left the Tribe?"

"Yes. My men and I are not going back. We took Baby Boy with us."

"The Iron Tribe will kill you for your crime against them."

"Maybe. Maybe not. But Marcus Graves must be stopped. If he is not, it is only a matter of time before we are all dead...or worse."

"What now?" asked Luna.

The driver handed her the truck keys. "Now *you* go to war."


Luna loaded weapons and ammo from Baby Boy into the airplane.

Donna remained unconscious. With care, Albert tucked his lab coat behind her head.

Jack read the airplane's gauges, then craned his neck to speak to Albert. "How's Donna doing?" he asked.

"Concussion. A few scrapes and bruises. Looks like a broken arm, too. I administered some heavy pain killers so she's probably feeling pretty damn good. She'll be okay, Jack."

Jack leaned back in his pilot's seat and sighed with relief. "Thank you."

"My pleasure."

Luna handed Jack two heavy metal pipes capped at both ends. "These are Iron Tribe pipe bombs," she said. "They've got enough pop to destroy our target without causing too much damage to the building. This isn't going to be like blowing up the ship. We don't need a skyscraper collapsing on a bunch of innocent people."

"Let me guess," said Jack. "Fly over the tower and drop it?"

211

"Once we get out of there, yes. And you've only got two, so make it count."

"How are we going to know you're safe?"

Luna switched on her tribal radio. "I'm sending a pulse to your plane now. Dial it up."

Jack switched on the cockpit radio and adjusted the receiver. After a moment of fuzz and squeals, he heard Luna's signal coming through. "Got yah. Frequency set."

"Good. Jameson and I are going to smash through Sable District and, with the help of the tribesmen, infiltrate the tower. We'll fight our way up until we find and rescue Carmen. Hopefully, we'll put a bullet in Graves' head while we're there, too. I'll let you know when we're out and you blast the Malad-X containment. If all goes well, we'll make it back to Albert's lab in time for breakfast."

"I like the sound of that," said Jack. "Be safe, Luna."

Luna returned to the colossal big-rig. She climbed into the driver seat and watched the red and white bush plane bounce across the grass, lift into the air, and disappear in the night sky.

# Chapter 17

The semi sped over the streets of Karma City, shaking the concrete and leaving a cloud of black smoke behind it. While Luna drove the rig, Jameson sat in the passenger seat wringing his shotgun and eyeing the gates of Sable District drawing nearer.

"Are you ready?" asked Luna.

She was always so good at feeling his tension, sensing his worry. He appreciated that and somewhere in his heart he wondered if he ever told her so.

"I'm ready," answered Jameson. And he always was.

"What about Brighton?"

"He's been silent since…"

"Since you almost killed Jack?"

Jameson's nostrils flared in regret.

"I'm worried for you, Jameson. Will you promise me something?"

"Okay."

"Promise me that you'll never forget who you are. I made that mistake." She reached out her hand.

Jameson closed his fingers over hers. "I promise."

Luna drove the rig straight through the main gates of Sable District. The iron bars bent over the truck's enormous grill and chunks of brick and stonework blew into the street. Sable Guard cruisers responded to the intrusion, chasing them with sirens shrieking. The tribesmen opened the trailer roof and raised the machine gun turret, locking the sights on the pursuing cruisers.

Luna radioed to the tribesmen in the trailer. "Give them a warning."

The machine gun sprayed a line of bullets ahead of the cars, blowing apart the concrete in lightning-like blasts.

The Sable Guard swerved away, abandoning the pursuit.

Jameson looked behind them from the side mirrors and muttered a curse. "Hey, Luna, I think we're going need more than warning shots to stop *them*." An impenetrable crowd of Sable

District citizens ran for their truck. He focused his Malad-X eyes to close the distance and noticed weapons of all types in their hands. Their contorted, enraged faces foretold their infection, but it was not Malady. He felt a surge pass through him, like a wave of subtle electricity. "They're all Malad-X infected," he warned. "I can feel it."

"I can tell…your eyes are glowing green again."

"Son of a bitch!" Jameson rubbed at his eyes. "I've become some kind of monster."

"Remember your promise," said Luna.

Jameson took a steady breath. *Whatever I am now, I'm still me. I can do things I couldn't do before, things no one can do. I can make this work.* He felt the heat of the green light fade from his eyes.

Luna shifted the gears and pushed the big-rig faster until she came to Sable Tower. She stopped outside the main entrance and took up her rifle, but she paused when dozens of armed Sable Guard soldiers poured from the tower's main entrance and surrounded the truck. Luna slammed her hand on the steering wheel in frustration. The mob of Malad-X infected citizens drew nearer. The soldiers triggered their small arms. Bullets sparked and chimed off the armored vehicle.

The tribesmen radioed to Luna. "Permission to fire?"

"Fire," answered Luna.

The giant turret swiveled, setting its deadly sights on the guards in black armor. The tribesmen shot down Graves' guardsmen but the wave of maddened citizens proved too great. They charged up the street and enveloped the truck. A hailstorm of bullets flashed white and yellow from the turret; blood sprayed and bodies collapsed. Jameson knew there were too many attackers to defend against. All he could do was watch as Graves' infected people scaled the truck and claimed the machine gun. The tribesman manning the weapon was thrown to the ground and ripped apart, as if fed to a pit of beasts. The entire truck shook as the horde focused its wrath against it.

"Get us out of here, Luna!"

Luna fired up the engine and shifted into gear. The semi-trailer rolled forward, crunching over the dead. The infected mounted the truck, beating against the hood. Luna slammed on the breaks; the men and women tumbled to the ground.

"There are too many of them! Graves has infected the entire district!" shouted Luna. "We're trapped!"

Jameson's heightened senses picked up a low rumble that slowly intensified, the resonance emanating from every direction at once. The droning roar soon filled the sky over the truck. Jameson looked up through the skylight in the cabin roof to see the shadow of Jack's bush plane swooping low overhead. Something small fell from the plane and a second later, an earsplitting explosion occurred in the street, devastating the mob. The citizens ran in terror, fleeing the sight of the strange object flying over them. The bush plane made a second pass, this time lower, clearing people from the street with the wail of its propeller. Jameson watched the plane touch down in the street and bob straight for the truck. Seconds before a devastating, head-on collision, Jack swung the tail around, angling the nose for take-off. Jameson saw Albert waving, hailing them to hasten to the aircraft now only a short run from the truck.

Jameson and Luna gathered their weapons and sprinted for the plane.

"You know," said Jack, as he pushed the plane forward, "I thought you two trying to infiltrate Sable Tower was a dumb idea." He pulled back the yoke and the plane took flight. "The vat of Malad-X is on the rooftop. Let's just fly over and drop the last pipe bomb before Graves infects the rest of the city."

Jameson leaned forward in his seat. "That will stop Malad-X, but not Graves. As long as he is alive, Karma City will never be safe."

"He's right," added Albert. "And we still need to rescue Carmen."

"I understand, but getting into the tower is impossible," said Jack. "Dropping the bomb on the rooftop is the easy part. It's not like we can drop Jameson and Luna out of the plane, too."

*Maybe that's it*, thought Jameson. He turned to Luna. "Remember when you and I jumped from the train before it exploded?"

"You're not thinking about—"

"Yes, I am. We can jump down to the roof."

"Falling from a speeding train to a river is one thing, but jumping from an airplane flying over Karma City to a skyscraper rooftop is insane. We'll be killed."

"No, we won't. My Malad-X makes me strong, Luna. Very strong. I used the new power to escape the hunters at the airfield. I was unstoppable. Even the electrocution from the hanger generator didn't harm me."

"I don't see you sprouting wings from your infection, Jameson."

"Luna, I'm serious. I can do this...*we* can do this. I'm not asking you to trust what I've become or what I can do. I'm asking you to trust *me*."

Luna sighed. "I trust you."

Jack looked over his shoulder as he guided the airplane through the sky. "You're all joking, right? Because from where I'm sitting, the conversation sounds ridiculous."

"Take us over the rooftop," ordered Luna. "We're jumping down."

"That's suicide!"

Luna looked at Jameson, who gave her a confident grin. "We'll be fine," she said.

"I can't land this plane on the roof," warned Jack. "If you're injured from the fall, I have no way of recovering you."

The sky lightened with the coming morning to a soft purple twilight draping over the cityscape of Karma. Jameson opened the airplane door. "I understand." The wind blew in, forcing the others to hold tightly to their restraints. Albert clutched his satchel and closed his eyes in fear. Donna remained asleep from the doctor's medication. Jack held the plane steady and angled it for a pass over the roof.

Jameson focused his powerful vision. "I don't see anyone on the roof," he yelled. "There's a chance we'll go unnoticed." He took off his backpack and tossed it to Albert. "Doc, there's climbing rope in there. Tie it to something. Jack, once we drop down, fly out of view so Graves doesn't hear the plane. We'll get Carmen, kill Graves and radio when it's safe for you to fly back for us. Albert, you lower the rope and I'll grab it. Luna will hold on to me and Carmen and we'll get off the roof. When we're all safe on the plane, we'll drop the bomb onto the Malad-X. Does everyone understand?"

"You don't have to jump!" pleaded Albert. "We can think of another way!"

"There isn't time. You know that. Now, do you understand the plan?"

"Yes."

"Good. This our last shot so let's do it right." Jameson took Luna's hand and positioned her near the open doorway. He looked into her eyes. "It's going to be all right."

"I know."

"I'll jump first," said Jameson. "Once you see me on my feet, jump. I'll catch you."

The bush plane flew over the rooftop of Sable Tower. Jameson closed his eyes and called forth a surge of Malad-X energy from the deepest chambers of his mind. He felt his eyes tingling with light and his body pulsed with a strange heat that only he could feel. He opened the aft doors and jumped, dropping fast like a stone falling to the bottom of a well. The surface of the rooftop slammed under his boots with tremendous impact. Bits of concrete cracked beneath him as if his body were solid iron, unbreakable and unbending. *Awesome!* The airplane circled high above. He waved for Luna.

Luna's fingers were talons digging into the frame of the airplane. The wind teared her eyes. The open sky pulled at her, breathed her in, while the screaming propeller stole away her courage. The rooftop waited far below and there, like a tiny toy soldier, stood Jameson, ready to somehow keep her from shattering like a porcelain doll. *This is madness. I'm going to die. The wind will drag me past the building, down to the street.* She imagined her body fluttering helplessly, like a dried leaf or lonesome feather. Shoot-outs, train jumps, even explosions felt normal compared to hanging from a flying airplane, toes on the edge of nothing. But Jameson had lived. He was okay. Just as he vowed. Luna nodded then, readying herself. *I believe.* She believed that this moment, this leap to freefall was right. It had to be. She knew she'd live because Jameson said so.

Luna let go of the doorway.

She thought of her sister.

She thought of the tribe.

She thought of the children of Karma City that woke up each day to a greater risk than falling from a plane. She took a deep breath, inhaling the cold, and outstretched her arms, not like a bird, not like a diver, but like a child trusting that unfailing hands would catch her. She thought of how much she loved Jameson Shoals and every minute with him on this deadly, insane and unbelievable adventure.

She jumped.

When Jameson saw Luna falling, he leapt upward, snatching her from the air and dropping back to his feet with cat-like grace. He held her in his arms, cradling her for a quiet moment. Luna stared into his eyes, in awe of his power.

"We made it," exhaled Jameson.

"We always do."

Jameson and Luna listened to the bush plane's engine trailing away in the clouds and set to work, quietly inspecting the rooftop. The cloudy white Malad-X cistern glowed in the center of the roof. A small control booth, with a power substation and control panel, hummed near the cistern. The equipment fed and monitored Graves' precious, parasitic brood.

They walked to the eastern edge of the roof and gazed as far as they could see. The sunrise threw streaks of orange, pink and yellow light behind the silhouetted cityscape. From the height of Sable Tower, every corner of Karma City could be seen. The East River sparkled with Oasis Hospital rising behind it. Central Karma was a cluster of blighted buildings surrounding Greely Park.

There, thin columns of black smoke stained the colors of morning. Beyond the city limits, the ravaged and hostile Void Lands rolled outward in all directions. Jameson could see the cruel highway, Route 88, running far to the west and vanishing over the horizon. Luna stood beside him.

"Look at that sunrise, Jameson. Whatever the world has been reduced to, whatever people hold on to, it matters. Every new day is a chance for something better. It's why we go on."

"I've seen a lot of sunrises."

Luna smiled. "But this is a good one." She took Jameson's hand. "I need to tell you something. This might be the last chance I get to give you something better."

"What is it?"

"Your father is alive."

Jameson's stomach knotted from her words. "How is that possible? You shot him...the vessel exploded."

"I shot him off you, hitting him the shoulder, and carried you both from the ship. You were so delirious from the Malad-X that you had no idea what was going on. Albert treated you both in his lab that night but your father slipped off while everyone slept. He was probably afraid. He probably thought he was about to be tested on again. I don't know. But we saved him and he's alive. He's out there, Jameson. I didn't tell you sooner because we've been going through so much and you've been suffering. I'm sorry."

"Thank you, Luna." A renewed hope ignited in his heart and he knew it wasn't because his father still lived. It was because of her. He held her face in his hands and looked deeply into her aqua-green eyes. "Luna Briggs...I love you."

Tears rolled down Luna's face. "I love you, too."

On the edge of the rooftop, with the Karma City sunrise burning before them, Luna and Jameson kissed long and hard. The small tears on Luna's lips tasted sweet and perfect. Jameson never wanted the kiss to end but in the far corner of his mind, he worried about holding her too tight. She banished the fear with her own crushing embrace. Her strength was incredible. Her hold on him, unbreakable. As his lips melted with hers, Jameson knew that Luna was right…whatever people held on to, it mattered. Nothing mattered more to him than her.

The clopping of hurried footsteps sent Jameson and Luna hiding behind a large air conditioning unit standing on the south facing edge of the roof. They listened and heard Dr. Marcus Graves speaking to Dr. Carmen Victoria.

"This is the real cure," said Graves. He ushered Carmen to the center of the rooftop where the vat of Malad-X loomed, effervescing with milky white bubbles. Graves gripped her hard above the elbow, keeping her close to his side; with her hands tied behind her back, there was little she could do to defend herself. "Malady proved stronger than mankind. And as you've seen, Malad-X is stronger than Malady. Malad-X is superior to all!"

Jameson clutched his head in both hands when Brighton's presence sharply returned in his mind. "*He's right*," said Brighton. "*Malad-X is superior.*"

Luna took Jameson's hands in hers. "Fight it," she whispered. "Remember who you are."

"*I really hate that burn-faced bitch*," snarled Brighton. "*I'd like to throw her off the roof.*"

"Stay focused, Brighton," said Jameson. "You've got bigger problems."

"*Oh?*"

"Don't you smell that?" Jameson sniffed.

"*I do smell it! Malady! Who is it?*"

"Dr. Graves. And he is in control of the last vat of Malad-X. Doesn't it just piss you off that a Malady-head is controlling your family?"

"*Yesssss!*" hissed Brighton. "*I won't stand for it! Kill him!*"

"I plan on it, but you can't get in my way. Leave this fight to Luna and I."

"*But you want to destroy the Malad-X. I won't let you!*"

"Relax, worm. We can figure out what to do with the Malad-X after Graves goes down. Deal?"

"*Swear to me that you will not harm my family.*"

"I won't. I swear it."

"*Very well. Kill the enemy swiftly.*" Brighton went quiet and released his mental grip on Jameson.

Jameson sighed in relief.

"Nice work," said Luna. "Ready to save the world?"

"Let's finish this. Cut behind them, to the left, and make for Carmen. I'll get Graves head on."

Luna slipped away, dashing silently to the west edge of the roof. Jameson watched Graves.

"I'm going to infect you, Carmen," said Graves. The white light from the Malad-X tank washed the shadows from Graves' face, smoothing his skin like a plastic mannequin. His marble eyes were wild with genius, crazed with scientific passion, hollow from designing murder, and lit by lust. "I'm going to study the effects that Malad-X has on a genius as beautiful as you. Will you go mad and seek to kill me? Or will the parasite awaken in you to serve me?" He caressed her frightened, tear-soaked face. Carmen tugged at the binds on her wrists. "Wolfgang was a lucky man. How I've longed for you to join me in my tower. To dine with me, to dance, to lay with me and—"

Carmen spat at him. "You're a fraction of the man that Wolfgang was and even less of a scientist. You're a disgusting monster!"

Graves wiped the spit from his face and smiled. "There is a sting to your words, Carmen. And it only thrills me. Imagine the ecstasy that minds like ours will know when evolved by my parasite. Imagine what you'll feel...what *we* will feel." He lowered his mouth over hers. She pulled away and kicked him under the ribs. Graves buckled from the blow and shoved her down. He pulled a long syringe from his black coat and leaned over her.

Jameson stepped out from hiding. "Leave her alone!"

Graves whirled around. "There's nothing worse than unexpected company. You must be Jameson. Tell me, where is your train-loving girlfriend?"

Luna's rifle fired into the air. "Right behind you, asshole."

Graves laughed. "You've come to kill me?"

"It's about time someone did." Jameson aimed his shotgun and slowly approached Graves. "Release Dr. Victoria. Now!"

"I don't think so." Graves pulled a black pistol from his side. Jameson paused. "Call off your partner and drop your weapon or I'll shoot Carmen."

"Do that, and we blow up your Malad-X. You'll have nothing left at all. No girl, no worms. Wouldn't that just suck?"

"Another step and I'll kill her!"

Carmen screamed in terror.

Jameson, only a few feet from Graves, lowered his gun.

"Drop it!" shouted Graves. "And call off your partner."

"Luna," said Jameson. "Do what he says." He dropped his shotgun in front of Graves.

Graves grinned. "Very good." He kept his firearm aimed at Carmen and the needle pointed at Jameson. Luna appeared with her rifle down. She slid it to Graves, who kicked both guns out of reach. "I do believe," said Graves, "that I've got enough parasites in this syringe for the three of you. It will be interesting to see what Malad-X turns you into, Jameson."

"I can show you right now!" Jameson's eyes became electrically charged emeralds. With blinding speed, he snatched Graves' wrist and lifted him off his feet. Graves' pistol flashed and boomed. The shot struck Carmen in the chest. She cried out, falling to her hands and knees, blood slowly raining to puddles beneath her.

Luna ran to her side and applied pressure to the wound. "Hang in there, Carmen. This will be over soon."

"His eyes…" gasped Carmen. "I saw his eyes!"

"Don't be afraid. We're going to get you out of here."

"Too much blood." Carmen's eyelids fluttered. "I don't have long." She gripped Luna's shoulder tightly. "Listen to me…. tell Albert he was right. Jameson's genetic chemistry is the answer. Albert can cure the people." She closed her eyes and wilted silently in Luna's arms.

Luna stared into the eyes of the dead woman in her arms. They looked like polished jewels reflecting back the light of the world but offering no light of their own. Carmen's death, was the death of an era and it stirred Luna's heart to sorrow. *I came so far,*

*Carmen, fought so hard; I believed in better days. But here I am, at the top of the world, and way up here where there should be peace, there's only suffering.* She held the body tightly, the way her sister probably held her dead husband, and Luna felt all of the sadness in the world crash over her. The wave of despair wanted to wash her away, it came to claim her, to devour her hopes and plans for a bright tomorrow. Her plans. *The plan. The fight isn't over. Jameson is fighting Graves right now.* He'd win, she knew he would, and in that knowing proved a hope that even the greatest wave of soul-crushing heartache could never steal away. *Keep moving, Briggs.* The details of their attack plan resurfaced, once more claiming the forefront of her mind. The final explosion would be next. She lifted Carmen and carried her away from the Malad-X cistern, taking cover inside the roof access bulkhead. There, in the enclosed stairwell, she'd be safe from the destruction of Dr. Marcus Graves' genetically altered parasite. Luna hunkered down, listening and waiting for the end.

Graves brought up his gun, but Jameson tore it from his hand, throwing it across the roof. The weapon slid over the edge. Graves thrust the needle toward Jameson's neck, but Jameson swung a tremendous punch that sent the scientist into the air.

Graves fell to his back, then rolled over spitting up teeth. He wiped his bloodstained mouth and lifted his head. He stared at Jameson, astonishment bulging his eyes. "What are you?"

"Shut up!" Jameson kicked Graves in the face, spraying blood over his boot "That was for my father." He kicked him in the stomach, cracking ribs. "And that's for the rest of the city." Graves, bellowing in pain and wheezing for air, clawed his way to the edge of the roof. Jameson followed the slithering scientist. "Too many innocents have suffered," barked Jameson. "Too many have died because of you. No more!"

Graves choked a laughed as he propped himself to his knees. "People suffer and die anyway. The city kills them or they kill themselves. You can't change the world, Jameson. Only science can do that!" Graves sprang forward and stabbed the needle into Jameson's thigh. Jameson cried out and lunged to grab the scientist, but Graves rolled to the side and kicked Jameson off the roof.

Jameson caught hold of the ledge, gripping it tightly with his Malad-X power, but numbness crawled up from the stab in his leg, coursing around his waist and tingling into his arms. The injection felt like Quell, and he couldn't guess how much longer his strength would last.

Graves appeared over him, holding Jameson's shotgun in his hands. Dark blood dripped from his shattered mouth. His greasy hair spiked from his head like the tangled feathers of dead crow. He knelt down, pressing the short barrel to Jameson's forehead, his finger lowering near the trigger.

The deafening whirr of the bush plane's propeller became thunder in the sky.

Graves' eyes widened in confusion.

Jameson seized the moment of distraction, yanking the shotgun and pulling Graves over the edge of the roof. The collar of Graves' black coat snagged on the roof's eave. He screamed, hanging helpless and frightened. The shotgun fell from view.

An earsplitting explosion shook the tower.

Volcanic, orange fire burst in all directions.

Shards of glass, chunks of concrete, and a hot spray of white Malad-X rained down as a plume of heavy, gray smoke swirled across the morning sky.

"What have you done?" screeched Graves as he dangled like a marionette.

"It's over. I told you...no more worms. Malad-X is gone."

"Is it?" Graves reached into his pocket and revealed a small, white vial.

Jameson noticed something black and metallic glinting on the eave near his right hand. *Graves' pistol.* He reached for it, fighting the numbness draining his strength and hooked the gun with his fingertips. He twirled it around in his hand, aiming it at Graves.

A terrible, crushing pain made Jameson scream. He looked up at his hand holding the roof. There, an apparition of Brighton loomed. The parasite in his mind ground his black boot atop Jameson's fingers. Hate and rage became a veil of betrayal.

*"You swore that you would not harm my family!"* yelled Brighton.

"And I didn't." Jameson snickered through his pain. "I wasn't the one who dropped the bomb, you stupid son of a bitch! How does it feel to lose control?"

*"I cannot let you kill Graves. He holds the last of the Malad-X. I warned you that I'd die for my family."*

"Then say goodbye!" Jameson focused the gun on Graves and pulled the trigger. The blast ripped through the scientist, knocking him off the building.

Jameson watched Dr. Marcus Graves fall to the city street one hundred and eight stories below.

Brighton wailed. The howling bush plane muffled his mournful screams. Jameson fought the searing pain in his hand as Brighton continued to crush his fingers.

"Let the rope out!" yelled Jack.

"It's impossible! He's going to fall! He's going to fall!" cried Albert in hysteria, his face mashed against the window.

"If you don't let out the rope, he has no chance! Do it! Now!"

Albert shoved open the aft door. The force of the wind knocked him back. He steadied and threw the coil of climbing rope into the sky. It unfurled, one end fluttering under the plane, the other tied off to one of the seats.

Jameson's fingers slipped. He'd fall any second. Jack's approaching plane swallowed the heavens in a mechanical roar. He looked over his shoulder to see the silver aircraft streaking toward him and from it dangled the rope, the last risk he had to take, the final chance.

*"You ruined everything!"* cried Brighton. *"There's nothing left to live for!"*

"I disagree."

*"You can't hold on much longer!"*

"I don't need to."

Jameson let go, shoving off the building with his legs and arcing back twenty feet. He knotted his arm around the airplane's rope. The plane lifted him upward and swooped low over the roof. Jameson saw Luna and reached for her outstretched hand; their arms locked.

Luna and Jameson hung from the bush plane as it flew high above Karma City.

# Chapter 18

*One week later:*

Dr. Albert Walker and the hospital staff organized a memorial service where thousands gathered in Wolfgang Commons outside of Oasis Hospital to honor the passing of Dr. Carmen Victoria. In addition, Albert was honored for his scientific advancements and formally credited for the treatment against Malady by Victoria's ASAM Team. His vaccine, derived from Jameson's unique genome, acted as an antigenic, dual-strain primer, enabling the human immune system to build defenses against Malady and Malad-X.

The new medicine ignited a wave of inspiration and drew people to Oasis from all parts of the city and the Void Lands. The Iron Tribe's locomotive rolled in and out of Karma Station every day, loading and unloading passengers by the hundreds, all of them eager to finally be protected from the mind-altering parasite and learn whether they, too, were Malady-Born. While vaccines were administered, blood tests were also conducted on individuals born from infected parents. In nearly all cases, Albert's theory of Malady-Born humans proved true. These people showed a natural resistance to common Malady.

Albert stood in the office that once belonged to Dr. Carmen Victoria. The wide windows let in the sun and overlooked the green campus grounds, lined with gardens, ponds, and willow trees. The office was his now. The desk. The conference table. The books. All of it. He was in charge. He'd become Karma City's final medical authority and lead scientist, yet he hardly felt the weight of it. He moved around the office with light steps, as if afraid to snag a trip wire that might suddenly drop the load of responsibility on him. He sat at the desk, bouncing for a second in the plush chair. *I got this. It's much cleaner than Undertown. I'll still run my lab there, though. Not gonna let this change me. There's still more work to be done.* A knock on his office door broke his thoughts. Jack Halligan and Donna Lynne stood together wearing warm coats and warmer smiles.

Jack stuck his head in the room and whistled. "Nice digs, Al!"

"Hey you two!" Albert chuckled, happy to see his friends looking so well.

"You wanted to see me?" asked Jack.

"Sure did. Thanks for coming by."

"No problem. How're you settling in?"

"I've been so busy that I haven't really had a chance to get comfortable." Albert stood from his desk and crossed the room to meet them at the door. "Donna, how are you feeling? How's the arm?"

"Just fine, Albert. Thanks to you and Jack."

Albert grinned. "We do make a good team, don't we Jack?"

Jack raised an eyebrow. "Alright...what is it?"

"Right, I won't keep you; I know you've got plans."

Donna squeezed Jack. "I'm really excited to fly today. It's going to be so beautiful up there."

Albert adjusted his glasses. "You won't get me back in that thing," he joked. "But in all seriousness, Jack, I'd like to put that airplane of yours to good use."

"What do you have in mind?"

"I want to send shipments of Quell and vaccinations out to the Void Lands. There's a lot of sick people out there. The railways have been doing a good job at getting meds out, but we can go farther. Help more."

Jack nodded. "I like it. Let's talk more about it tonight, okay?"

"Okay."

Donna gave Albert a kiss on the cheek. "You're a good man. Never change."

"Don't plan on it."


The cold autumn air blew through the trees in the Commons, sweeping up orange and brown leaves in swirling ribbons. Jack held Donna close to keep her warm as they walked to the bush plane resting in the middle of the grassy field. Tucked under his arm was a notebook, already filled with notes about the demise of

Graves Enterprises and the rise of the new Oasis Wellness Center overseen by Dr. Albert Walker. Families grouped around the plane, marveling at its incomparable beauty. The children regarded Jack with excitement and praise.

"I want to fly like you someday, Mr. Halligan," said a young girl. Her sparkling eyes shined a hero's light on Jack.

"You're going to need an airplane," replied Jack. He tore a blank page from his journal and knelt beside the child. "Watch carefully." Jack folded a small paper plane and handed it to the girl. "Now, toss it straight and gentle."

The little girl flung the plane and a light breeze scooped it high into the air. She laughed and ran to catch it as it whirled and soared.

Donna pulled Jack in for a kiss. "I'm very proud of you, Hun."

"And so am I," said a man near the bush plane.

The hallucination of his dead father stood near the cockpit door. Jack looked closer at the vision. No longer did a grotesque corpse stand in grave-tattered rags. There, in a crisp blue flight suit, combed brown hair and light morning stubble covering his cheeks, stood Mark Halligan, just as he looked when Jack was a boy.

"What is it, Jack?" asked Donna. "Is it your dad again?"

"Yeah, but this time, I wish you could see him, Donna. It's him. The way I remember him...the way I need him."

"I can see him, Hun...in you."

Jack blinked away the tears of happiness and walked Donna to the airplane. "Ready to fly?"

"As long as you remember how," she teased.

Jack smiled at his father. "I don't think I'll ever forget again."

In her guest room at Oasis, Luna Briggs looped the old half-moon pendant around her neck and stuffed her combat vest into her bag. She tied the bag closed and slung it over her shoulder. Jameson waited in the doorway.

"Are you sure you don't need company?" he asked.

"It's better if I do this alone. I think it needs to be that way. Besides, Albert says you need to rest."

"I'm certainly fine with relaxing a while. How long are you going to be?"

"A week or so." She looked down.

Jameson knew she was scared. He lifted her chin with the knuckle of his thumb. "It'll be fine. Your sister is going to be real happy to see you again."

"Thanks. Are you going to be all right?"

"Doc's got me on some tweaked version of Quell. Haven't heard the worm since the tower. It's been nice."

"Good." Luna kissed him. "Time to catch the train. I'll see you soon."

Luna started down the hall. Jameson called to her. "No rifle?"

"Not this trip."

When she was gone, Jameson looked back into Luna's room. Her sketch book rested on her bed. A small folded paper sat beside it. Unfolding it revealed a note.

*Jameson,*

*There's a lot of room left in my journal. The empty pages are reserved for the memories we'll make together. I left a new drawing for you. Hope you like it. It's my favorite. Stay well and strong while I'm away. I love you.*

*Luna*

A loose paper waited under the front cover. Jameson felt his heart swell to see the sketch of a man and woman standing atop a skyscraper, locked in a tight embrace, kissing with the sun rising behind them. With a smile, he tucked the drawing into his coat pocket.

The late afternoon clouds drifted in tangerine tufts over the Oasis Campus. Jameson decided on a walk and some fresh air to clear his head. The stress of the ordeal lingered in him, as if there was some hidden lesson he needed to unravel or some experience he needed to contemplate to gain strength...a post-hardship habit of a hardened survivor.

He walked the campus, stopping at the courtyard playground. The wind rocked the swings and the merry-go-round squeaked on its rusted pivot. Jameson sat on the bottom of the metal slide and lit a cigarette. He stared at the worn picture of his father, the picture he'd carried with him every day of his journey. The corners were torn, the edges creased and the color faded, but the memories of the man remained vibrant. *And here I am again. Full circle.* He had traveled so far, gone to immeasurable lengths to find answers to a mystery that proved darker than he could have imagined. What was gained? *Still alone...the journey is over and I'm still...*

The patter of approaching steps alerted Jameson. He sprang to his feet with his hand hovering over the knife on his hip. "That's close enough," Jameson warned the man who now stood in front of him.

"I'm sorry to bother you."

Jameson eyed his clean-shaven face, almond-brown eyes and tired gait. The man didn't appear to have any weapons, and his left arm rested in a sling. Jameson relaxed. He took a drag from his cigarette and blew the smoke through his nostrils. "What do you want?"

"I'm here to pick up my boy. He was playing here, last I knew."

"Well, there aren't any kids here."

"I guess I'm pretty late, huh, Jamie."

Jameson dropped his cigarette to the sand.

"Luna told me I might find you here. She knows you well." The man stepped closer. "I've missed you, son."

Father and son, two tired survivors longing for better days, embraced; neither wanting to ever let go. Jameson and Eric Shoals shared quiet tears of joy. When Jameson pulled away, he looked deeply into his father's aged face and saw a man that had endured torturous hell yet somehow prevailed, somehow stood strong and well enough to have come back for him, to care, to love and want to continue being his dad. Here was Jameson's lost hero, the sole reason why Jameson pressed on as the years eroded everything around him; and Jameson knew that he must have been his father's reason, too. *Together again. So much to say. Where to begin?* He wiped his eyes and asked the same question he did as a boy. "Are you okay, Dad?"

"Yes. I am."

Brighton screamed a murderous war-cry, robbing Jameson of control. He drew the knife. Eric stepped back, but Brighton was too quick. He slashed the blade across Eric's throat, spraying a cloud of crimson over Jameson's face. Eric's body collapsed to the sand, wheezing, gurgling, then lifeless.

"NO!" Jameson bawled. The horror disintegrated his heart. He fell to his knees beside his father. "WHY?"

Brighton laughed. "*You killed my family. I killed yours.*"

\*\*\*

The setting sun blazed in rose-gold banners. Jack brought the airplane out of the lavender clouds, looking down at the rolling landscape of the Void Lands. Tent towns of drifters and nameless settlements sprawled around the long and mysterious Route 88 that ran forever to the west. Pockets of abandoned suburbs and decaying towns served as monuments to lives long forgotten. Jack looked over at Donna seated beside him, who gazed at the world through binoculars. "What do you think?" he asked.

"It's so pretty up here but there's not much out there," she commented. "It can be tough living in Karma but people really do have it hard outside of the city; don't they?"

"There's no easy living anywhere. The Void Lands, and the 'Strange Highway' as they call it, are very dangerous."

"Hey, Hun," Donna's voice became serious. "I see a man running."

"That's odd. Let me have a look." Jack lowered the altitude and brought the binoculars up to his eyes. He gasped. "It's Jameson! He's covered in blood!"

Jack lifted the radio and switched the frequency from the Oasis to Luna's tribal radio. "Halligan to Briggs. Halligan to Briggs. Do you copy?"

The radio static seemed to last forever. Finally, Luna answered the call.

"Copy. This is Luna Briggs. What is it, Jack?"

"We have a problem. Jameson is running into the Voids. He's a mess. Blood all over him!"

"Shit! Where are you?"

"Roughly five miles west of Lobos."

"My train just left Lobos station; I'm not far. I'll take the big-rig off the rails and ride out there. Stay in communication, Jack. Don't lose sight of him!"

Jameson ran as fast as his Malad-X power allowed. Brighton taunted him.

*"Keep running, Jameson, because if you stop, I will kill Jack and Donna. I will set fire to the airplane. And when Luna Briggs returns to save you from yourself, I will rip out her heart."*

"I won't let you near them!" Jameson yelled.

Fear, larger than any he'd ever felt in all his life, devoured him. Even with Albert's formulated Quell in his veins, Brighton had still taken over. The parasite in his mind was now beyond his control and understanding. With the murder of Jameson's father, Brighton had proven that he could do what he vowed. Luna would never be safe.

With glowing eyes, Jameson looked up at the airplane, now wishing he had a radio to tell Jack to go back for help, to get Albert, to tell Luna to stay back until he—what?—he didn't know what he meant to do, couldn't think that far ahead. Too afraid. Desperate, he waved for Jack to turn back; it was all he could do and perhaps all Brighton would allow.

The airplane drew nearer.

Jameson pushed his legs to run faster.

Ahead, the remnants of a dead neighborhood appeared. A chain-link fence surrounded the perimeter of the long-abandoned community. Decades of thick overgrowth claimed the streets and clusters of houses. He leapt high over the fence, dashing into the dense ruins, hoping to hide from the plane.

"Halligan to Briggs…"

"Go ahead, Jack."

"I lost him."

Karma City

Gardner M. Browning

# Acknowledgments

A group of friends, with strange imaginations, helped bring this story to life. Special thanks to: Alan Ouellette, my best friend; Brittany Blazich, the real Luna Briggs; Patrick McGonagle, the man behind Jameson Shoals; Phillip Thibault, who is Dr. Walker; Chris Brownell, gamer elite and my creative consultant; and Jimmy Gilbert, a friend I can always count on.

Heartfelt appreciation to Michael Neff, my editor and friend. Thank you for believing in me and my work. I'm a better writer because of you.

Many thanks to literary agent, author and friend, Paula Munier. Your help made this story shine.

Thank you, Sharon Arsenault. Your intelligence and creativity brought me inspiration and I'm grateful beyond words.

And beautiful Devin, my wife, my love, thank you. This one wasn't easy. It took a lot of years. Yet, there you were, encouraging, smiling, and making me feel like I am special…you always do that. It makes the difference every time. I love you.

G. M. Browning

Gardner M. Browning

www.ingramcontent.com/pod-product-compliance
Lightning Source LLC
Chambersburg PA
CBHW031722170626
46808CB00005B/1848